EXTRA KILL

Dell Shannon is an American author who is fast becoming famous as the 'Queen of Police Procedurals'. Well-known and read by thousands of people on both sides of the Atlantic, her books show an accurate knowledge of police practice and also a sympathetic skill in drawing her central character, a detective of Mexican heritage called Lieutenant Luis Mendoza, who, together with his colleagues in the Los Angeles Police force, has attracted a great deal of popular support.

Books you will enjoy from Keyhole Crime:

PILOT ERROR by Bill Knox
CRUEL AS THE GRAVE by Helen McCloy
PRUDENCE BE DAMNED by Mary McMullen
THE LEEDS FIASCO by Angus Ross
THE TWELVE DEATHS OF CHRISTMAS by Marian Babson
MOTIVE IN SHADOW by Lesley Egan
CHILL FACTOR by Aaron Marc Stein
FATAL SWITCH by Ian Stuart
DEATH IN A COLD CLIMATE by Robert Barnard
DON'T OPEN THE DOOR! by Ursula Curtiss
THE BEADED BANANA by Margaret Scherf
DEATH IS A DRUM . . . BEATING FOREVER by John Wyllie
THE BEAUTIFUL GOLDEN FRAME by Peter Chambers
STAR TRAP by Simon Brett
THE FAMILY VAULT by Charlotte MacLeod

EXTRA KILL

Dell Shannon

KEYHOLE CRIME
London · Sydney

Reissued in Great Britain 1977 by
Victor Gollancz Limited

This edition published 1982 by
Keyhole Crime, 15–16 Brook's Mews,
London W1A 1DR

ISBN 0 263 73790 X

Set in 10 on 10½ pt Times

Photoset by Rowland Phototypesetting Ltd
Bury St Edmunds, Suffolk
Made and printed in Great Britain by
Cox & Wyman Ltd, Reading

Jaques: And then he drew a dial from his poke,
And, looking on it with lack-lustre eye,
Says very wisely, "It is ten o'clock.
Thus may we see," quoth he, "how the world wags.
'Tis but an hour ago since it was nine;
And after one hour more 'twill be eleven;
And so, from hour to hour, we ripe and ripe,
And then, from hour to hour, we rot and rot;
And thereby hangs a tale."

—*As You Like It*, Act II, sc. 7

CHAPTER ONE

That he was making history was an idea that didn't enter the head of the rookie cop Frank Walsh. He was riding a squad car alone for the first time, which made him more conscientious than usual. He saw this car first when they pulled up at a stop light alongside each other on Avalon Boulevard; he'd never seen one like it and was still looking for some identification when the light changed and it took off like a rocket. He was going the same way, and it was still in sight when they passed a twenty-five-mile zone sign; it didn't slow down, and Walsh happily opened up and started after it.

The bad old days of quotas for tickets, all that kind of thing, were long gone—and Frank Walsh was twenty-six, no starry-eyed adolescent; nevertheless, there was a kind of gratification, a kind of glamour, about the first piece of business one got alone on the job. In time to come, he would have kept an eye on that car for a while, clocked it as only a little over the legit allowance and obviously being handled by a competent driver, and let it go. As it was, a mile down Avalon he pulled alongside and motioned it into the curb.

It was quite some car, he thought as he got out and walked round the squad car: a long, low, gun-metal-coloured job, a two-door hardtop. This close he made out the name, a strange one to him—Facel-Vega, what the hell was that? One of these twenty-thousand-buck foreigners, probably with a TV director or a movie actor or something like that driving it, just to be different and show he had the money. Walsh stopped at the driver's window. 'May I see your operator's licence, please?' he asked politely.

The driver was a slim dark fellow with a black hairline

moustache, a sleek thick cap of black hair, a long straight nose, and a long jaw. He said just as politely, 'Certainly, officer,' and got out his wallet, correctly slid his licence out of its plastic envelope himself, and passed it over.

There was a woman beside him, a good-looking redhead who seemed to be having a fit of giggles for some reason.

Walsh checked the licence righteously, comparing it with the driver. A Mex, he was, and quite a mouthful of name like they mostly had: Luis Rodolfo Vicente Mendoza. The licence had been renewed within six months and matched him all right: five-ten, a hundred and fifty-five, age thirty-nine, eyes brown, hair— Walsh said, 'You know, Mr Mendoza, you were exceeding the limit by about fifteen miles an hour.' He said it courteously because that was part of your training, you were supposed to start out anyway being polite; but he felt a little indignant about these fellows who thought just because they had money and a hot-looking expensive car the laws weren't made for them.

The driver said, 'You're perfectly right, I was.' He didn't even point out that practically everybody exceeded the limit in these slow zones; he accepted the ticket Walsh wrote out and put his licence back in its slot, and Walsh, getting back in the squad car, was the least bit disappointed that he hadn't made the expected fuss.

It wasn't until his tour was over and he reported back to his precinct station that he found out what he'd done. It was the car that had stayed in his mind, and he was describing it to Sergeant Simon when Lieutenant Slaney came in.

'. . . something called a Facel-Vega, ever hear of it?'

The sergeant said it sounded like one of those Italians, and the lieutenant said no, it was a French job, and what brought it up? When he heard about the ticket, a strangely eager expression came over his face. 'The only Facel-Vega I know of around here—what was the driver like, Walsh?'

'He was a Mex, sir—why? I mean, his licence was all in order, and the plate number wasn't on the hot list. Shouldn't I—?'

'And his name,' asked Slaney in something like awe, 'was maybe Luis Mendoza?'

'Why, yes, sir, how—'

'Oh, God,' said Slaney rapturously, 'oh, *brother*, this really makes my day! Walsh, if I could christen you a captain right now I would! You gave Luis Mendoza a ticket for speeding? You don't know it, but you just made history, my boy—that's the first moving-violation ticket he's ever had, to my knowledge.'

'You *know* him, Lieutenant?'

'Do I know him?' said Slaney. 'Do I—? I suppose he had a woman with him?'

'Why, yes, there was a redhead—a pretty one—'

'I needn't have asked,' said Slaney. 'There always is—a woman, that is, he's not particular about whether it's a blonde or what. He looks at them and they fall, God Almighty knows why. Do I *know* him, says you. For my sins I went through the training course with him, eighteen years back, and we worked out of the same precinct together as rookies. And before we both got transferred, the bastard got a hundred and sixty-three dollars of my hard-earned money at poker, and took two girls away from me besides. That's how well I—'

'He's a *cop*?' said Walsh, aghast. He had a horrid vision of riding squad cars the rest of his life, all applications for promotion tabled from above. 'My *God*, I never—but, Lieutenant, that car—'

'He's headquarters—Homicide lieutenant. The car —well, he came into the hell of a lot of money a couple of years after he joined the force—his grandfather turned out to've been one of those misers with millions tucked away, you know? Oh, boy, am I goin' to rub his nose in this!' chortled Slaney. 'His first ticket, and from one of *my* rookies!'

'But, Lieutenant, if I'd known—'

'If you'd known he was the Chief you'd still have given him the ticket, I hope,' said Slaney. 'Nobody's got privileges, you know that.'

Which theoretically speaking was true, but in practice things weren't always so righteous, as Walsh knew. He went on having gloomy visions for several days of a career stopped before it started, until he came off duty one afternoon to be called into Slaney's office and introduced to Mendoza, who'd dropped by on some headquarters business. Slaney was facetious, and Walsh tried to balance that with nervous apology. Lieutenant Mendoza grinned at him.

'Cut that out, Walsh, no need. Always a first time for everything. The only thing I'm surprised at is that it was one of Bill Slaney's boys—I wouldn't expect such zealous attention to duty out of this precinct.'

'Why, you bastard,' said Slaney. 'Half your reputation you got on the work of your two senior sergeants, and I trained both of 'em for you as you damn well know.'

'Yes, Art Hackett's often told me how glad he was to be transferred out from under you,' said Mendoza amiably.

All in all, Walsh was enormously relieved; despite his rank and his money Mendoza seemed to be a regular guy.

That happened in January; a month later, the memory of this little encounter emboldened Walsh to go over Lieutenant Slaney's head and lay a problem before the headquarters man.

'I've got no business to be here, Lieutenant,' said Walsh uneasily. 'Lieutenant Slaney says I'm a damn fool to waste anybody's time about this.' He sat beside Mendoza's desk, stiffly upright, and fingered his cap nervously. He'd called to ask if he could see Mendoza after he came off duty, and was still in uniform; he was on days, since last week, and it was six o'clock, the day men just going off, the night staff coming into the big headquarters building downtown with its long echoing corridors.

'Well, let's hear what it's about,' said Mendoza. 'Does Slaney know you're here?'

'No, sir. I've got no *business* doing such a thing, I know. I asked him about it, sir, and he said he wouldn't ask you to waste your time. But the more I got to thinking about it . . . It's about Joe Bartlett, sir, the inquest verdict yesterday—'

'Oh?' said Mendoza. He got up and opened the door. 'Is Art back yet?' he asked the sergeant in the anteroom.

'Just came in, want him?' The sergeant looked into the big communal office that opened on the other side of his cubbyhole, called for Art, and a big broad sandy fellow came in: the sergeant Walsh remembered from last Friday night and yesterday at the inquest. He wasn't a man to look at twice, only a lot bigger than most—until you noticed the unexpectedly shrewd blue eyes.

'I thought you'd left, *now* what d'you want? I just brought that statement in—'

'Not that. Sit down. You'll remember this young fellow, he's got something to say about the Bartlett inquest. You handled that, you'd better hear it too.'

'Bartlett,' said Sergeant Hackett, and sat down looking grim. Nobody liked random killings, but the random killing of a cop, cops liked even less.

'I don't think that inquest verdict was right,' blurted Walsh. 'I don't think it was those kids shot Joe. Lieutenant Slaney says I'm talking through the top of my head, but—I tried to speak up at the inquest yesterday—maybe you'll remember, Sergeant, I was on the stand just before you were—but they wouldn't let me volunteer anything, just answer what they asked.'

'What was it you wanted to say? Didn't you tell your own sergeant about it?'

'Well, naturally, sir—and the lieutenant—and they both think I'm nuts, see? Sure, it looks open and shut on the face of it, I admit that. Those kids'd just held up that market, they were all a little high, and they weren't sure they'd lost that first squad car that was after them—maybe they thought we were the same one, or maybe they didn't care, just saw a couple of cops and loosed off at us. We were parked the opposite direction, but they might've figured, the way the coroner said, that that first car had got ahead and gone round to lay for them.'

Which had been the official verdict, of course: that those juveniles, burning up the road on the run from the market job, had mistaken the parked squad car for the one that had been chasing them and fired at it as they passed, one of the bullets killing Bartlett. They'd already shot a cashier at the market, who had a fifty-fifty chance to live.

'They say, of course, that they never were on San Dominguez at all, never fired a shot after leaving the market,' said Hackett.

'Yes, sir, and I think maybe they didn't. I—'

'Giving testimony,' said Mendoza, 'isn't exactly like talking to somebody. Before we hear what brought you here, Walsh, suppose you give me the gist, in your own words, of just what did happen. I know Sergeant Hackett's heard it already, and I've read your statement, but I'd like to hear it straight.'

'Yes, sir. We were parked on the shoulder, just up from Cameron on San Dominguez. That's almost the county line, and one end of our cruise, see. We'd just stopped a car for speeding and I'd written out the ticket. Joe was driving then and I was just getting back in, and in a second we'd have been moving off, when this car came past the opposite way and somebody fired at us from it. Four shots. It must've been either the first or second got Joe, the doctor said, by the angle—and it was just damned bad luck any of them connected, or damned good target shooting, that's all I can figure. The car was going about thirty. The shots came all together, just about as it came even with us and passed, and the way things were I hardly got a look at all. Joe never moved or spoke, sir, we know now the shot got him straight through the head . . .' Walsh stopped, drew the back of his hand across his mouth. He'd liked Joe Bartlett, who'd been a good man for a rookie to work with, easy and tactful on giving little pointers. Ten years to go to retirement, Bartlett, with a growing comfortable paunch and not much hair left and always talking about his kids, the boy in college, the girl still in high school. Also, that had been Walsh's first personal contact with violence, and while he'd kept his head it hadn't been a pleasant five minutes. 'He slumped down over the wheel, I couldn't get at the controls until I'd moved him, it was—awkward, you can see that. I think I knew he was dead, nothing to be done for him—I just thought, got to spot that car . . . I shoved him over best I could to get at the wheel, but by the time I got the hand brake off and got her turned, my God, it wasn't any use, that car was long gone. I was quick as I could be, sir—'

'It was just one of those things,' agreed Hackett.

'I got the siren on, and I went after it, but no use, like I said. I saw that, and I pulled into the side and reported in what had happened. They told me to go straight to Vineyard and Brook, there was an ambulance on its way there already, so I did. That's where they'd finally picked up the kids, you know, just then. Price and Hopper, I mean, and Gonzales and Farber in the first car that'd been after them were called in too—they were there when I got there. Price had to fire at the car to get it to stop, and one of the kids was hit, not bad—you know all that, sir.'

Mendoza nodded. 'That's all clear enough. What's in your mind about it now? Your own sergeant and Sergeant Hackett had your story then, and you said, if I recall rightly, that it must have been those juveniles. Something changed your mind?'

'It looked,' said Walsh, 'like it must've been, sure, because what *else* could it have been? I mean, it's not as if there were a dozen cars around that area that night with somebody taking pot shots at squad cars out of them. When we came to sort it out, the times looked tight, but it could have happened like that, and how *else* could it have?'

'We went into it as thoroughly as possible,' said Hackett.

'Yes, sir, I know. And I don't want to make out that I was mistaken in anything I told you, it's not that. It's just that when I came to think about the whole thing afterwards—as a whole, if you see what I mean—well, it's nothing to get hold of, nothing definite, but the more I thought about it—And I told Sergeant Simon, and Lieutenant Slaney too, but I guess the reason it sounded crazy to them is just that—how else could it have happened?'

'What bothers you about it?' asked Mendoza patiently.

'The main thing is the times. Sure, it could have been, but it's tight figuring. Look, here's Cameron and San Dominguez, where it happened. I don't see how I could have been more than thirty seconds getting under way afterwards, even call it a minute before I got the car turned and got up speed after that car—and it didn't take me another minute to see it was no go. All right,'—in his urgency Walsh was forgetting some of his nervousness—'there's two minutes, and I'm about half a mile down San Dominguez. Give me another ten minutes to pull in and start to call. I couldn't get through right away, they were busy that night, but it couldn't've been more than another twenty seconds before I was reporting in. Say that's three minutes, even four, after the shots were fired—I don't think it was four, actually, but give it that much leeway—and I was talking maybe another twenty seconds or half minute, and the girl had me wait another ten, twenty seconds while she checked on where that ambulance call was from—Price reported in just before me. So I'm sent to Vineyard and Brook where they got the kids, and that's about half a mile from where I was then, or from where the shots were fired—it makes a kind of triangle, see, with the point at Vineyard and Brook. O.K., now when I got there, which was maybe two and a half minutes later, the first squad car'd already got there, that's Gonzales and Farber, who'd been the first to go after the kids, and they'd been called up *after* Price and Hopper were on the kids' tail. Look, I even made a diagram of it, and this is how it works out in my book. Call it five past nine when the shots were fired at us and Joe was killed. Say it was the kids, they've got to get over to Vineyard—which runs the same way as San Dominguez, it's not a cross street—and be going west there hell-bent for election when Price and Hopper spotted them two-three minutes later. Because Price's call in, saying they were on them, was clocked at seven minutes past nine, and Gonzales and Farber got the word where to join them a minute later. The ambulance call Price put in, same time as he reported arresting the kids, came over at eleven minutes past nine. And at about that time I was calling in about Joe. I can't figure how it could've been more than four minutes between Joe's getting shot and Price and Hopper picking up those kids. And you know, I don't suppose they gave one look at the car and spotted it, bang, right off—they'd take a closer look to be sure it *was* those kids, which cuts down the time a little.'

'Mmh, yes. You've really gone into this, haven't you?' Mendoza tilted back his chair, regarding the opposite wall thoughtfully. 'That sounds like a very short space of time, but a lot of things can happen in three or four minutes, and you're not absolutely sure of the times on your end, are you? Even if you'd just happened to look at your watch before Bartlett was shot, it could have been off a bit from the clocks in the radio room here.'

'Yes, sir, I know. But another thing, as I don't need to tell you, Price and Hopper didn't just slam bracelets on the kids and rush right back to report in, there'd be a couple of minutes there, getting the kids out of their car and so on . . . Well, I don't know, it just seems to me—'

'Look,' said Hackett, rubbing his jaw. 'Leave all this thirty seconds, twenty seconds business out, what you're saying is, it seems to you that by the time you got sent to meet the ambulance, the kids had been busy with Price and Hopper a little too long to have been over on San Dominguez when Bartlett was killed. Now I've got just this to say. Time's funny—when a lot's happening, sometimes it seems to go faster and sometimes slower—you've had that experience?' Walsh nodded silently. 'I agree with you that it all happened damn fast, but we've got no check on exact times, and nobody can say just on that account it couldn't've been those kids. And the gun checks—as much identification as we'll ever get. I don't need to remind you it was a homemade gun with a smooth bore, so, sure, Ballistics can't say definitely this bullet came out of that gun—but the market cashier and Bartlett both had .38

caliber bullets in them, and the kids had half a box of 'em left. It looks pretty open and shut.'

'I know,' said Walsh helplessly. 'All I can say is, even making every allowance for the way you do lose track of time in the middle of a thing like that—well, I still feel it's too tight. And, Sergeant, why did they turn off San Dominguez if it was them?'

'Why shouldn't they?'

'It's the main drag,' said Walsh, 'the best road along there. They were all from that section, they'd know the streets. They must've known that if I was on their tail after they'd fired at us, their best chance of losing me was to stay on San Dominguez, because it's a divided highway and not much traffic that time of night. They would make tracks and still do enough weaving in and out of what traffic there was to throw me off. They'd know I couldn't have got their plate number—it's dark as hell along there, those arc lights are so high—and they'd blacked out their taillight. Look, you get off the main drag along there, most of the cross streets are full of potholes and not all of 'em go through to the next main street, Vineyard. They'd be damn fools to turn off right away, and take a chance on getting to the next boulevard—they couldn't be sure I wasn't on them when they'd turned off, the way they must've if they were going to be spotted where we know Price and Hopper spotted them, on Vineyard just west of Goldenrod going about sixty.'

'Well, now,' said Hackett. 'They weren't exactly thinking very clear, you know, right then.'

'They'd just shaken off Gonzales and Farber, Sergeant, after a twenty-minute chase—and Lieutenant Slaney says Farber's the best damn driver out of our precinct.'

Mendoza laughed. 'That's a point—he's got you there, Art. Of course,'—he sat up abruptly—'they wouldn't have us after them if they weren't damn fools to start with, and damn fools have a habit of acting like what they are. And like the rest of us they have good luck and bad luck.' He brushed tobacco crumbs off his desk tidily, straightened the blotter, lined up the desk tray with the calendar as he spoke; but automatically, like a persnickety housewife, thought Walsh. Even in the midst of his earnest effort to get through to them with this, Walsh couldn't help noticing. One of those people who went around straightening pictures, he figured Mendoza was: the orderly mind. He looked it too, very natty and dapper in an ultraconservative way, like an ad in *Esquire*—the faintest of patterns in the tie, and that suit must have cost three hundred bucks if it cost a dime. Of course, all that money Lieutenant Slaney said he had . . .

'And if it wasn't the kids?' asked Mendoza. 'What else?'

'It's crazy,' said Walsh, 'I know. But suppose it was somebody who wanted to kill Joe as—well, who he was. Not just a cop in a squad car. A—a specific cop.'

'Now let's not reach for it,' said Hackett dryly. 'You know anybody who might have wanted Bartlett dead? Who might try it like that?—not just the easiest method, by the hell of a long way. I manage to keep up enough of a score on the board myself so I don't come in for extra practice, but I'd think twice about trying a target shot like that, practically in the dark and at thirty miles an hour.'

'I know,' said Walsh again, humbly. 'It sounds crazy to me too, Sergeant. If it wasn't those kids, I don't know who it could've been, or why. But I just can't figure it as the kids, when I think back over it. The way I told you, I didn't get any kind of look at the car, I had my head down sliding into our car beside Joe. I couldn't say if there was just the driver or three kids or a dozen blue baboons in it. And when I *did* look up, at the shots, it was already almost past, and all I could tell was it was a sedan—but two-door or four-door I couldn't see—and a dark colour, and it had fins, so it was a fairly late model. That's all I can honestly say, sir, for sure. I only had it in sight for about two seconds. So I know it doesn't count for much when I say that, thinking back, I get the impression that looking at those tailfins side on, the way I saw the car as it went past, they curved up at the ends.'

'The car the kids were driving,' said Mendoza, 'was a

two-year-old four-door Mercury. I don't keep up with all these little changes in design—' He looked at Hackett.

'Straight fins,' said Hackett tersely. 'When did all this begin to come to you, Walsh—in a dream?'

'Look, sir, I'm just trying to be honest about it. Maybe I was slow on the uptake, but, like you say, a lot happened all at once, and it wasn't until I had a chance to sit down and think about the whole thing in—in retrospect, you know, that it added up like this. Or didn't add up. And by then you all had my statement and the inquest was set—and the sergeant said I was crazy, because how *else*—and the coroner wouldn't let—'

'You did quite right coming in to tell us,' said Mendoza.

'Second thoughts—' began Hackett, looking a little angry.

'*Tómelo con calma, chico,* if we don't like a little new piece of truth we can't shove it under the rug because we like something else better. Which you know as well as I do. And another thing we all know is that sometimes you get a clearer picture of a thing looking back on it. No, you were quite right to pass this on, Walsh—you needn't be afraid you'll get in any trouble over it.'

'Do you think—?'

'I don't think anything right now,' said Mendoza. He put out his cigarette carefully in the brass tray. 'We haven't got enough to think about. But maybe it wouldn't do any harm to take a little closer look at this thing. *Todos cometomes errores*—we all make mistakes—and peculiar coincidences do occur, no denying.'

'Now *look*,' said Hackett, 'if you've got one of your hunches, Luis, tell it to go away. Of all the far-fetched—'

'No hunch,' said Mendoza. 'I'd just like to look at it a little closer. To be sure.' He looked at Walsh. 'We'll keep this quiet for a while. If it turns out you've been exercising your imagination, I don't want it to get round that you fooled Mendoza for a minute—everybody knows I'm never wrong! But if there seems to be something in it, I'll want to see you again.'

'Yes, sir,' said Walsh, grinning and then cancelling the grin as he remembered Bartlett.

Hackett shut his eyes and said, '*Lo mismo me da*—all the same to me—I'm only the wheel horse that'll do all the work. The games you think up, Luis! Working a case twice, just to be sure.'

'Well, this is one we'd like to be very damned sure about, isn't it?'

'That's why,' said Walsh. 'I mean, I thought I ought to tell somebody, sir, on account of those kids. That cashier's still alive. If he doesn't die, it wouldn't be a homicide charge—except for Joe.'

'Oh, that,' said Mendoza. He got up, straightening his tie, yanking down his cuffs; his cuff links, Walsh noticed, were heavy gold monogrammed ones. 'What the hell, about the kids? They're no good to anybody and the chances are very small they ever would be. They're all under eighteen and wouldn't get the death penalty anyway. This way or that way'—he took down his hat, a rather high-crowned black Homburg, and brushed it—'they'll be around quite a while to make work for us and deviltry for a lot of other people. It's not on that account I'd like to know more about this. I just want to know what really happened. I'm told I've got as much irrational curiosity as a dozen women, which is maybe why I'm a cop in the first place.

CHAPTER TWO

He happened to have a date that night with his redhead, Alison Weir. It was a little different thing, with Alison—he hadn't troubled to figure why—just, maybe, because she was Alison: he could be more himself with her than with any other woman. So over dinner he told her they'd take a little ride out towards Long Beach—something he wanted to look at—and without much prodding added the whole funny little story.

'This boy,' said Alison thoughtfully, 'he's not just trying to build up something, get into the limelight?'

'I don't read him that way,' said Mendoza. 'And these days rookies aren't always as young as that—he's twenty-five, twenty-six, old enough to have some judgment. No, I don't know that there's anything in it, and to tell you the truth I've got no idea where to start looking to find out.'

'But— Well, say for a minute it's *so*, Luis, though it sounds perfectly fantastic—if it was someone who wanted to kill this Bartlett specifically, surely something would show up in his private life, if you looked?'

Mendoza lit cigarettes for both of them and looked consideringly at his coffee. 'Not necessarily. You take a policeman, now—he gets around, and in a lot of places and among a lot of people the ordinary person doesn't. You might say, if you're looking for motives for murder, a cop has a little better chance of creating one than most people. The difficulty is—' He broke off, took a drag on his cigarette, laid it down, drank coffee, and stared at the sugar bowl intently.

'*¡Siga adelante!*' said Alison encouragingly.

'Well, the difficulty is that if it was anything like that—something he'd heard or seen on his job—big enough to constitute a reason for killing him, he'd have known about it himself and made some report on it. And if it was something that had happened just on that tour of duty—which, if we accept the whole fantasy, I think it may have been—young Walsh would know about it too. Because, although some people still cling to the idea that most cops aren't overburdened with brains, we are trained to notice things, you know. And while I've never met a motive for murder that was what you might call really adequate, still nobody would think it necessary to kill the man because he'd seen or heard something so—apparently—meaningless to him that he hadn't mentioned it to anybody. But this is theorising without data . . .'

An hour later he pulled up on the shoulder of that stretch of San Dominguez, just up from Cameron. He switched off the engine and the headlights, switched on the parking lights, and gave her a cigarette, lit one himself.

'And what do you expect to find out here?'

'I don't expect anything. I don't know what there is to find out. You've got to start a cast somewhere.'

'Like fox hunting. You just turn the hounds loose where you think there might be a fox? I thought crime detection was a lot more scientific than that these days.'

'*Segun y como*, sometimes yes, sometimes no.' He was motionless shadow, only the little red spark of his cigarette end moving there; he stared out at the thinnish passing traffic. 'I'll tell you something funny, *chica*. With all the laboratories and the chemical tests and the gadgets we've got to help us—Prints and Ballistics and the rest of it—like everything else in life it always comes back to individual people. To people's feelings and what the feelings make them do or not do. Quite often the gadgets can give you an idea where to look, but once in a while you've got to find out about the people first—then the gadgets can help you prove it.' He went on staring out the window.

Alison slid down comfortably against his shoulder and said, 'Oh, well, at least there's a heater to keep my feet warm. Pity I don't knit, I could be accomplishing something . . . I have a theory about policemen. Just like musicians, they come in two types—the ones who learn the hard way, by lessons and practice, and the ones who do it by ear, just naturally. You play it by ear. You do it in jumps, a flash of inspiration here, a lucky guess there. What you're doing now is waiting for your muse to visit you, *¿no es verdad?*'

He laughed. 'You know too much about me. A ranking headquarters officer, he's supposed to work by sober routine and cold scientific fact, not by ear.'

'Never mind, I'll keep the dark secret,' she said sleepily. 'Then when your hunches pay off and everybody says,

"The man's a genius," you can look modest and say, "Just routine, just routine."'

Mendoza went on staring at the boulevard. No place within twenty miles of downtown L.A. was thinly populated, but there were stretches here and there, and this was one of them, where the contractors hadn't got round to planting blocks of new little houses or new big apartments, or rows of shops and office buildings. Half a mile up, half a mile down, half a mile away to each side were close communities, blocks of residence and business, and the port of Los Angeles; here, only an occasional grove of live oaks at the roadside, and empty weed-grown fields beyond. The arc lights on the boulevard were high but adequate; the effect of darkness came from the lack of other lights to supplement them, the neon lights of shop fronts along built-up sections. And from the shadow of the trees, along here.

He wondered if Walsh and Bartlett had been parked under these trees.

Five minutes later a black-and-white squad car came ambling along, hesitated, and drew in ahead of the Facel-Vega. One of the patrolmen got out and came back to Mendoza's window, and he rolled it down all the way.

'Not a very good place to park, sir,' said the patrolman tactfully. 'Unless you're having trouble with your car, I'll ask you to move on.'

'It's O.K.,' said Mendoza, 'not what your nasty low mind tells you. I can think of at least three better places to make love than the front seat of a car. I'm more or less on legitimate business,' and he passed over his credentials.

'Oh—excuse *me*, sir.' The man in uniform shoved back his cap and leaned on the window sill. 'Anything we can do for you?'

'I don't know. This is about where Bartlett got it, isn't it?'

'Auggh, yes, sir.' The voice was grim. 'By what Frank Walsh says. That was the hell of a thing, wasn't it? A damn good man, Joe was. I'm Gonzales, sir, Farber and I were in on the arrest, maybe you'll know. There when Walsh come up with Joe. I tell you, it was all we could do, keep our hands off those goddamned smart-aleck kids, when we heard . . . The hell of a thing.'

'Yes, it was. Walsh much shaken up? He hasn't been in uniform long, has he?'

'No, sir, but he's a good kid. Sure, he was shook, but he'd kept his head—he acted O.K. I tell you, Lieutenant, I guess I was the one was shook—and I've been in uniform seven years this month and that wasn't the first time I'd picked up some pretty tough customers who happened to be Mexican—but I tell you, with *those* kids, it was the first time I ever felt ashamed of my name.'

'*Vaya, amigo*, we come all shapes and sizes like other people—good, bad, and indifferent.'

'Sure,' said Gonzales bitterly, 'sure we do, Lieutenant, but a lot of people don't remember it when the names get in the paper on a thing like this.'

Alison sat up and said that it was a pity, while all this research was going on about a cure for cancer and the common cold, that nobody was looking for a cure for stupidity: it was needed much more. Gonzales grinned and said it sure was, hesitated, and added, 'Excuse me, Lieutenant, but—the inquest was yesterday, I mean I was wondering if there was anything—'

'More?' said Mendoza. 'Like maybe have I heard a little something from Frank Walsh?'

'Oh, he *did* see you? I didn't want to stick my neck out if he'd got cold feet.' At which point Farber up ahead got impatient and came back to see what was going on.

When he heard, he said, 'Walsh is O.K., but he's really reaching on this one, Lieutenant. Overconscientious.' He was an older man than Gonzales, compact and tough-looking in the brief flare of the match as he lit a cigarette.

'Well, boys,' said Mendoza, 'they say better safe than sorry. It won't do any harm to take another look. But there's no need to—mmh—worry Bill Slaney about it unless it appears there's something to tell him. I don't want him breathing fire at me for encouraging one of his rookies in a lot of nonsense, and I don't want him coming down on Walsh for going over his head. I'll square him when the time comes, if it's necessary. Meanwhile, could one of you do me a little favour? You're on night tour, I see—Walsh is on days right now. Could one of you get a copy from him of his record book of last Friday night, and bring it to me tomorrow morning? I'll meet you somewhere near the station, or anywhere convenient.'

Farber was silent; Gonzales said, 'Sure, I'll do that, Lieutenant. If you think there's anything to be looked into. Frank talked to us about it, but it sounds—'

'Crazy, I know. I'm not saying yes or no yet. Just looking. Where and what time?'

'Corner of Avalon and Cole, say about ten-thirty?'

'O.K. Thanks very much. I'll see you then, Gonzales.' As the two men walked back to the squad car, Farber was seen to raise his shoulders in an expressive shrug. Mendoza murmured, 'Overconscientious . . . I wonder,' and switched on the ignition. Then he said, 'Better places, yes, but just to be going on with, as long as we're here—' and postponed reaching for the hand brake a minute to kiss her.

At ten forty-five the next morning he sat in his car at one end of that cruise Walsh and Bartlett had been riding on Friday night, and read over the terse history of what jobs they had done between four-thirty and nine. It hadn't been a very exciting tour up to then. On Friday night, he remembered, it had been raining: grey and threatening all day, and the rain starting about three, not a real California storm until later, but one of those dispirited steady thin drizzles. Californians were like cats about rain, and that would have been enough to keep a lot of people home that night.

In the four and a half hours Walsh and Bartlett were on duty, up to the murder of Bartlett, they had responded to four radio calls and handed out seven tickets. At four-fifty they had been sent to an accident on Vineyard; evidently it had been quite a mess, with three cars called in and an ambulance, one D.O.A. and two injured, and they hadn't got away from there until five thirty-five. At six-three they'd been sent to another accident, a minor one, and spent a few minutes getting traffic unsnarled there. At six-forty they'd rescued a drunk who'd strayed onto the freeway, and taken him into the station for transferral to the tank downtown overnight. At seven thirty-five they'd been sent to an apartment on 267th Street, a drunk-and-disorderly. Apparently the drunks hadn't been very disorderly, for they were back on their route again by eight o'clock. At eight-twenty they'd stopped at a coffee shop on Vineyard, and were on their way again at eight thirty-five.

The tickets had all been for speeding, except two for illegal left turns.

Mendoza started out to follow their route. He went to the scene of the first accident, and parked, and looked at it. It said nothing to him at all, of course: just a fairly busy intersection, with nothing to show that four nights ago it had been a shambles of death and destruction.

He went on to the place of the second accident, and that said even less, eloquently. Again, of course . . . What the hell did he think he was doing? Waiting for his muse, Alison said. Waiting for that cold sure tingle between the shoulder blades that told him the man across the table was bluffing hard, or really did hold a full house. Or for that similar, vaguer sensation that for want of a better word was called a hunch.

Nothing said anything to him. An hour later he had got as far as the place where they'd subdued the D.-and-D., and had reached the conclusion that he was wasting time. It wasn't an apartment building, this, but a one-storey court built in U-shape around a big black-topped parking area. There were four semi-detached apartments on each side, in two buildings, and across the end a fifth building also with two apartments; at the street side of the first two buildings were double carports, and a single one at each end of the fifth. All the buildings were painted bright pink, with white door-frames and imitation shutters; they looked curiously naked standing there in the open, not a tree anywhere around, or any grass: only the blacktop and in the middle of it a large wooden tub in which was planted some anonymous shrub, which obviously wasn't doing very well—thin and anaemic-looking. Six television aerials stretched importunate arms heavenward; presumably the other tenants possessed newer sets of the portable type.

In his exasperation with himself, Mendoza thought he'd never seen a more depressing place to live. Even a slum tenement gave out a warmer sense of life than this sterile, cheap modernity.

There was no parking lane along here, and he turned up onto the blacktop to make a U-turn, start back downtown, and quit wasting time. As he swung around by the twin front doors of the building across the end of the court, the left one opened and a woman bounced out in front of the car; so he had to stop.

'Was it about the apartment? You're lucky to catch me, I was just goin' to market. You're welcome to see over it, won't take a minute to get the key—' She might have been sixty; she was an inch or so short of five feet and very nearly as wide, but every bit of her looked as firm and brisk and bouncy as a brand-new rubber ball. She had pug-dog features under a good deal of wild grey hair, and her cotton housedress was a blinding Prussian blue with a pink-and-white print superimposed.

'Not about the apartment, no,' said Mendoza. Oh, well, as long as he was here . . . He got out of the car and introduced himself. 'You, or someone here, put in a call to the police last Friday night complaining about a drunk—'

'Mrs Bragg, that's me, how-do. Mex, hey? Well, I don't mind that, you're mostly awful polite folk, I will say, nor I don't mind the police part either—matter of fact it might be sort of handy sometimes, with them Johnstones. Now there, if I haven't *got* the key, musta picked up the wrong bunch—it's this apartment right here, what'd-you-say-the-name-is, and a bargain if I do say so—'

'I'm not interested in the apartment.' But he had to follow her to the door to say it, and she prodded him inside before he got it across. 'This call you put in—it was you?—'

'*And* what about it?' said Mrs Bragg. 'Got a right to call the police, I hope, I pay taxes, and not the first time either since them Johnstones've been in Number Three. I don't mind folk taking a drink now and then, and it's none of my business are they really married or not, which I don't think they are, but when it comes to getting roaring drunk three nights a week average, and taking 'em both as it does, him trying to beat her up and her yelling blue murder, well, I've got my other tenants to think of, I hope you can understand that—'

'Yes, of course, why don't you get rid of them?'

'Oh, well, she's a nice woman when she isn't drunk, quite the lady, *and* the rent on the dot first of every month. Funny thing is, it never lasts long, you see—half an hour and they quiet down. Beats me what fun they get out of it, but there it is, it takes all sorts. Thing is, it went on a bit longer Friday night, and I thought it might kind of bring them to their senses if I called the police, *which* it did as it has before—they quieted down soon as they come and the older one, he gave 'em a good talking-to, and never a peep out of them afterwards.' She eyed him speculatively. 'Might be real handy, have one of you here all the time. You're sure you don't want to move? It's a real nice apartment—now you're here you might's well see over it, just on the chance. Three and a half rooms, all utilities, *and* furnished real nice if I do say so—just take a look around—and only ninety a month. The gentleman I've just lost out of it, he was a *real* gentleman, if he did have a funny name—Twelvetrees it was, Mr Brooke Twelvetrees, kind of elegant-sounding at that when you say it, isn't it?—and he took real good care of everything, I was sorry to see him go. You can see he left everything in apple-pie order, to tell the truth I haven't got round to cleaning it up myself since, except for emptying the waste-basket and so on. *Which*, however, would be done before you moved in, even to windows washed. Handy to everything, market two blocks away, and thirty minutes to downtown. Now you can see—'

Submerged in the flood, Mendoza was swept ruthlessly across the tiny living room (pink flowers in the rug, Prussian blue mohair davenport, blond step-table beside a maroon-upholstered chair) into an even tinier bedroom, in which there was just room for a double bed of blond finished pine, a bureau enamelled cream, and a straight chair. The bed bore a pink chenille spread with fringe, and there was a small bedside table with a lamp about nine inches high which wore a madly ruffled shade very much askew. The rug here had maroon flowers.

Mrs Bragg pounded the bed vigorously. 'Good mattress, good as new, you can see. Oh, I tell you, I was sorry to see Mr Twelvetrees go—a real gentleman he was, and finicky as a lady, you can see by the way he left everything so neat. Here's the bathroom, shower *and* tub if they *are* all together so to speak, and real tile, not that plastic stuff.' It was mauve, and the shower curtain was embellished with improbably blue fish.

'I'm really not interested—'

'Plenty of closet space, even for a man like Mr Twelvetrees and he had as many clothes as a woman, you shoulda seen—a real snappy dresser he was. And the kitchen, if I *do* say, is all nice and modern as anybody'd want—' Mendoza was prodded back across the living room to the kitchen, to admire a very small table with chromium-tube legs and a rose-coloured plastic top, chairs to match, real blue tile on the drainboard, a practically new refrigerator and stove. Mrs Bragg pounded the table to illustrate its sturdiness, and it rocked violently.

'There now, he's got it over the trap—you don't need to worry about *that*, it's just what they call access for the plumber, case they have to get at the line underneath, and it don't hardly show a bit, you can see, covered with the same linoleum. You see, it's steady as a rock, you get it in the right place. Everything handy. I don't deny it's small, but arranged very convenient, as you can see—' She made a sudden dart at the narrow kitchen door and snatched up an object from the threshold: a shiny new trowel. 'So that's where my trowel got to—he musta been at that Tree of Heaven again. Real helpful he was, and quite the gardener, I often said to him, "You oughta have a place of your own." He even got me some special plant food for the blamed thing, but it didn't seem to do no good. Well, now, you can see what a bargain the place is at ninety—'

'But really I'm not interested in another apartment—'

'—And I'm not one of those fussy landladies, either. Men will be men, single ones, that is, *and* some of the others, and women I don't mind, none of my business and live and let live I always say, as long as everything's quiet and no rowdy parties. The only thing I *do* draw the line at—just in the interests of my investment here, as you can understand—is pets and children, *that* I can't have—'

Mendoza, between fascination and the feeling that he might willy-nilly find himself signing a lease on the spot, perceived that Providence was rescuing him. He said in that case the apartment would never do, as he had some cats.

'*Cats!*' exclaimed Mrs Bragg, recoiling a step.

'Three cats,' said Mendoza. 'That is, a cat and two kittens.'

'*Cats* I will not have. I'm afraid if you want the apartment you'll have to get rid of them.' She looked at him disapprovingly; he had disappointed her. Something peculiar about a man who kept cats, and three at that.

'I'm only curious,' said Mendoza, recovering his equilibrium, 'but do you say that to prospective tenants with children?'

'Tenants with children *or* pets I don't take. I'm sorry, but you should have explained that to start with and I needn't have wasted time showing you over the place. I'm very sorry, but I can't make any exception.' She all but pushed him out the door. 'I'm sure you can understand that it's *ruination* on a furnished place.'

Mendoza got back into his car as she banged her own

front door. '*¡Quiá!*' he said to himself. 'And my grandmother asks me why I don't marry a wife! *A ningun precio*—not at any price, take such a chance!'

CHAPTER THREE

He looked, in the places indicated to look, and found nothing. If there was anything funny anywhere, it didn't show in any way. He saw the kids again, the insolent, sullen kids who didn't clearly understand that they'd done anything wrong, just resented the cops for putting them in jail. Who said sullenly, insolently, that the cops were making scapegoats of them (though they didn't use that word) on the Bartlett thing—probably had some reason to put Bartlett away themselves and were covering for the real killer.

He even thought about that, but not for very long, because while all cops in uniform and out, who carried guns at all, carried .38's, they weren't smooth bores and Ballistics would have spotted it right away.

He looked back in the records over Joe Bartlett's career, and at the family, and it was all one big blank.

Hackett went to see everybody again, and it all sounded just the way it had before. Hackett said, 'I told you so. Walsh, he hasn't had the experience, that's all, and it shook him—only natural.'

Mendoza began to agree. You just didn't run into the kind of thing it would be if it wasn't those juveniles—the fiction-plot thing, the obscure complexity.

Walsh had come to see him on Tuesday, and by Thursday, having taken his closer look at it, Mendoza stopped looking. He saw Walsh again on Friday, and told him it looked like a mare's nest. And after Walsh had thanked him for listening anyway, and gone, he sat there with a couple of day's work in front of him and felt uneasy about it.

He didn't know why. It wasn't a hunch; it wasn't the kids' stubborn denial, although there was a little something there, all right: it had made them feel like big-time pros to have shot that cashier; that one they hadn't tried to deny—of course they couldn't, there were witnesses. And the cashier hadn't died after all: the homicide charge depended entirely on Bartlett.

It wasn't anything he could put a finger on—that made him wonder if he hadn't missed something . . .

After a while he put it forcibly out of his mind and went back to the several cases on hand when Walsh had first come in.

The day after that he happened to drop in at the same restaurant for lunch that Woods and Goldberg had picked. Federico's, where a good many of the headquarters officers habitually went, was closed for redecoration, and this was a hole-in-the-wall place which opened out unexpectedly into several large dining rooms. It wasn't fancy, but the food was good and not too expensive, and there were no jukeboxes or piped-in music: you could eat in peace. Consequently it was crowded, and he wandered through the first two rooms into the third looking for a table. There, at the back, he ran into Goldberg and Woods just sitting down, and joined them principally because the only empty chair was at their table. Lieutenant Goldberg of Burglary and Theft he knew, but Sergeant Woods he didn't. Woods was young for a sergeant, not more than twenty-eight; he looked more like an earnest postgraduate student of something like anthropology. He was tall, thin, and gangling, with a pale face under already thinning dark hair, a rich bass voice, and a very quiet manner.

Goldberg asked how life was treating Mendoza these days, and Mendoza said he couldn't complain. The waiter took their orders and went away, cigarettes were lit, and after a little desultory conversation Goldberg asked suddenly, 'Say, what should you do for a cat that has fleas? Is the stuff for dogs too strong?'

'Fleas? Cats that are properly cared for don't have fleas. Where does she sleep—or he?'

'She, we've still got a kitten we couldn't find a home for. In the garage, at least I fixed a box with an old blanket, but half the time—'

'*Entendido*, there's your trouble, leaving her outside at night to roam all over. Keep her in—I know people think they're nocturnal animals, but when they live with us they keep our hours, you know.'

'Well, I suppose I could bring the box into the service porch.'

'You can, not that it'll do much good,' said Mendoza. 'She'll pick her own bed, and quite likely it'll be yours or one of the kids'. Let her. If you've been feeding her things out of cans, stop it, and get her fresh liver and beef. Wheatgerm oil twice a week, and lots of brushing with a good stiff brush.'

'Look,' said Goldberg, 'I've got a living to earn, I can't spend all that time waiting on a cat, and my wife's got the house and the kids—neither can she. Do you know what beef liver's gone to now? Of course it's an academic question with you. All I asked was about flea powder.'

'And I told you what to do. Let a vet de-flea her now. Fresh meat only, horsemeat'll do, and meanwhile brush half a can of talcum into her every day.'

'Look,' said Goldberg, 'she's only a cat.'

Mendoza put out his cigarette as the waiter came up and said, 'You shouldn't have a cat, Goldberg, you've got the wrong attitude entirely. Cat people say, "*We're* only human beings."'

Woods uttered the deep rumbling laugh that sounded so surprising coming from his weedy-looking frame and said, 'Reason I don't like cats around much—like a lot of people, I think—not that I don't like them exactly, but they make me feel so damned inferior.'

'Isn't it the truth,' agreed Mendoza. 'Yes, if they'd only

admit it, I'm convinced that's the reason some people say they can't stand cats. Now I'm an egotist myself, I admit it, but it certainly hasn't cured me. Right now I've got a cat that's crazy—in a devilish sort of way—and even he makes me feel inferior.'

'Is that so?' said Woods. 'A crazy cat?'

'Possessed of the devil. I intended to keep one of the kittens, but I ended up with this El Señor as well because nobody else would put up with him. He's got no sense at all except for planning deliberate mischief, and that he's very damned smart at. I call him El Señor for convenience—sometimes it's Señor Estúpido, and sometimes Señor Malicioso, and other things. I believe he must have been a witch's familiar in another incarnation. But even when he's being stupid, he can look down his nose at me as superior as the other two.'

'Madame Cara,' said Sergeant Woods, regarding his Beef Stroganov thoughtfully, 'says that the highest point of animal reincarnation is represented by cats, and they're all of them superior human souls on the way—er—up the ladder again.'

'And who in hell is Madame Cara?' Goldberg wanted to know.

Woods grinned. 'This thing I'm on now. That embezzlement. I suppose I should say "alleged," like the papers—I've got no proof he did it, and as far as I can see I never will unless I catch up to him—and it looks as if maybe he borrowed one of the spells and made himself invisible.'

'Oh, that Temple of Mystic Truth thing,' said Goldberg.

'What is mystic about the truth?' asked Mendoza.

'There you've got me, Lieutenant,' said Woods. 'All I know is what it says on the sign out front. Myself, I thought at first it ought to have been handed over to somebody in Rackets, but of course however the Kingmans came by the money it did belong to them—that is, to the—er—church, which is officially incorporated as a nonprofit organisation—'

'Now there's what they call laboured humour,' said Goldberg.

'—And this Twelvetrees hadn't any title to it just as their treasurer. Yes, I thought,' said Woods, looking intellectually amused, 'that I'd learned pretty thoroughly what damned fools people can be, but Madame Cara Kingman and her husband's given me another lesson. Twenty-three hundred bucks, if you'll believe me—one month's take.'

'Good God,' said Goldberg, 'I'm in the wrong business. Just for telling fortunes?'

'Well, it's dressed up some. Quite fancy, in fact—fancy enough to attract people with money and—er—more sophistication than the kind who patronise the gypsy fortune teller at the amusement pier. But nine out of ten people are interested in that sort of thing, you know, it's just a matter of degrees of intelligence.'

'Twelvetrees,' said Mendoza meditatively. 'He absconded with the take?'

'That he did, at least he's gone and the money's gone, and at the same time. Where I couldn't say. I've been looking for six days, and not a smell. Mr Brooke Twelvetrees has pulled the slickest vanishing act since vaudeville died.'

Mendoza laid down his fork. 'Mr Brooke Twelvetrees. Elegant-sounding name. Did it really belong to him, I wonder?'

'Your guess is as good as mine. Sounds almost too good to be true, doesn't it? And sort of gratifying in a way—you know, the biter bit and all that—the Kingmans seem to have trusted him absolutely. Yes, he's done a very nice flit, overnight—left a note for his landlady and not so much as a bag of dirty laundry to provide a clue, and disappeared into the blue.'

'I suppose you've looked at his recent quarters, then—as well as elsewhere. Out on 267th Street.'

Woods stared at him, also laid down his fork, and said, 'How d'you come to know that, Lieutenant? I didn't know

Homicide was interested in Twelvetrees. What—'

It ran a small finger up between Mendoza's shoulder blades, the feeling he'd waited for before in vain. 'Woods—when did he go?' he asked softly.

The sergeant cocked his head at him curiously, and then, as if divining his urgency, answered, terse as an official report. 'A week ago last night. Last seen four in the afternoon by the Kingmans. They came in Monday to lay a charge.'

Mendoza said, '*Donde menos se piensa solta le liebre*—isn't it the truth, things happen unexpectedly . . . Indulge me a minute, Sergeant—he's just vanished, no sign at all of his leaving for anywhere, even in disguise?'

'Not a smell. We've been working our tails off looking. His car was found abandoned down near the Union Station—nothing in it. None of the personnel there could identify his photograph, and he's a man you'd remember if you'd seen him—especially a woman. Nobody remembers him at an airport or a bus station either. Or any of the places he might have gone to buy a disguise—false whiskers or something. If he dyed his hair, he didn't do it with anything he bought at a drugstore near where he lived or near this—er—Temple. Oh, yes, we've looked in all the indicated places, but maybe he's been too smart for us. And now, why?'

'*Aquí está*, wait for it—wait. Now what *is* this, what could it—? What kind of a car—did it have long tailfins that curved up at the ends?'

Woods opened his mouth, shut it, and said, 'Well, no. It's a two-year-old Porsche, an open roadster.'

'You don't tell me,' said Mendoza slowly. 'You *don't* tell me. Now, I wonder . . . A two-year-old Porsche. And twenty-three hundred dollars. That cancels out in a way, doesn't it? Not like a battered ten-year-old heap not worth fifty bucks on a turn-in. And he couldn't retire on twenty-three hundred. Not a very big job, was it?—worth all the trouble of a disguise, covering his tracks so thoroughly—leaving the car—? I mean, surely he could have accumulated a bigger take than that if he'd planned to steal any money at all . . .' What was it in his mind, struggling up to the surface? He sat very still, letting it find its own way out. 'Woods—when and how did you take a look at that place Twelvetrees lived?'

The half-untouched food congealed on their plates. Goldberg went on eating, watching and listening interestedly. 'Mix-up about that,' said Woods. 'We couldn't get the address for a while—the one the Kingmans had was three years old, the place he'd lived when he hooked up with them nearly four years ago. They knew he'd moved, they thought they had the address somewhere but couldn't find it. There'd evidently been no occasion to contact him at home. Thought they had the phone number too, but couldn't find that. That kind of people—or making out they are—unworldly, you know. In the end we got it from one of the—er—members of the sect, the phone number that is, and that was Wednesday morning. When I got the address from the phone company, I went out there, of course—Wednesday afternoon—and I looked it over. Well, I didn't take the floors up, but—'

'You didn't take the floors up,' said Mendoza. 'Maybe you should have done just that, Sergeant. Maybe. That—that perpetual talking machine Mrs Bragg—she didn't follow you around pointing out all the amenities, I take it.'

'I don't,' said Woods, 'encourage people to watch me work, no. I shut the door on her. And just how do you know about Mrs Bragg and 267th Street? What's your interest in Twelvetrees?'

'I don't know that I've got any—yet. But I think you and I and my Sergeant Hackett will go out there right away and take a closer look at a couple of things. I'll explain it to you on the way, it's a funny little story—and I may be seeing ghosts, but it just occurs to me that maybe, just maybe, Mr Twelvetrees is being slandered . . . All that blacktop, so inconvenient. And a trowel. Of all things, a *trowel* . . . *Vaya*, I *must* be seeing ghosts—it's even more far-fetched than what Walsh— But no harm to make sure.'

* * *

They stood in the middle of the little living room, the three of them, at two o'clock that afternoon, and Hackett said, 'You haven't got much to make this add up, Luis.' They had got rid of Mrs Bragg by sheer weight of numbers and official supremacy, but she might well be lurking outside, suspicious of their intentions towards her good furniture and rugs. 'If you're just relying on a hunch, and the damndest far-fetched one I ever knew you to have, at that—'

'Not at all,' said Mendoza. 'Sober deduction from sober fact, it's just that I happened to have a couple of facts Woods didn't have. I admit to you I've had a little funny feeling that something's fishy—it's been growing on me—but the facts are there to be looked at, and very suggestive too. Anybody could add them up. I don't say it's impossible Twelvetrees didn't decide to decamp with a month's take when he could have made it the whole bank account, and we all know from experience that people can disappear without trace. But it's odd he should go to so much trouble for a relatively small amount, when it involved abandoning an expensive car and the promise of more opportunity to come—after all, he'd been with this racket for four years, didn't you say, Woods? Evidently it paid off. Why should he walk out on it just for twenty-three hundred he wasn't entitled to? It isn't reasonable—I know crimes get committed for peanuts, but not by people of this kind.'

'Which,' said Woods, 'did occur to me, Lieutenant, but there's a couple of ways it could have happened. Maybe some skirt was making things hot for him and he had to get out. Maybe he was afraid the Kingmans were going to fire him, or somebody was threatening to tell them the tale on him, and he'd be out anyway—and he figured he might as well take a little something along. Maybe it was just impulse. People aren't always reasonable, in fact I'd say very seldom.'

'I know, I know,' said Mendoza. 'But look at a couple of other things to add up. Why a note to tell Mrs Bragg he was leaving? All he had to do was go six steps from his own front door and tell her in person. She was home that Friday night, we know. He didn't leave in that much of a hurry, not when he took time to pack up all his personal belongings. Why in hell should he thumbtack that note to his front door instead of ringing her doorbell? And if he was in such a hurry, why did he take time out from his packing to do a little desultory gardening on that anaemic-looking Tree of Heaven out there? She says she *had* her nice new trowel about noon that day, she knows, because she used it to pry open a can of paint.'

'A trowel,' said Hackett in exasperation. 'A *trowel*, for God's sake.'

'All right, all right, it won't take long to look!' Mendoza turned and went out to the kitchen. 'I couldn't help remembering it, we get in the habit of noticing things automatically, that's all. Damn it, look—the man had lived here for nearly three years, and if he didn't cook his own meals he made coffee in the morning anyway, he used this table for something sometimes.' He laid a hand on it; it was steady, but when he moved it to any other angle it rocked at a touch. 'How does a table get shoved around out of its usual place? In the process of cleaning the floor, something like that. I doubt if Twelvetrees was that good a housewife. A bachelor living alone, mostly if he doesn't hire it done it doesn't get done—what the hell? But the table was in the wrong place on Wednesday morning—before you got here, Woods—and Mrs Bragg said she hadn't got round a cleaning here yet. And that trowel was over there by the kitchen door. Why?' He shoved the table clear away from the trap door in the floor at this end of the kitchen. It was about two feet by two and a half, the trap, and covered with linoleum like the rest of the floor; only a little dark line round it, and the small flat hinges, betrayed its presence. One of the makeshift arrangements to be found in such jerry-built new rental units, in a climate where jerry-building wasn't always detectable at once. Mendoza reached down and pulled up the trap by its dime-store bolt, which slid back and forth easily. 'Who's going down?'

'Not you, obviously,' said Hackett, 'in that suit. I'll go.'

'You've been gaining weight, I don't think you could make it. All right, it's my idea, I'll do the dirty work.' Mendoza sat down and slid his legs through the opening.

'That's a lie, a hundred and ninety on the nose ever since I left college. Be careful, for God's sake, don't go breaking a leg—hell of a place to haul you out of.'

'Hell of a place to get anything into,' added Woods to that, gloomily.

'He gets these brainstorms,' said Hackett, squatting beside the trap resignedly. 'About once in a hundred times he's right, just by the law of averages, you know, and that convinces him all over again to follow his hunches. *Well?*' he bellowed down the hole, where Mendoza had now vanished.

'*¡No me empuje*—don't push me! I've just got here.' Mendoza's voice was muffled. 'I need a flashlight, hand one down . . . *¡Válgame Dios y un millón demonios!*' That came out as he straightened too abruptly and hit his head on the floor joists. Like most California houses, this sat only a little above a shallow foundation; the space underneath the floor was scarcely four feet high.

Hackett laughed unfeelingly. 'He wants a flashlight—why didn't he think of that before? You got a flashlight, Woods?'

'I seldom carry one in the daytime,' said Woods.

'That's funny, neither do I. Use your lighter!' he advised Mendoza heartlessly.

There followed a period of silence but for the muffled sounds of Mendoza moving around cautiously down there; then another curse and a longer silence. Suddenly Mendoza straightened up through the trap and demanded an implement of some kind. 'Failing the trowel, a soup ladle or something—look in the drawers. The place is furnished, there ought to be tablespoons, a cake server—'

Hackett rummaged and offered him a tablespoon, a hand can opener, and a long wooden fork. '*¿Nada más?* A big help you are,' and Mendoza vanished again with the spoon and fork.

'Does it come on him often?' asked Woods sympathetically, offering Hackett a cigarette.

'Thanks. Five days out of seven he's as sensible as you please. I've thought tranquilisers might help, but on the other hand, just once in a while he does hit pay dirt. I got it figured that it's because essentially he's a gambler—he's in the wrong line, he ought to have been a cardsharp. He calls himself an agnostic, but that's a lie—he's superstitious as hell about his hunches, whether he'd admit it or not.'

'Well, we all have foibles,' said Woods. 'I knew a fellow once who collected paper bags, had a closet full of them. Card player, is he? I kind of fancy myself at bridge, does he go in for it?'

'I think that's a little genteel for Luis, he likes poker. But he won't play for the kind of stakes you and I could stand.'

Mendoza's upper half appeared through the trap; he rested an elbow on the ledge and laid the fork and spoon tidily on the floor. His shoulders had collected a good deal of dust and his tie was crooked, but he looked pleased with himself.

'If you've finished slandering my character, and the phone's still working, *chico*, you can go and call the rest of the boys.'

'Hell and damnation,' said Hackett incredulously. 'You don't mean he *is* down there?'

'Didn't you hear me fall over the suitcases? Give me a hand.' Mendoza hauled himself out of the hole up into the kitchen, and began to brush down his clothes fastidiously. 'You can stop looking for your embezzler, Woods, and hand over what you've got on him to us.'

'Holy angels in heaven,' said Woods mildly. 'No wonder I couldn't find him. How, when, and where exactly, Lieutenant?'

'Not being a doctor and having only the lighter, I'll pass that one. He's not very deep, only six inches or so on top of him, and I just dug away enough to be sure. The hell of a job it must have been to get him there—and of course I'm premature in saying it *is* Mr Twelvetrees, but it's somebody, and in male clothing, I think. And, at a guess, he's been there just about the time Mr Twelvetrees has been missing. About four feet from the trap, say under the door to the living room. And three suitcases alongside him, not buried.'

'I *will* be damned,' said Hackett. 'This one you really got by radar, boy. And I suppose from now on you'll quote it every time anybody laughs at your hunches.' He looked at the gaping black hole of the trap— 'And how the boys are goin' to love that job.' He went to call headquarters for a homicide detail.

CHAPTER FOUR

It was six o'clock before they were finished at the apartment. Mendoza went down again with the surgeon and the men to fix up some kind of light; all of them let out frequent curses, crowded together down there. Woods went down to look at the corpse when its face emerged; he provoked an outburst of profanity on his way up by inadvertently pulling out the wire from the nearest outlet down the trap, and plunging the labourers into darkness. He shoved the plug back in and said to Hackett tersely, 'Twelvetrees, all right.'

Down below, Mendoza could be heard telling someone to keep his clumsy paws to himself, they'd get to the corpse all in good time, but if there was any little something buried with it by accident, he'd like to see it before it got buried again. 'Well, well,' said Hackett. 'It is, is it? How?'

'Surgeon thinks a bang on the head, or several bangs.'

Hackett grunted. They sat smoking, carefully sharing the ashtray out of the Facel-Vega to avoid using anything here, until Marx and Horder climbed out of the hole laboriously with all their equipment and Marx called back down, 'What d'you want up here, Lieutenant?'

'Everything, everything! And don't forget the bottoms of window sills and the tops of doors!'

Marx sighed and shrugged at Horder; they went into the bathroom to start. Mendoza came up and hauled out the suitcases, one by one, as they were handed to him. 'O.K., boys, now we get busy.' He sat down on the davenport and produced a folded envelope. 'Treasure-trove from the grave.'

They looked at the thing he shook out into his palm—a small round pearl-finished button. 'Could've fallen down the trap any time and rolled,' said Hackett dubiously.

'Don't think so. It was about an inch under the surface, in the loose dirt shovelled over him. Couldn't have been there very long, either, by the look of it, even if it just happened to be there when he was covered up. And I think it tells us what we're going to find out anyway—someone was smart enough to wear gloves.'

'Why?'

'It could be off a number of things, this shape and size and colour.' It was flat on top like a stud, not rounded, it had a shank, it was amber-coloured. 'A woman's blouse. A man's sport shirt. A dress, even a skirt, though I'd say it was too small for that. But what I think it came from was a glove—a glove with a button, or buttons, at the wrist.' He put it away carefully. 'Now, the suitcases. They've all been printed outside, and they're clean. Which is very odd indeed, only not in this case, of course.' He laid the first one beside him on the couch, brought out a key ring—'From the corpse, I haven't searched him, except for these, when I found the cases were locked'—and opened it. Clothing, neatly packed: six solid-colour sport shirts, in two layers, on top—just back from the laundry, by the way they were folded and pinned: the kind of shirts that sold for fifteen dollars and up. Two of them monogrammed. Another half-dozen less expensive white dress shirts underneath. A leather case with eighteen or twenty ties neatly folded in it.

Clean socks rolled up in pairs. Shorts and undershirts, almost all of knit nylon. Three pairs of silk pyjamas, all of exotic colours. Two pairs of shoes, on trees and wrapped in paper: one pair tan suede, the other black.

'Thirty bucks at a guess,' said Mendoza, setting them down carefully without touching the shoe trees. Under the tied-down flap of the lid was a leather case containing an electric razor, a manicure set, and a number of jars and bottles, all bearing the same green-and-gold label and, in tortured script, the words *Flamme d'Amour*.

'*¡Qué hombre!*' said Mendoza, removing the top from a bottle of cologne with handkerchief-shielded fingers, and sniffing.

'He wouldn't like himself much right now,' commented Woods.

Another fitted case with hairbrushes and comb. Six belts, tidily rolled up. A flat leather jewel case containing half a dozen pairs of links, tie clasps, a monogrammed sterling buckle.

'Don't,' said Hackett to Woods earnestly, 'ask him for any deductions or we'll be here all night. One of the things he's an expert on is clothes.'

'Nobody needs to be an expert to deduce from all this that he was a man of no taste,' said Mendoza. 'The latest fashion, the expensive, but'—he lifted his lip at the cologne bottle—'Main Street masquerading as Beverly Hills.' He opened the second case, which was of the tall and narrow kind designated a fortnighter; it contained four suits, six pairs of slacks, and four sport coats, all carefully arranged on the hangers, and four more pairs of shoes.

'However,' said Mendoza, 'all this has something to say besides that,' and he looked at the two cases thoughtfully before opening the third.

This was older than the others, of scuffed brown leather instead of plane-weight aluminium; it looked as if it had seen hard usage. When Mendoza lifted the lid, all of them stared in silence, and then Mendoza called Marx and Horder. '*Pronto*, let's see if there's anything on this.'

'Very pretty,' said Woods. 'Never saw one quite like it—looks kind of antique, would you say? But he wasn't shot, was he?'

'It's an old one,' agreed Hackett. 'Look at the length of the barrel. A six- or seven-shot of some kind—open cylinder like one of those old Colt six-shooters, but not quite the same—' They watched the two men from Prints lift it out carefully and set to work.

Mendoza looked at Hackett pleasedly. '*¿Cuanto apuestas*—how much do you bet it's a smooth bore?' he asked happily.

Hackett fingered his jaw. 'Walsh's business. You want to hook it up to this. I don't know that I'd lay any bets, Luis, but I can't see any connection offhand.'

'Can't you? Well, it's all up in the air yet, nothing solid, but I can see a couple of little things to build a plot on, you know—stories to tell ourselves about it.'

'You don't suppose that any surgeon's going to be able to say, this man died at eight o'clock P.M. on Friday the thirtieth? After all this time? What are you trying to make out—that Bartlett saw this murder done and just forgot to mention it to Walsh, and the killer followed them and an hour and a half later shot Bartlett? I used to like fairy tales, about thirty years back, but they don't thrill me any more.'

'*Tengo paciencia*, I'm not filling in that plot yet—we'll just file it for reference. But I'll say this about the Bartlett business. Here we've got a homicide that isn't fresh enough so the surgeon can say within a day or a day and a half when it started to be a homicide. Isn't it a little helpful that we've got this other thing nailed down as to time? Coincidences do happen, but this is just the least little bit suggestive, or it could be. We can't operate on the arbitrary premise that these two things must be hooked up, but let's keep it in mind, because if they are, we've got a much narrower time limit for the corpse than the autopsy could possibly give us. And now let's look at the rest of this.' He turned back to the third suitcase.

The top layer here consisted of soiled shirts,

handkerchiefs, underwear, and socks, crowded in haphazardly; several ties in need of cleaning, also crumpled together and shoved into a side pocket; clean handchiefs, rumpled out of their folds and stuffed into every crevice; two pairs of soiled pyjamas and a clean pair crushed in together; a pair of leather slippers. In the bottom was a dressing-gown of scarlet silk moire; it had been neatly folded.

'Yes,' said Mendoza, feeling delicately in the pockets of the robe and coming up with another soiled handkerchief and nothing else. 'Yes. It all says a little something, doesn't it? What elementary deduction occurs to you, Art?'

'That Woods hasn't been slandering Mr Twelvetrees,' said Hackett absently. 'Or at least, if he wasn't planning any embezzlement, he *was* planning to leave. With all his *lares* and *penates*. Because—'

Mendoza said parenthetically to Woods, 'Speaking of foibles, you notice he forgets his favourite role now and then—the big dumb cop. You catch him off guard, he can actually pronounce three-syllable words.'

'*Estése quieto*, I'm deducing,' said Hackett. 'He didn't do all that packing in fifteen minutes, and the way he's been so careful to sort and fold everything all neat and tidy, it was him did it. He expected to be using all this stuff for some time to come, it represents quite an investment. It looks as if he'd been packing, he'd got almost everything in, except the stack of clean handkerchiefs and all his dirty laundry, and at that point something happened to put him in the hell of a hurry all of a sudden. He just shoved everything else in, cramming it down any old way—'

'Or somebody did it for him,' said Mendoza. 'You may get to be a lieutenant someday after all. Yes. You know, I think somebody finished his packing for him. Because from the state of the other cases, he was a finicky customer. Like me. We can't help it, it's an automatic thing, like—like cats washing themselves. I don't, maybe, go quite so far as this one did with his flame-of-love cologne and his nail buffer and his—*vaya por Dios*, are these bath salts?—but I'm enough like that myself to guess at the kind of thing he'd do or not do. And however much of a hurry this one was in, I think he'd have put all that soiled laundry into a bag for packing. I think he'd have had that bag handy, laid out ready for when he wanted it, and so he wouldn't have had to waste time getting it and skipped it for that reason . . . I wonder what happened to it, that bag. It wasn't in the bedroom on Wednesday morning . . .'

'Let's look,' said Hackett, 'for clues that might exist, friend, not ones we dream up ourselves, hah?'

Marx said from the other side of the room, 'The gun's clean, Lieutenant. Not a thing on it anywhere.'

'Yes, of course,' said Mendoza. 'I don't know why we bother to take you boys out on a job at all any more. Even those six-year-old shoplifters Juvenile's getting these days know about fingerprints.' He got up and wandered into the bedroom. 'A large stout paper bag,' he murmured to himself, 'or a bag made for the purpose—a cotton laundry bag, with a slit in it, or drawstrings. You see them at dime stores, with stamped patterns for embroidering.' He lay down prone and looked under the bed. 'My grandmother has one, a hideous thing, with a design of hollyhocks on it. Red and orange. And *Laundry* spelled out underneath.' He went into the closet.

'I get the general idea,' said Hackett patiently. 'But there are things called hampers too.'

'Not here.' Mendoza came out of the closet looking dissatisfied. 'The bathroom isn't big enough.'

'You were just saying a while ago that bachelors living alone don't pay much attention to these things. Now you want to make out—and it's a piddling little thing anyway, what does it matter?'

'It may not matter a damn, I'd just like to know. You miss the point. It's a personal thing. You take me, I wouldn't notice about the kitchen floor needing waxing or the mirrors needing to be washed, it's only me and my personal things that have to be just so—and he was like that, by his clothes and packing . . . What do *you* do with soiled laundry?'

'I've got a drawer for it. Easiest thing. Logical thing. Probably he did too.'

'No. Not here. Not enough drawers, with all the stuff he had.' Mendoza gestured at the one bureau. 'And *not* logical, but slipshod, that is. You ought to get married, be taken care of properly.'

'Give advice, never take it,' said Hackett.

'But that's just it, *I* don't need a wife for that, which is the only reason to acquire one in the long view. I'm much more particular at looking after myself than most women, and I can afford to hire the housekeeping done. *Caray*, dirty clothes in a drawer, I'm surprised at you.' He looked in all the drawers; Marx and Horder had left them liberally covered with grey powder, and a number of nice prints had showed up: with very little doubt they would prove to belong to the dead man, or Mrs Bragg. All the drawers were empty except for sheets of clean newspaper. 'I take it,' he said to Woods, 'that Mrs Bragg hadn't got round to cleaning in here between my visit and yours, and that you hadn't let her in since?'

'This is all very interesting,' said Woods, sitting down on the bed and looking more like an earnest postgraduate than ever. 'You've got Twelvetrees down pat, Lieutenant, by what I've got on him. The Kingmans and a couple of other people—members of that, er, sect—they all say he was a sharp dresser and finicky about himself. One woman said to me, and it kind of stuck in my mind as an apt description, you know—this Miss Webster it was, the only one I've talked to who didn't like him—she said he was like a big black tomcat preening himself . . . And that's right as far as I know, about Mrs Bragg. I told her on Wednesday afternoon not to touch anything here. But it didn't seem important enough to put a seal on the door. Matter of fact, of course, there wasn't anything here really useful to me, I just wanted to keep it open a day or so, maybe have a closer look. But it's her property and she's got a key, I couldn't say whether she's been in or not.'

'Yes. A paper bag she might have taken away—we'll ask.

But I don't think an ordinary laundry bag.'

'What does it matter?'

Mendoza stood in the middle of the room, hands in pockets, and stared vaguely at the maroon flowers in the rug. 'Well,' he said, 'well—it might just be—yes, I can see it happening—that somebody wanted to carry away something—and for some reason wanted something to carry it in. Like that. Because it was, say, a lot of little somethings awkward to carry unwrapped—or revealing somehow—or because the somebody didn't have any pockets to carry it in. Or a handbag big enough. And there was the bag ready to hand . . . A big black tomcat, you said, Woods? Tomcat that way as well as this?'

'Oh, well, I wouldn't say definitely. Myself, I think he'd have liked people to think so, and that's about the extent of it. You've seen his picture?' Woods hauled out the photograph again and handed it to Hackett. It had been blown up from a not-very-good snapshot and was a little fuzzy, but the subject had distinctive enough features that that didn't matter. On the back were noted his vital statistics. Brooke Twelvetrees, if that was his real name, had been just a little too handsome, with fair skin, blue eyes, wavy black hair, a strongly cleft chin, a consciously winning smile showing even white teeth: five-nine, a hundred and sixty, age estimated as thirty-two or thereabouts. 'Quite the ladies' man, *in* that sense only. I'd say.'

Mendoza looked over Hackett's shoulder and laughed. 'Oh, yes, I see. The arm-patter and door-holder—not necessarily the bed-jumper. These collar ads, usually not much else to them but front. And the same goes, of course, for the female of the species. They get by so easily on their looks, no reason for them to develop in other directions. So let's hear something about the Temple set-up.'

'I wouldn't like to say whether it's a planned racket,' said Woods. 'Maybe the Kingmans are seriously sold on this Mystic Truth business. I didn't pay much notice to the ins and outs of it, but this Madame Cara—er—missionises at everybody, and I gather it takes in a little bit of everything, from astrology to something called Pyramidology. I went and saw Arnhelm in Rackets, but he's got no record of complaints, they've kept within the law. It's been a going concern for about five years, and it started on capital given to the Kingmans—outright gift—by half a dozen wealthy people, all of whom are still members of the sect. That—' He paused as the preparations for bringing up the body reached a climax. The ambulance men tramped in with their basket; Dr Bainbridge hoisted his tubby middle-aged self out of the trap with some difficulty. Dwyer and Landers below heaved the body up to reaching hands, head first; it was an awkward thing to handle in that space, but they got it into the basket at last and took it out in a hurry. The burial and the clothes had helped, but it had still been dead a week or so.

As they went out, the men inside heard a long pleasurable sound from the little crowd gathered. A couple of men were questioning the other tenants, those who were home, and a number of the neighbours had drifted over to watch.

Dr Bainbridge sat down on the other end of the couch, wiped his brow, and lit a large black cigar. 'Next time, Luis, let's make it in a more accessible place, shall we?'

'Not my idea. What have you got to give me right now?'

'Not a great deal. Don't know that I can tell you much more after an autopsy, except odds and ends like what he had for his last meal. Though the body's very well preserved. He was killed by a blow on the head, several blows were struck and it may have been just one that did for him or a combination of all of them. Blows were struck from the front and side, the left side—his, that is. Nearest I can say as to time of death is between five and seven days. Say between a week ago yesterday and last Sunday.'

'Could he have died round about seven-thirty that Friday night?'

'Certainly. Or the next night. Or ten o'clock Sunday morning. You pays your money and you takes your choice.'

Dwyer, who'd gone back down the hole, emerged again with a lidless carton and presented it to Mendoza. 'Contents of the pockets. I labelled 'em for you.'

'Ah,' said Mendoza, but he didn't look at them immediately. 'Tell me, Bainbridge, just to reinforce my own opinion—about getting him down there, would it have taken great strength? Could a woman have done it?'

'Oh, well, you *have* presumably heard of the law of gravity,' said the surgeon. 'Always easier to get a thing down than up. If he was put down there more or less at once after death, when he was still limp, it wouldn't have been much of a chore, no—question of dragging him to the trap and sliding him through. And anybody can dig away enough dirt, even with a trowel, to cover a body as thinly as he was covered. It'd take a little time, and it's an awkward place to work—especially without light—though the kitchen light would have penetrated down the trap some, of course. But it'd just be a matter of patience and care. Certainly, a healthy woman could have done it.'

'Mmh, my own idea. Apologies to interrupt you, Woods, just go on talking while I look at this.' Mendoza regarded the little collection interestedly.

'. . . That,' Woods calmly picked up where he'd left off, 'hadn't really a thing to do with Twelvetrees and the money, I just had a look because I was curious. But anyway, you can say that this Mystic Truth is a profitable business, because evidently it's attracted people with more money than sense, whether the Kingmans planned it that way or not. Judging from the fact that an average month's gross was twenty-three hundred bucks. Twelvetrees and this old Miss Webster—I say old, but she's sharp as they come—even if she did fall for the Mystic Truth—were the only—er—officers of the Temple aside from the Kingmans. Have some fancy titles for themselves I don't recall offhand.'

Left trouser pocket, where the keys had been, forty-eight cents in change, a half-used packet of matches from some place called the Voodoo Club on La Cienega. Right trouser pocket, a slightly soiled handkerchief, a small automatic pencil, and a cigarette case, a handsome affair of rolled gold plate, alternating bands of dull Florentine finish with bright modern: it had a lighter in the top, and on the inner left side was a line of engraving in script: *Brooke, affectionately, Mona*. It was half full of Pall Malls.

'. . . Miss Webster, who I gather is fairly well off, doesn't take any salary for whatever she does—she volunteered that herself—but Twelvetrees was getting five hundred per for whatever he did, which seems to have been banking the take every week. Miss Webster wasn't at all surprised that he should run away with money that didn't belong to him. She never trusted him, a young man out for what he could get if you asked her, and not particular how he got it.'

Breast pocket: clean handkerchief. Inside coat pocket: used handkerchief, wallet. Mendoza looked at both thoughtfully. And nothing in the other pockets except another handkerchief in the shirt.

'The—er—church property is owned outright—former store building way out on Wilshire. They've fixed it up some, and no makeshift do-it-yourself job either. The Kingmans live on the premises, there's a second storey done up as an apartment—I didn't see that. The whole business is incorporated, as I say, and the Kingmans take a very comfortable living out of the net. They bank at the Security on Western. As of right now there's $14,840 in the term savings account, and a little over $7000 in the checking account. All four officers had access to the accounts, as representatives of the Temple.'

Dr Bainbridge sniffed loudly. 'Most successful con game ever put over on the human race, organised religion. Infallible. You'd think we'd have seen through it in a quarter of a million years or so, but most people never seem to.'

'*¡Me lo cuenta a mí*—you're telling me!' said Mendoza. 'And essentially as crude a con game as the old pigeon drop, too.' But he said it absently; he picked up the wallet and began to go through it.

'Twelvetrees,' said Woods, 'became a convert to the sect about four years ago, in its early days. He'd then just landed here from some place back East, the Kingmans aren't sure exactly where, and was trying to break into the movies, without much success. Everybody liked him—except old Miss Webster—in fact he ingratiated himself so well that within a couple of months he was appointed treasurer at this comfortable salary, so he quit his job as a clerk in a men's store to devote all his time to the Temple.'

'From rags to riches,' said Mendoza. 'Country boy makes good. Only he wasn't a country boy. Not when he habitually carried his wallet in his inside breast pocket.'

'Did he?' said Hackett, interested. 'Yes, that's the smart place—I do myself, so do you—but a lot of men don't, even city livers. He'd been around some, to do that.'

'I went,' said Woods, 'to the place he'd been working, to see if I could get a line on where he was from, references he might have given, and so on. But it's a small shop, not a chain, and they don't keep such records that long. The manager remembered vaguely that Twelvetrees said he was from some place in New England. The studio agency he'd put himself on file with didn't have anything on that at all, all they were interested in was his physique and experience. For what it's worth, Twelvetrees had had a little vocal training and played the piano. He'd stayed on the agency's books, and got a little extra work now and then. And that's just about all I can give you.'

'And a few possible helpful points there, thanks very much.' Mendoza had all the contents of the wallet spread out before him. Not too many contents, compared with the usual clutter a man accumulates in this substitute for a woman's bag. Everything had been fingerprinted, and the only prints were the dead man's, at first glance. Two fives, a ten, three single bills. Driver's licence; and that lacked the optional thumbprint. Nothing too odd about that, of course: some people still connected fingerprinting solely with criminal records, and refused to give the D.M.V. a print. Social Security card. In the plastic slots, two snapshots, one of himself with a blonde woman, the other of a dark woman alone.

The blonde was very blonde, very Hollywoodish in a strapless gown. Brooke Twelvetrees was conscious of the camera, smiling his white winning smile, head tilted to show off the cleft chin and the wave in his dark hair. That was an interior shot, by flash, and showed the pair of them sitting at a table; Mendoza deduced one of those cheap night-club photographers. The woman in the other picture, a bad snapshot taken on a beach somewhere, was dark, slender, consciously posed.

Mendoza looked at the second picture longer than the other, but finally put them both back into the wallet and everything back into the carton. 'Yes. Well, if you think of anything else, hand it on.'

'Oh, certainly,' said Woods. 'I'm only too pleased to be rid of this one, Lieutenant—we were getting nowhere fast, and I've got a couple of other things to get busy on. Not that I won't be interested in what you find out.'

Hackett sighed and said gloomily, 'We're not exactly casting around for something to keep us occupied either. I don't know why the hell you had to look in your crystal ball and find this one, Luis. There he was, peacefully moldering away, doing no harm to anybody. And now you've dug him up, *I've* got a hunch he's going to be a tough one to untangle.'

'Maybe—and maybe not,' said Mendoza.

CHAPTER FIVE

It was almost eight o'clock when he ended his block's walk from the nearest parking space and looked up at the sign over the door. Quite a modest sign, and unlighted. This wasn't the most glamorous stretch of Wilshire, but it *was*

Wilshire, valuable business property; the building taken over by the Temple of Mystic Truth looked as if it might have started life as a small furniture showroom, or as duplex shops. It had been remodelled, and presented a rough fieldstone front with the entrance at one side, severely modern. A small board beside the front door, discreetly lighted from below, bore the legend:

Sabbath Celebration, Renascence of Atman
Weekly Saturdays 8 P.M.
Novitiates 10-4 Tuesdays and Fridays
Ceremony of the Constellations, 3 P.M. Wednesdays
Ceremony of the Inner Chamber, 8 P.M. Fridays

'Vaya, vaya,' said Mendoza to himself, and went in. There was a very small brick-floored foyer, and double doors standing open at the right let him into a large, darkish place which must comprise nearly the whole ground floor. It was half chapel and half theatre—very appropriate, he thought: padded folding chairs in rows like theatre seats; a carved wooden fence round what was probably meant for an altar, pulpit, proscenium, or what-have-you; niches in the walls for statuettes—he noticed an Egyptian ibis, the inevitable horned bull, a goddess crescent-crowned in white alabaster.

No usher or attendant: he sat down in the last row. There was a fair crowd already gathered, perhaps sixty or eighty people, and in the next five minutes a dozen more came in. He remained the lone occupant of the last row; everyone else settled as near the altar as possible.

There was just enough light from the lobby and a couple of wall fixtures along each side that he had a fairly good look at the late arrivals; among them he was gratified to spot the Hollywood blonde of the snapshot. She was, in fact, the last comer, and he had the feeling that in better light and a different place it would have been quite an entrance. She glided past him, erect and confident, in something dark that rustled and showed a good deal of white throat, the shining blonde hair, to advantage: and she trailed behind her an invisible cloud of spicy, heavy scent.

Mendoza inhaled thoughtfully and said to himself, '*Flamme d'Amour*, female species?' Something like chypre, anyway. Very interesting, but she would keep . . . A number of the congregation seemed to know her; she seated herself amid subdued rustlings and whispers of greeting.

Almost immediately the ceremony began. He paid little attention to it beyond remarking that it was handsomely staged. Impossible to gather much about the Kingmans at this distance: thin, ethereal Madame Cara, in a Grecian robe, and Kingman, looking distinctly odd with his naked bald head rising out of a voluminous black cassock. Several other people similarly clad took part. There was an elaborate ritual of procession about the altar; there was a tall gilt chalice, and an invocation pronounced by Madame Cara; there was chanted response from the congregation. There was mention of the great All-Parent, the cycles of the gods, the perfect circle of the four trinocracies, and the lesson of the Great Pyramid.

Mendoza sat back and thought about Brooke Twelvetrees, what they had on him so far, what they had on that Friday night, and about Joe Bartlett.

He couldn't help thinking about Bartlett, at least: he didn't like ragged edges to things, and it would be so much neater if Bartlett and Twelvetrees *were* hooked up somehow. But as he'd said to Hackett, they couldn't proceed on the arbitrary premise that Twelvetrees had been killed that Friday night—it was just something to keep in mind.

Mrs Bragg indignantly denied that she had removed anything from the apartment, even a paper bag. She had been *in* it, of course: finding the note announcing Twelvetrees' departure, she had checked the supply of linen and dishes, and had placed an ad in the *Times*, first appearing on Monday, which had brought several prospective tenants to look at the place before Woods had showed up. There had been no bag of any kind left—so she said.

The note, of course, had been thrown away with the trash on Monday. She could not recall the exact wording, but remembered that it apologised for his sudden leaving, gave only a vague reason of 'important business.' As it happened, of course, to be the end of the month, he was paid up to date; having paid the customary two months' deposit when he came in, he was in fact due a rebate, and she had assumed that she would receive an address from him later on to send it to. She hadn't seen his signature or writing before—he always paid the rent in cash—and consequently she could offer no opinion as to whether the note was a forgery.

She had first noticed the note, neatly tacked in its envelope to the outside of Twelvetrees' door, late on Sunday morning as she left for church. It might have just been put there, or it might have been there for two days—she couldn't say: she hadn't set foot out of her own place since Friday night, having been trying to come down with flu and warding it off with rest and various potions. And as her door and Twelvetrees' were in the rear building, and no other tenant had had occasion to call on her those two days, there was no evidence on when the note had been tacked to Twelvetrees' door.

The apartments, of course, shared a party wall, and she admitted that loud noises were audible through it now and then, but remembered nothing of that sort on that Friday night. 'Of course, with them Johnstones kicking up a row again, and I was over there to Number Three twice before I called the police, well, you can see there might've been something going on in Mr Twelvetrees' place I just didn't hear.' Of course, of course. And Saturday, nothing; Sunday morning, nothing.

His key had been enclosed in the envelope with the note, and she had naturally handled it, not that it was likely to have borne any helpful print. The same could be said of the bolt on the trap, which Mendoza himself had handled.

All the prints in the place belonged to her or to Twelvetrees; but a few places where one might expect to find prints had been polished clean, which was neither very helpful nor interesting—the table in the kitchen, the top of the bureau, the bedroom chair. If that said anything, it said that whoever had cleaned those places probably had not visited the apartment for long (or often), if those had been the only things touched.

The trowel, she said, was kept in a box sitting on the small bench inside her carport, along with a few other tools. She didn't think any of the other tenants were likely to know that: they hadn't any occasion. It was account of Mr Twelvetrees taking interest the way he had in her Tree of Heaven that *he* knew.

Ballistics would, Mendoza hoped, tell him something about that gun in time.

All those handkerchiefs . . .

The alcoholic Johnstones admitted frankly that they remembered little about that Friday night, and were suffering hangovers all day Saturday. Sober, they were very sorry they'd disturbed everyone. None of the other tenants who'd been home could recall anything helpful at all: nobody remembered whether or not there had been a light showing in Twelvetrees' apartment, or whether his car had been in his carport, either on Friday night or any other . . .

The congregation gabbled a long response to a cue from the altar, and Mendoza muttered profanely to himself. The car—damn it, he should have thought of that before. Phone in and get an inquiry started right away. Because Twelvetrees' Porsche must have been taken away immediately afterwards; whoever had finished arranging his planned departure could not know that Mrs Bragg wouldn't be out and about, that somebody else wouldn't notice the car unaccountably still there after he had supposedly left. The car had been abandoned near the Union Station, and that was quite a trip from 267th Street. Unless there were two people involved, it must have meant that someone had to take a taxi back to 267th, or thereabouts, to pick up his or her own car. The question of public transportation didn't enter in: he doubted very much that there was any out there, after six or seven o'clock, and in any case it would be infinitely slow. No problem at all if there were two people in the business, of course.

There was also that snapshot. That dark girl, something teasingly familiar about her. Leave it at the back of his mind, it would come to him eventually . . .

And that seemed to be the last outburst from the congregation; the robed figures had vanished from the altar, and—ah, of course—now came the important part of the whole business, the attendants passing down the aisles with little velvet bags, taking up the collection. Not much audible jingling of hard money; there wouldn't be, by the sum missing from Twelvetrees' keeping.

Missing?

And, *Dios mio*, of course, what had happened to the bankbooks?

The attendants missed him there in the last row; the congregation began to drift out. He let it go past him until the hall was empty, and wandered out after it. What was probably a nucleus of—could one call them?—charter members was gathered in the little lobby around the Kingmans. The blonde; a scrawny old woman in rusty black; a buxom hennaed female with a foolishly loose mouth and a mink stole; a scholarly-looking middle-aged man, others more nondescript.

Mendoza leaned on the wall and lit a cigarette, watching and listening—principally to the Kingmans. He was interested in the Kingmans. He didn't listen long: the lobby was too small for anyone to go unnoticed, and he began to collect curious glances. So he detached himself from the wall, went up to them, introduced himself, and asked for a private word with them.

'Dear *me!*' exclaimed Cara Kingman, opening her eyes very wide on him. 'A policeman! What *can* we have done?' He put her down as nearing fifty. She was so thin she looked haggard; her fair hair in its thick coronet of braids had only lost colour, not turned grey. She had very pale china-blue eyes, and wore, apparently, no cosmetics: she was a ghost-figure head to foot, colourless, still in her white robe bound with a velvet rope at the waist. Round her neck dangled a long silver chain with a medallion, and her long fingernails were enamelled silver.

'About Mr Twelvetrees . . .' said Mendoza gently.

'*Ah*—poor Brooke,' she said deeply, lowering her eyes. 'Of course, of course. For a moment I had forgotten—do forgive me. One must put all these worldly matters aside during the Renascence. Martin—' She turned to her husband gracefully.

'We must put ourselves at your service, sir,' said Martin Kingman gravely. He had a fine rich baritone, eminently suited to public speaking; Mendoza had noted it during the ritual. He conveyed a kind of ultimate respectability, of upper-middle-class conventionality, which must be worth a great deal in this business. He looked like a reliable family lawyer or doctor: bald, a little paunchy, very neat in a navy blue suit—he had removed his cassock—a white shirt, a sober tie. He had intelligent brown eyes behind rimless glasses. 'Anything we can do to help you, of course, Lieutenant. My dear, we'll ask these good people to excuse us—'

A general murmur, curious glances at Mendoza; they began to drift away politely.

'*Dear* Madame Cara,'—the buxom lass—'such a dreadful disappointment for you—we must all *concentrate* on forgetting it—'

'So unworldly, so trusting,'—the scrawny old lady—'There's such a thing as too *much* faith, Martin. Indeed!' Snapping black eyes darted toward Mendoza; she didn't seem to think much of him. Evidently the watch-word on Twelvetrees was forgive-and-forget, and also don't-mention; they muttered goodnights as embarrassedly as if he had brought up something obscene.

The blonde touched cheekbones with Madame Cara,

delicately. 'We must try to remember only the good, isn't that so, dear?'

'The only charitable thing, dear Mona. Now do come and see me for a cosy little private chat, *soon*.'

'Won't you come up to our quarters, Lieutenant?' invited Kingman. 'Quite a draught here, and we must think of my wife's health, she takes cold so easily. Now I don't recall meeting you before, do I? There was a very polite young man—er—Wilson, Williams, Woods—that was it—'

'Yes, the case has been handed on to me.' Mona. That was nice to know, he thought.

'Oh, I—er—see. If you'll just step this way, the elevator—' Yes, money had been spent here . . .

'Dead?' exclaimed Kingman. '*Dead*—Brooke?' He sounded incredulous; his rich voice trembled with all the proper emotion. 'And in such a way— But then, how we have maligned him!' He sat back in his chair, whisked out a handkerchief, and blew his nose loudly. 'This is dreadful news, dreadful.'

'My very thought, Martin,' said Cara Kingman mournfully. 'We found it hard to believe,' her pale eyes turned on Mendoza, 'that dear Brooke would do anything dishonest—and to steal from the Temple treasury, of all dishonourable things. I said at once—you remember, Martin—there is *some* other explanation, which will be revealed to us in time.'

'And you were right, as you so often are. I fear it was my more—um—worldly suspicion, Lieutenant Mendoza, which prompted me to issue the charge. You understand, we had trusted Brooke absolutely, but when he so unaccountably—um—absented himself from the Sabbath service, and a check with the bank on Monday informed us that he had not deposited the collection . . . Really, to my mind it seemed foregone, incredible as it appeared. But now—'

'Ah, the *money*,' said his wife. She shut her large, light eyes with the effect of switching off headlights. 'The *money*—quite unimportant—we must only *share* the awful responsibility, Martin, that it was because he had the money that he was killed in this terrible way. Some violent, greedy person—a young, *young* soul—knowing he had the money, breaking in, and dear Brooke struggling with him to protect the Temple's property—' She shuddered delicately.

'Well, you know, we don't think it happened quite like that,' said Mendoza. 'A casual thief would scarcely take the trouble of burying him.'

She gave no sign that she heard, lying back on the couch, robe trailing, graceful. A comfortable living indeed they took out of this: it could almost be called a luxurious apartment, with its wall-to-wall carpeting, furniture not from a bargain basement, everything the latest and best. And entirely impersonal. Mendoza deduced a decorator service from one of the better department stores, and nothing added to the decorators' choice. He did not feel somehow that, left to herself, Cara Kingman would choose to live with beige tweed carpet, champagne-coloured curtains, eighteenth-century-reproduction mahogany, and parchment lampshades.

'But how else could it have happened?' wondered Kingman. 'Ah, now I think, of course I see the fallacy—you men trained to reason acutely about such things, I daresay the notion of a thief never occurred to you, but I confess I should have accepted that solution at once, myself. How *else*? I assure you, I find it inconceivable that anyone who *knew* the boy—'

'That's what we'll find out. I understand you saw Mr Twelvetrees for the last time at about four o'clock on the afternoon of Friday the thirtieth?'

'Ah—that's correct,' said Kingman. 'I—we, my wife and I, had just finished conducting the—um—afternoon class for novitiates. We came out of the sanctuary—ah, that is what you would call the chapel, where our services are held—we have a very modest establishment here, you see, there is only a small robing room besides on the ground floor—together, on our way to the elevator, and met Brooke just leaving. He had been working on the Temple accounts in the robing room, which also serves us as an office.'

'I see. What conversation did you have with him?'

'Why, none—none at all, Lieutenant. It was quite casual. I believe I said something like, "Finished for the day, my boy?" and he replied that he was. He was—um—just going out as my wife and I entered the elevator.'

'If I had *known*,' she said, opening her eyes again, 'that it would be the last time I should see him—on *this* plane, of course! But my mind was still with our dear novitiates, and I daresay that prevented any presentiment I may have had.'

'My wife,' said Kingman, adjusting his glasses with a precise gesture, 'is a gifted psychic, you see.'

'But one *cannot* control these things, and I never pretend to do so. That is why I have given up such childish efforts as the *séance*. It is all so false, so forced. One must only *accept*, as it comes. Doubtless it was not intended that I should receive warning, or I should naturally have told Brooke to be on his guard against the forces of evil. Destiny . . .' She lifted a hand, let it fall limply.

'As it was, you exchanged no words with him at all, Mrs Kingman?'

'None—none. I was tired, I went straight into the elevator. But tell us, Lieutenant, what explanation can there be, if it was not a thief? As my husband says, no one who knew Brooke could have wished to harm him.'

'It is,' said Mendoza, who was rather enjoying himself, 'a little early in the investigation to make any guesses.'

'Ah, yes, one would want to be *sure*.' She sat up and widened her eyes fully on him. 'Now do tell me, Lieutenant Mendoza, what is your birth date?'

'February twenty-eighth.'

'Ah, Pisces—of course,' she murmured. 'I should have guessed it, I feel from you that nuance of understanding. You have great sympathy for people, great insight—but you must always guard against trusting your emotional judgment too much—don't you find that? All you Pisceans, *so* prone to being sadly misunderstood by those less acute of mind. And that fatal pride, so apt only to add to others' misunderstanding of you—a sad handicap—*however*, undoubtedly you find your native Piscean intuition for people most useful in your work.'

'My dear, we must not take up the lieutenant's time, when he is—um—occupied on this sad matter so near our hearts. If you would tell us, sir, what else we might do to help you—'

'I would like a list,' said Mendoza, 'of your members here.'

'Oh dear, oh dear,' said Kingman, removing his glasses and beginning to polish them vigorously, 'surely you cannot be thinking that any of these good people, our little flock—? But it's not my place to question, of course. I can easily supply you with that, if you'll accompany me down to our office— No, no, my dear, you must not stir, all this has tired you, you must rest.'

'One must *not* give in,' she said bravely. 'Anything we can do to help you at any time—please do not *hesitate* to ask. But if you will forgive me now, I do feel quite exhausted—'

'My wife,' said Kingman as they stepped into the elevator, 'is a very sensitive woman—very sensitive. She is an Aquarian herself, of course.'

Mendoza let himself into his apartment at an early hour by his usual routine. Bast, the russet-brown Abyssinian, and her five-month-old daughter Nefertite who had taken after the Abyssinian side of the family and was also russet-coloured with black trimmings, came to meet him with shrill welcome. He switched on all the lights and began to look about automatically to see what mischief the unpredictable El Señor had got into in his absence.

The magazine rack was still upright, but quite empty, and all the magazines were spread out on the floor with the morning paper neatly on top of them.

'Now how in the name of all devils does he *do* these things?' Mendoza wondered. He was beyond asking himself why. He looked further, and located El Señor gazing coldly down at him from the top of the kitchen door. El Señor was also five months old, but twice the size of his sister; he had inherited his father's Siamese points in reverse, like the wrong side of a negative, and was nearly black all over except for blond eyebrows, paws, nose, and tail-tip. He had large almond-shaped green eyes. 'Señor Misterioso!' said Mendoza. 'Do you grow hands when my back is turned?' He began to pick up the magazines.

El Señor leaped gracefully down to the narrow mantel from the door, and abruptly became Señor Estúpido; he lost his balance, blundered into the electric clock and knocked it flat, and began trying to climb the wall.

'I put up with you only for your mother's sake,' Mendoza told him. He plucked him off the mantel and let all the cats out, went to the kitchen and cut up fresh liver pending their return, and made coffee. He carried a cup with him into the bedroom; with his tie off and shirt half-buttoned he paused to study those snapshots in Twelvetrees' wallet again.

That girl. What *was* it that made her familiar?

Studio agency. Twelvetrees had ambitions towards a screen career. He had done work as an extra, he had met other such people. This girl, maybe. Have I seen her in a film? wondered Mendoza. But he never went to film theatres. He never watched TV.

He shook his head and went on undressing. He had a bath, and all the while that vague familiarity teased at his mind. He got into a robe and went back to the kitchen for more coffee. He let the cats in and fed them.

Damn it. She stood there on an anonymous beach, in a white bathing suit, shoulder-length dark hair tossed in the wind—features too indistinct to identify individually, but something indefinable in the stance, the frozen gesture . . .

He finished the coffee and washed the pot and cup.

It was like a hangnail, he thought, he couldn't leave it alone. He—

Hangnail. Hands. Manicure.

'*¡Por todos angeles negros y demonios de Satanás!*' he exclaimed aloud. Of course, of course. He must be getting old.

Marian Marner . . .

CHAPTER SIX

'. . . A special kind of model,' he said to Hackett the next morning, 'it was only her hands they used. You know, for soap advertisements, hand lotion, wedding rings, and so on. But that was nearly twelve years ago, whether she's still in that job is anybody's guess. I'll have a look at the agencies. And the damn funny thing is, I don't even remember where she lived—not that she'd likely still be in the same place, of course. And I didn't, I will say, know her very long. But it's odd how the mind operates sometimes.'

'I wouldn't say odd in your case that you mislaid one little wild oat out of the field of them you've sown,' said Hackett.

'True. You know the only other thing I remember about her at all is that she had a funny-shaped appendix scar, with a little hook at one end.'

'Now that's real helpful,' said Hackett. 'We'll just camp out on the beach until some day she comes by in a Bikini and we can identify her. I think the agencies are a better idea. I don't suppose she'll be much use when we find her.'

'*¿Por que no?*'

'Oh, well, I was just thinking of the snapshots—not what you'd call really good portraits, but the best is that one of him with this blonde. If he was really much interested in this Marner girl, he'd have provided himself with a better picture, wouldn't he? This thing'—Hackett looked at it again—'it might be any woman with dark hair.'

'Something in that, sure. I'll have a look around for her

anyway, and we'll see. I wanted to go after this blonde myself—'

'*¡Como no*—naturally, naturally!' said Hackett.

'—But I also want to see Arnhelm and get whatever he may have on this Mystic Truth and the Kingmans, as well as following up Marian Marner—and I think I'll let you handle the blonde. You might see this Miss Webster too. The blonde'—Mendoza consulted the list of members Kingman had given him—'is one Mona Ferne, at least I deduce she's the one, the only Mona on the list. Whether Miss or Mrs it doesn't say. She lives out in West Hollywood, here's the address.'

'O.K.' Hackett stared at it absently. 'Mona Ferne. That rings a faint bell in my mind—'

'Don't tell me this is one of *your* wild oats intruding on the same case. Coincidence has a long arm, but—'

'My past is pure as a virgin's dreams—compared to yours, anyway. No. It's—Mona Ferne, now what does it say to me?—up in lights, sure, there was a star by that name a while back. Quite a while back it'd be, I seem to remember I was just a kid when . . . Wouldn't be the same, I shouldn't think, not young enough for this one.'

'Well, go and find out.'

'I'm going, I'm going. Enjoy yourself with your old girl friend if you find her.'

The address, when Hackett found it on one of the older residential streets out west of La Brea, proved to be a single house. This was a neighbourhood of solid money, twenty-thousand-a-year-and-up class: the houses were bigger than most California houses, many of two storeys. This was one of them. It tried to look like the traditional Southern mansion: it was white, it had pillars, but on a city lot there was space only for a strip of lawn, and the enormous blue spruce in the front yard dwarfed it, towering the height of the house again above the roof, and probably darkening all the front rooms. The wrong tree, as it was the wrong house, for a city lot.

But plenty of parking space. He parked and walked up the path indicated by sunken steppingstones to the low brick porch. The woman who opened the door to him was obviously a domestic; her only association with this house would be strictly the dollar-and-a-half-an-hour kind. She was middle-aged, plain, neat, and dowdy, with a mouth like a steel trap.

'Miss—or is it Mrs?—Ferne,' said Hackett. 'I'd like to—'

'*Miss* Ferne, and she's not here, but she don't buy at the door.'

'I'm not selling anything.' He produced his credentials. A detective sergeant of police made no more favourable impression on her than a salesman; she looked down her nose at him.

'Miss Ferne ain't got nothing to do with the police. If it's a traffic ticket—'

'Detectives,' said Hackett, 'don't have anything to do with that part of the business. I happen to be from Homicide, and it's important that I see Miss Ferne. When will she be home?'

The maid retreated a step. '*Murder*, you mean—'

'Well, that's not the legal definition but it'll do in this case.'

'Miss Ferne couldn't have nothing to do with a murder—'

'We all have opinions. When will she be home?'

'I couldn't say,' snapped the maid. 'I guess you better see Miss Carstairs.' She retreated farther in tacit invitation and shouted, 'Oh, Miss *Angel*!'

Hackett went into the entry hall. He was right: the tree made all these rooms so dark that you'd want the lights on even at noon, to avoid the furniture. The several open doors off the hall looked like entrances to caves. Only the open front door shed any light here, on a polished parquet floor, a couple of fussy little pedestal side tables bearing knickknacks, a grandfather's clock, a carpeted stairway.

'Well, what is it *now*?'

'The police,' said the maid succinctly.

Hackett couldn't place the girl coming down the stair. No

housekeeper or secretary or—were there still such things as governesses?—would hold her job a day looking like that. She looked about twenty-five, and she didn't have bad features but she hadn't done anything about herself at all, for a long time. Lank brown hair was pinned back carelessly to straggle, overlong, past her shoulders; she wore no make-up, even lipstick was missing; she had on a drooping black skirt too long for her and an ancient darned grey sweater too large, no stockings, and flat-heeled brown shoes.

'Oh,' she said. She stopped at the foot of the stair and looked at him, neither surprised nor much interested, apparently, by her flat tone.

'*Homicide,*' said the maid. 'He wants to see your—Miss Ferne.'

'Has she killed somebody?' asked the girl. 'That'd be a little change, and very nice too, if they put her in jail.'

'You oughta be *ashamed*,' said the maid viciously. 'A nicer, kinder, sweeter woman I never—and *you*—'

The girl said detachedly, 'You're hired as a maid, Winter, not a nursemaid. I'll talk to the policeman.' She jerked her head at him. 'You can come in here.'

It was, when she switched on the lights, a big, stiffly formal, cold sitting room. She threw herself into a chair and told him ungraciously to sit down. 'What do you want to see Mona about?'

'A murder, Miss Carstairs. Someone she knew has been murdered, and we'd just like to hear a few little things, like when Miss Ferne last saw him and so on.'

'She's just left, what a pity—she'll enjoy *that* like anything.' Evidently she wasn't interested in who had been murdered. 'A man hanging on her every word—even a policeman. Heaven knows when she'll be home, she's gone to see her agent. I suppose you could find her there if it's all that urgent—Stanley Horwitz, two doors from the Cha-Cha Club on the Strip. She'd be *delighted* to be chased down.'

Hackett watched her curiously. 'Thanks very much, I

may do that.' She was thin enough, even a little too thin: she might have a nice figure under that sloppy outfit. It wasn't the deliberate sloppiness some girls affected, thinking they achieved the casual air: it was just carelessness. Uncaringness. 'You haven't asked who's been murdered.'

'Well, I know it wasn't Mona, more's the pity, and if it was one of her friends, it's not likely to make any difference to me.'

'It was a gentleman by the name of Brooke Twelvetrees.'

She sat up from her ungraceful slouch and stared. 'Brooke? Who on earth would want to murder *him*? He's not—not *important* enough.'

'Somebody evidently thought he was.'

'Funny,' she said. 'And you have to go round asking questions to find out who and why. What a dull job. But I suppose you're used to it. Do they pay you much for sorting through other people's dirty laundry?'

Hackett didn't often get mad, and he was used to overlooking insults from people he questioned, but unaccountably he felt his temper beginning to slide with this girl. 'It's a living,' he said shortly.

'And gives you that *nice* feeling of power, I suppose, you can b-bully witnesses and beat up gangsters whenever you pl—'

'Oh, for God's sake!' said Hackett angrily, and then stopped. Belatedly it came to him that she hardly knew what she was saying: she was caught up in some violent emotional maelstrom, and he'd just walked into the middle of it. She was trembling convulsively; now she sprang up, crushing both fists against her mouth, turning her back on him.

'Here,' he said, anger dropping away from him, 'what's the matter?'

She just stood there shaking. He went up and laid a hand on her shoulder. She was taller than he'd thought; unlike most women, she'd reach above his shoulder if she straightened up. But too thin.

'Look, don't do that,' he said helplessly. 'You'll go working yourself up into hysterics in a minute, and that prune-faced maid'll think I'm murdering you.'

She gave an involuntary, half-tearful giggle. 'I'm s-sorry. Just a minute. I'll be—all right—in a minute.' She groped blindly for a handkerchief, blew her nose; after a minute she turned around and sat down again. 'I'm sorry,' she said more steadily. 'I've been saying horrible things, I didn't mean— Not your fault . . . You'd better try Mr Horwitz's office if you want Mona, and if she's not there I think she was going to the Fox and Hounds for lunch.'

She sat stiff and upright on the edge of the chair and said it like a child reciting a lesson. A child with nobody to see her hair was combed and her face washed and her nails scrubbed. Hackett was curious and oddly irritated: what was wrong with her? She wouldn't be bad-looking at all if she'd fix herself up a little. She had a small straight nose, nice teeth, a clear pale complexion; her eyes were good hazel-brown with black lashes, and if she was tall for a woman she wasn't all that outsize. And she sat there looking like hell, like some female in one of those funny sects where they thought coloured clothes and short hair and lipstick were engines of Satan—worse, because those people did comb their hair and wash their hands. Her nails were like a child's, short and unpainted, and her hands weren't very clean, and that straight limp hair falling stringily down her back . . . And the maid had called her Miss Angel. Angel, my God, what a name, and for this one.

He got up and said, 'Thanks very much, I'll see if I can find her there.'

She went to the door with him. 'I'll give you a little tip,' she said, and her flat voice was metallic. 'You just start out by telling her you remember all her pictures and think she's the greatest actress since Bernhardt, and she'll fall over herself to oblige you.'

'I thought I remembered the name—Mona Ferne—she's the same one who used to be in pictures, then?'

'Oh, goodness, don't say *that* to her. Used to be. She's

just taking a little rest between jobs, according to her. A little twenty-year rest.' In the merciless light, from the open door, of pewter-grey cold daylight, she looked awful: she looked grey and cold as the sky, and her eyes were too bright, too expressionless on him. 'She'll like you, she likes big men. What's your name? . . . Oh, yes, that'll be all right too, a nice American-sounding name. Now I look at you, you look quite nice, because I like big men too. I've got to, haven't I, being so big and clumsy myself, but it's rather an academic question, of course, because it doesn't work the opposite way—nobody ever looks twice at me, no reason. Will you do me a little favour, Sergeant Hackett?'

The little fixed smile on her colourless mouth was somehow terrible. He said carefully, 'Well, now, that depends on what it is, Miss Carstairs.' Something very wrong here.

'Oh, it's nothing difficult. Just, when you *do* locate Mona, and talk to her, or should I say listen to her, I'd like you to remember that she's my mother, and I'm twenty-six years old, and she was thirty-four when I was born—it was fashionable to have a baby that year, you see. Will you do that?'

'Yes, I'll do that.'

'Thank you very much,' she said. 'I'm sorry I said nasty things to you, before. Goodbye.' She still wore the fixed smile when she shut the door after him.

Hackett got out a cigarette and lit it, and was surprised to find that his hand was shaking. That one, he said to himself, is just about ready for the men in white coats. But it didn't pass through his mind academically or cynically. And as a cop he'd seen a lot of trouble and grief and evil and lunacy, and he'd learned to shut off much feeling about it because that got you nowhere—you'd just tear yourself to pieces over it and accomplish nothing. But right now he felt something, he couldn't help it, about that girl—he felt so damned sorry for her he could have wept—and that surprised him all over again.

* * *

'I just had the feeling,' said Mendoza, 'that Mr Martin Kingman is a little too smooth and slippery to be entirely unacquainted with the law. Of course there's a very thin line there, I admit it—that kind is always very smooth. The same essential type, it goes in for politics and the church and show business, as well as legally dishonest jobs, and you've got to separate the sheep from the goats . . . But it was all very pat, rather like a pair of professional gamblers sitting in with a pigeon, you know—I had the distinct feeling there was a cold deck rung in.'

'Not surprising,' said Lieutenant Arnhelm, and sighed. He looked like someone's jolly and indulgent grandfather, bald, round, and amiable, but in reality was a bachelor and a complete cynic. 'They get that way. After all, it's six of one, half dozen of another whether they keep inside the letter of the law or not—it's still a racket. It's still a front they're putting up, and it gets to be like a seasoned vaudeville act, the automatic routine.'

'I wish you could give me something else on them.'

'I've got just so many men and there are still only twenty-four hours in a day,' said Arnhelm. 'We can't go looking every place there's a possibility of fraud. Keeps us busy enough investigating complaints. Sure, we keep a little list, just on the chance we'll be looking into this or that some day—another fortune teller takes out a county permit, another funny cult gets set up, we file what information shows up on the applications and so on—but that's as far as it goes, unless somebody comes in with a complaint.'

'Yes, and what are the odds on the information being false? It's like income tax returns, you can't check them all. I know those applications for permits, those affidavits—*Have you ever served a prison-term, Have you ever been known by another name*, and so on. Like asking when you stopped beating your wife. Nobody in his right mind is going to put down *Yes*, and give chapter and verse, but so long as he scratches in *No* with a post office pen and signs any name that occurs to him, it gets duly approved.'

'I tell you,' said Arnhelm, 'you go out and recruit the force about five thousand more men, nice bright boys with superior I.Q.'s, and we might begin to do things the really efficient way. Check up on every single application for every kind of permit, among other things.'

'All right, all right, I know the problem. And at that, those recruits would do more good walking beats the old-fashioned way—and five thousand just a drop in the bucket for that job, in this town.'

Arnhelm agreed gloomily. 'And the point is here, what's the difference? It's a way to milk the public, sure. So is any business, in the long view, except that some businesses sell things the public needs. Mostly it's things they just think they need, which is what's called human nature. You've got to gull the public in *some* way to sell anything, but the law draws a line as to how bad you can gull them. As long as people like the Kingmans keep inside the line, we can't go poking our noses into their private racket, any more than we can into the cosmetic business, or the automobile factories, for instance. And if we did it wouldn't do any good, they'd just find more pigeons. People are such damn fools. Why d'you think women go on buying some new brand of face powder? Because the ads say it'll make them look younger. Why do men go on buying hair restorer? Because they're damn fools. We can't cure that situation.'

'All true, but it doesn't stop me wishing you had something more on the Kingmans,' said Mendoza. 'However, thanks very much for the lecture.' He started back to his own office thinking about the little he'd got from Arnhelm. The Kingmans, according to the affidavits they'd supplied in the process of incorporating the Temple, hailed from Philadelphia, where Kingman had been in the hardware business. He was fifty-nine, she was fifty-one. References consisted of the people here who had supplied capital for establishing the sect. And that was just about the sum total of usable information.

Sergeant Thoms, who sat at Sergeant Lake's desk on Lake's days off, was still patiently working his way through the phone-book list of model agencies. He shook his head silently at Mendoza.

The autopsy report wasn't in yet. Ballistics was silent on the gun. Mendoza went out for coffee, and at the drugstore counter found Goldberg sneezing violently into Kleenex over a half-eaten sandwich.

'The very man I wanted to see,' and he climbed onto the adjoining stool. Goldberg emerged from the Kleenex long enough to say that it was supposed to be his day off but something had come up.

'Whad cad I do for you?'

'Allergies,' said Mendoza. 'Everybody talks about them but when it comes down to it I don't seem to know much about them, except that they hit you different places. What are the symptoms?'

'Are you kidding?' said Goldberg. The paroxysm over, he put the Kleenex away. 'We could sit here until tomorrow while I told you. Almost anything. Me, I've read all the books and spent a lot of money on specialists, and I've come to the conclusion that nobody knows anything about it for sure. They can tell you what you've got—sometimes—and sometimes what to do about it, but by the time you've got one allergy cleared up you've developed another one. What are *your* symptoms?'

'I haven't got any. What I want to know is this. If you find somebody using about three times as many handkerchiefs as the normal person, used handkerchiefs stashed away in every pocket, isn't it likely to be a symptom of an allergy? That's the way it takes most people?'

'That it does,' said Goldberg. 'Some people have hives too, and some people itch, and various other things, but you can say that practically anybody with allergies is going to have, to start with, the nasal drip and the stuffed-up sinuses, and so he's going to be using a lot of handkerchiefs. Or Kleenex. Why?'

'Yes, I thought so. My latest corpse did, I think. I wonder if he was going to an allergy specialist.'

'If he was crazy or a millionaire, he was,' said Goldberg.

'Don't they say it's psychosomatic?'

'Listen, damn it, you say it if you want a good punch in the nose—go on, say it's all emotional. That's what they tell you when they mean they don't know and can't do anything else for you. So I'm allergic to about forty things, see, like whiskey and cat hair and the glue on postage stamps; all right, so I get hay-fever when I haven't been near any one of the things I'm allergic to, so what do they say? They say, well, well, Saul my boy, you must have grown another allergy, maybe your wife's nail polish, we'll find out—but if I haven't got the ten or twenty or thirty bucks for more tests, *then* they say, it's psychosomatic, maybe you'd better see a head doctor. Passing the buck. The hell with them.'

'I see. I suppose I can get a list of specialists from the Chamber of Commerce or somewhere.'

'And I wish you joy of them,' said Goldberg, beginning to sneeze again.

When Mendoza got back to his office Sergeant Thoms had finished calling the agencies, without result. 'But being it's Sunday, I couldn't get hold of only about half of them, sir, and at most of those places it was an emergency number, not their office, and they couldn't say for sure without checking records. We're to check back tomorrow on those.'

'Damn Sunday,' said Mendoza. 'I suppose none of the doctors' offices would be open either.' It would, of course, be easier to check with someone who had known Twelvetrees: always providing they told him the truth. But there couldn't be much in it . . . 'When Frank Walsh comes, shoot him in.' He had called Slaney to borrow Walsh for more questioning. He went into his office and called the Temple, got Kingman, and asked him if Twelvetrees had had an allergy problem. Why, yes, so he had. Was he going to a specialist? Yes, Kingman thought so, but couldn't tell him which one definitely—it had been a doctor on Fairfax Avenue, he remembered that, and the name was something like Grass or Glass.

Mendoza thanked him and had recourse to the phone

book; and there was a Dr Graas on Fairfax Avenue. Child's play, and what did it mean? Very likely nothing. Nevertheless, he'd ask. Just on the chance that there was something.

He called Alison. 'Would you like to visit a place called the Voodoo Club tonight? I'll pick you up about eight. Preferably in that amber silk thing.'

'I can't say the prospect thrills me. Of the Voodoo Club, that is. You know I don't like night clubs—neither do you—why this sudden passion to be conventional?'

'I just want to take a look at it, it may be mixed up in a case.'

'That doesn't reassure me,' said Alison. 'The first time I went out with you it was the same sort of thing, a place you just wanted to look at, and it ended in our getting shot at and my ruining a brand-new pair of stockings.'

'*Mi carina bella*, not that sort of thing at all. I hope. I'll take good care of you. Eight o'clock.'

'Oh, damn,' she said suddenly in his ear. 'No, that's not for you, but that devilish kitten you insisted on giving me—Sheba, no!—I've been painting the view out the bedroom window, and she's got into the rose madder—Sheba, get down, *not* on the bed, darling—' The receiver crashed in his ear and Mendoza laughed.

Sergeant Thoms put his head in the door and said Walsh was here. 'Fine,' said Mendoza, 'bring him in and go get some coffee for all of us.'

CHAPTER SEVEN

'No, you're not lucky to catch me exactly,' said Mr Stanley Horwitz. 'I keep legit show business schedule—dark on Mondays—fancy of mine. Usually get a lot done on Sundays too, but it's been slow lately . . . So you want to know something about Mona Ferne? I could write a book.

Homicide—has she killed somebody?'

Hackett said he shouldn't think so but you never knew.

'Pity,' said Mr Horwitz. 'Offer you a drink? . . . You boys don't *have* to be so damn moral about rules, you just do it to annoy. No pleasure drinking alone—but I will.' He got out a bottle of Scotch, flicked down the lever on his intercom, said, 'Milly, I'm busy for the next half hour or so, if that nance who thinks he's America's answer to Sir Laurence Olivier comes in, he can wait. And wait.' Mr Horwitz, who was edging sixty, five-feet-four in his elevator shoes, and possessed a shock of curly grey hair, poured himself a drink and slid down comfortably in his upholstered desk-chair. 'I wish you'd have a drink, Sergeant. Nice to see somebody approximately normal in here, for a change.'

'Don't you usually?'

'Dear God, these people,' said Horwitz. 'These *people*. Nobody, Sergeant, nobody at all is mixed up in show business to start with—or wants to be—unless he, she, or it has an exhibitionist complex. Just in the nature of things they're all egotistic as hell, and that's *right* where you can get into the hell of a lot of trouble with them, because they're so very damn smooth in covering that up, you know? You got to keep it in mind every minute, that they're just front. It gets tiresome.' He swallowed half of the drink. 'And maybe you better keep it in mind about me, because God knows I don't suppose I'd be in this rat race of a business if I wasn't a little bit like them. Just a little bit. Right now, of course, they're all busy overcompensating for the granddaddy of all inferiority complexes, and that makes 'em a little quieter than usual.'

'How's that?' asked Hackett.

Horwitz eyed him in faint surprise over the glass. 'You grow up in this town?'

'Pasadena,' said Hackett.

'Don't you notice what's going on? Time was they *were* this town—this was the capital of honky-tonk, the Mecca for all faithful pilgrims who never missed the change of show at the Bijou. Time was, all the money in this town, the real money, was theirs—show-business money. Everything important that happened here was show-business kind of important. Sure, the legit folk back on Broadway kept their noses in the air, but, brother, when one of 'em got the nod from Goldwyn or De Mille, he came a-runnin'—and for why? The folding stuff, the long green. Oh, this was quite a town in those days, Sergeant. And them days is gone forever. The real money behind this town now, why, all the studios together never used or made money like that—they're just a drop in the bucket of capital now, since the aircraft and missile plants moved in, all kinds of business, and since all this irrigation made us, what is it, second highest in agricultural production of the nation? *They're* just peanuts now, and tell the truth, I figure the people in this town've got fed up with 'em too. It's time. Not surprising. You don't have to know one of 'em personally very long before you find out what they're like—personally—and I guess it just took a little longer for the public to learn, living in proximity as you might say. The gimmick doesn't work any more, not the way it did. The old glamour's dead. They don't get in the headlines—even local—any more, for losing a diamond necklace or marrying a European aristocrat. The gossip columns about the stars are shoved into the second section and a back page at that—there's too much interesting news about Cape Canaveral and the new government contracts at Lockheed and Douglas and what big companies are moving out here with all their personnel, building ten-million-dollar offices and so on. Too many vice-presidents and union officials riding around in Rolls Royces, too many of their wives in sable coats leading French poodles—*and* losing diamond necklaces at the opera—nothing to exclaim about any more, nothing to mark them as royalty, way they used to be. See? Notice how quiet they act these days, trying to pretend they're just like other people, plain down-to-earth folks. That's one of the symptoms. And, brother, how they hate the whole business! How scared and indignant they are, and *how* loud they deny it's happened!' Mr Horwitz retired into his glass.

'They do, hm? I can see how that'd be. Never thought much about it before.'

'You're not in the business—and for that you can thank God. Oh, yes, they're wearing a chip on the shoulder all right—can't do this to *us*, you know?—and at the same time trying to pretend nothing's happened at all, that it's still their town . . . But you were asking about Mona. Case in point. One of the worst ones. I don't mind gossiping about Mona Ferne, if you've got time to listen—'

'I've got time.'

'—And I got the feeling,' said Horwitz dreamily, 'I might do just that even if you were somebody from TV thinking of hiring her—because she annoyed the hell out of me just before you came in, and that was just once too often she did. To start with, in case you're curious, her real name was Minnie Lundgren, and she came from some place in South Dakota. Won some sort of piddling beauty contest back there, and right away made tracks for Hollywood—read "Mecca"—to join the royal family . . . You remember any of her pictures?'

'Hardly. I think I was about three when she was in her heyday as a star. I wasn't noticing females much yet. But I've seen her in bit parts, later on, when I was just a kid. Just vaguely remember the name.'

'You didn't miss an awful lot,' said Horwitz. 'She never could act—she took direction, that's all. They built her up, like they built up a lot of others who didn't really have much on the ball. And you've got to remember that comparatively speaking it's a new medium—anyway it still was thirty-five years back—and fashions in these things, they change like other fashions. She was a star, sure, they made her one. And don't you forget either, Sergeant, that's just the end of one long road, and she nor nobody else gets there, usually, without the cold guts to kick anybody in the teeth who gets in their way. You married? . . . Well, when you come to get married, take my advice and don't pick a beautiful woman *or* an actress. The two don't always coincide. Point is, anybody naturally good-looking, they're awful apt to be—what's the head doctors' word? —narcissistic. Me, me, me, twenty-four hours a day. And some of it's other people's fault, building 'em up all the time, you know?—because they got looks. Which is damn silly, because they hadn't a thing to do with it, didn't have to lift a finger, just came that way. You take Mona. She lands here with a short-term contract—part of the take from the beauty contest, a publicity gimmick—they did that in those days. Nine out of ten cases, the girl'd turn out to be about as photogenic as I am, and they'd just let the option drop. But Mona was one of the ones with the guts and the drive to push herself and keep on pushing until she got where she wanted to go. Because she figured it was just her due. And she had a little *something* usable, in those days, you know. She could take direction, like I say, and she had the kind of looks that were popular, right then. Baby-faced blonde. They gave her dancing lessons and singing lessons and so on, and the big build-up—latest discovery—and she went down pretty good at the box office for awhile. She did a couple of Class A Westerns to start—just to break her in—not second-feature stuff, the historical kind where the brave pioneer lassie helps the hero fight Indians out of a covered wagon, you know—and then she did some light dramatic stuff . . . But it's the damndest thing, how things change. There was a picture Fox made, not more than fifteen years back, I thought it was the greatest—and last week I saw it's being rerun at a neighbourhood house, so I dropped in to see it again—and I'll be damned if it wasn't *the* hammiest piece of schmaltz I'd ever sat through. Just shows you. I got a sneaking hunch if Davy Garrick and Edwin Booth and some of those other great legits came back today, we'd laugh 'em off the stage. Fashions change, like I say. Along about twenty-five years back, the public fancy for women like Mona took a drop. In the middle of a depression, whether that was the reason or not, baby-faced blondes began to sort of pall, and so did the kind of pictures she'd always made. Sentimental light stuff, you know—sure, the public always *goes* for it—there's never a time you can't sell corn—but it depends on how it's done, and Mona's style was just getting obsolete. She made a couple of flops, and then they put her in four-five Class B things to run as second features, and about that she got mad and walked out on her contract. Of course she said to me—and anybody else who'd listen—it was all the studio's fault, if they'd give her a decent part and decent support they wouldn't have laid those eggs. Fact was, like I say, she'd just stopped being box-office. She never had much to offer besides looks, and when the fashion came in for smart sophisticated gals in tailored suits, Mona just wasn't in the running. If you get what I mean.'

'I get you. Husbands and/or?'

'If I had to guess,' said Horwitz, 'and I'd have to—I've been strictly her business agent, God help me, for thirty-three years, since I've been in the business—I'd say no and/or's. I just told you these people are all front, and all me-me-me. They can look sexy as hell, but they very seldom really are, because they're so busy admiring themselves and thinking how to get something else they want, they've got no time or room for any other feelings. Sure, she was married. Twice. Number One was Bobby Ryan—he'd been a kid star and was trying for the gold ring again about that time, but he didn't make it—and when he naturally got jealous of her because she did, they split. Number Two was Bill Carstairs, who was in the production end—how long that'd have lasted I couldn't say. Bill was a nice fellow and fairly smart, he might have seen through her in the end, only he got himself killed in a plane crash before that happened.'

'There's a daughter,' said Hackett.

'Oh, you know that? God, that *creep* of a girl,' said Horwitz. 'Sure, so maybe it's Mona's fault, I don't suppose she was ever much of a mother to the kid, but the kid's over twenty-one, she could do *something*, you'd think. Would you believe it, there was a time Mona wanted to get her in pictures. Pestered the life out of me. That was about the time she did her last stint. *I* couldn't do anything for her—Mona, I mean—when she started slipping. I was damn pleased to get her options taken up, and then it was out of my hands, if they gave her sweet mothers or spinster aunts or a walk-on as a clerk or something, what could *I* do about it? She lost her last contract nearly twenty years ago, and nobody'll touch her now. For one thing, she's got nothing to offer, like I say—she looks pretty good across a room, she's had her face lifted and so on, she fights damned hard, I'll give her that—but you see her any closer, you can tell it's the hell of a long time since she played ingenues. And she can't do character stuff, never could and never will. And for another thing, she's never stopped acting like a star, thinking of herself as one of the royalty, you know?—*and* a star who can throw her weight around any way she pleases, and never get slapped on the wrist for it because she's valuable property. And that's the story on Mona Ferne. She comes in here a couple of times a week—I can't stop her—what am I doing for her, when can she expect a new contract?—good God in heaven, I've given it to her straight enough times, but it just doesn't penetrate. Hear her talk, you'd think she'd had a couple of pictures gross a million in the last six months, and it's just a little legal fuss with the studio leaves her without a contract. Every once in a while she threatens to get another agent, and I wish to God she'd try, but she never will—she knows damn well, if she'd admit it, nobody else would ever put her on the books.'

'I suppose she's living on what she used to make—investments?'

'Mostly, I *think*, on Carstairs' money—she spent most of hers as it came in. Maybe he'd begun to see through her at that, he'd tied it up in trust—in two trusts actually, one for the girl. They'd only been married a couple of years, the kid was just a baby, when he crashed. Sure, Mona's got plenty to get along on, but that's not enough for her.'

'She is,' said Hackett, 'a member of a funny cult called

the Temple of Mystic Truth. Know anything about that?'

Horwitz shook his head and shrugged. 'Can't say I want to. This town used to have a reputation for that kind of thing too, and when you come to think of it, it's natural. You take these people—they're people without roots, you know?—and most of 'em are suckers for that kind of thing. Especially, you might say, as they get older. They feel a lack somewhere, they look around for something solid, for an answer, and because they're the kind of people they are, the orthodox doesn't attract them.'

'Yes, I can see that. She'd been going around some with this fellow who got knocked off, Brooke Twelvetrees.'

'Oh, *that* one, was it? And that's why you're interested. I remember *him*. She brought him in, pestered me to take him on. Well, you never know where you'll find something good, I looked him over. He had looks, the kind a lot of women go for, but don't get me wrong when I say, like I did about Mona, that's the first and only thing. It's important, but you and I could both name a dozen top stars without much in the way of looks. Mona and some like her, both sexes, got to the top on looks alone, but that doesn't hold you there. It's a thing there's no word for—showmanship, I guess that comes closest to it. Nothing to do with talent. I can name you people'—he did so—'who've been on top for years, without having anything but a lot of gall, *and* showmanship. It was that, even a little bit of it, this Twelvetrees didn't have. The personality didn't project, he couldn't've held an audience with the doors locked and safety belts to fasten 'em down. I said nothing doing, and Mona was mad as hell . . . No, that was the only time I ever met him, it'd be about two years ago . . . I heard later Meyer and Hanks took him on, don't know if or where they'd got him anything.'

'Well, thanks. Where's that outfit?' Hackett took down the address. 'You don't think there'd have been anything serious about their going around together? Just as an opinion.'

Horwitz laughed. 'Because Twelvetrees was maybe twenty-five years younger? Look, you don't need to be a psychiatrist to read these people. One of the damndest awful things about them is that they never get past a certain stage in life. They're kind of fixed at the mental age where parties and clothes and boy friends and girl friends, and all the—the froth, you know, is all that's important in life. It can have sad results. You take anybody fifty-five, sixty years old, even if he's got good health, nothing chronic, he's glad to let down once in a while, take things easier, stay home Saturday night and read a book. He's got a long way past being interested in kids' things—he's got to other things just as much fun. He's found out he doesn't have to be twenty-five years old and handsome as a movie star to get a kick out of making love to his wife, and she doesn't have to be Marilyn Monroe. He doesn't—you know—have to keep up a front. These people, the front's all they've ever had, and it's the most important thing in the world to them—they can't *let* themselves let down, ever. The front of perpetual youth. In looks and every other way. I tell you, once in a while I find myself in a night club or somewhere like that, not by choice but on business, and I don't know any sadder sight. These people like Mona, hell-bent on having a good time the same way the twenty-five-year-old kids are having a good time. Out of the fronts of things—good looks and clothes and going to parties . . . Mona and this Twelvetrees? She always has a man in tow, to be seen with. Whatever she can pick up. She's got to. By the only rules she knows, if she didn't have something in pants to be seen with at the good-time places, it'd mean she was dead—as a female. And there are, in this town, enough men like her that she can always find one. But of course she'd always prefer one like Twelvetrees, to the ones her own age working just as hard as she is, with their toupées and expensive false teeth and corsets. Shows she's still an attractive, *vital* female—that's a word they like—to pick up a young man. You want my opinion, well, Twelvetrees was one of these people too, and he probably took up with Mona thinking she could do him some good in the way of contacts. Or just maybe because she paid the bills at the good time places. I wouldn't say she'd gone down quite as far as that, to pay a fancy man to squire her around, but maybe—and there are nuances in these things, even with people like Mona.'

'So there are,' agreed Hackett. 'Well, thanks very much for your help. Don't know that any of it's much use to us right now, but you never know—and anyway it's interesting to get the inside view on them.'

'You find it interesting?' said Mr. Horwitz sadly. 'Seems funny to think I ever did. These goddamned awful people . . . like reading the same page in a book over and over. Someday I got to get out of this business . . .'

Walsh didn't know yet why Mendoza was asking him about that D.-and-D. call; he was doing his best to be helpful, but it had been such a routine thing . . .

'I don't want to prompt you. But just visualise it in your mind—a big blacktopped area with apartments on two sides and across the rear. The one where the drunks were was Number Three, that's in the front of the second building on the right as you drive in. It was about seven-thirty, and it was raining. It was the landlady called in, and she was waiting for you—'

'Funny little fat lady in a man's raincoat,' said Walsh suddenly. 'Yeah, I got it, Lieutenant. We pulled up where she was, I guess it'd be in front of her place, she was waiting there on the porch, I remember that—and we both got kind of wet going across to the drunks' apartment—left the car where it was, see, it was just a step really but it was coming down pretty steady then.'

'Yes, go on.'

'Well—I don't know just what you want, sir. There wasn't anything *to* it. It's funny how just the sight of the uniform'll quiet 'em down sometimes. There was this big bruiser of a fellow and a little blonde woman, going at it hammer and tongs—you could hear 'em half a block away, the landlady needn't've come out to tell us where. Soon as Joe knocked and said who we were, they stopped and the man let us in. We talked to 'em a few minutes, you know the sort of thing: hadn't they better quiet down, have some consideration for the neighbours, and that's all it took really.' He stuck again there, and was prodded on. 'Well, let's see—Joe gave me the nod, I knew what he meant, and I went out to the car to report in. See, Joe figured, and I guess he knew from experience—he was a good cop, Lieutenant, the best for my money—'

'I know he was.'

'—He always said, about a deal like that, where they aren't really slum people who just naturally distrust cops, that you don't have to go acting tough, and a lot of times they'll listen to a good stiff talk from a man in uniform where they'd just get mad with somebody like the landlady or the neighbours. That's what he meant, see. We could see they wouldn't make any more disturbance, and so like I say I went back to the car to report in, and Joe stayed to talk to 'em, so maybe they'd think twice the next time.'

'Yes. And then?'

'Well—that's all,' said Walsh blankly. 'I sat in the car and waited for Joe, and pretty soon he came out—with the landlady—she'd stayed in the drunks' apartment with him—and she thanked us and we got back on our route again.'

Mendoza made a few marks on paper, shoved the page across the desk. 'Look, here's the set-up, let's get it clear. The apartments numbered Five and Six are in the building across the end of this court. The landlady lives in Number Six. Numbers Three and Four are in this second building from the street, at right angles to that. Show me where your squad car was in relation.'

Walsh hesitated, finally pointed. 'I'd say just about in front of this rear building, I mean not in front of either of the apartment doors there but sort of in between them.'

'Damn it, I don't want to force this,' said Mendoza softly, 'if there *is* anything . . . When you both got out of the car, you went straight across to Number Three? Bartlett was with you?'

'Why, sure, of course.' Walsh stared.

'He was in Number Three how long?'

'I guess about fifteen, twenty minutes—no, say eighteen. Altogether.'

'You'd gone back to the car and reported in what it had turned out to be. How long did you sit there waiting for him?'

'About ten minutes, I guess. I remember I smoked a cigarette, it was just about finished when Joe came. I don't get what this is about, Lieutenant, it was just a routine—'

'Yes. Now when Bartlett came out of Number Three, did he come straight across to the car?'

'Yes, sir—at least, I'd think so. Wouldn't have any reason to do anything else, would he? I guess if you pinned me down I couldn't say I *know* he did, because I had my back to that side of the court, you know—he just came up and got in and said, "O.K., Frank, let's go." The landlady came up behind him, with that funny raincoat over her head, and hopped up on her front porch and yelled "Thanks" at us and—well, that was that.'

Mendoza sighed. 'And if Bartlett didn't come straight from Number Three to the squad car, the landlady would know . . .' He could ask, but he had the feeling this was a dead end. Call it what, a minute, two minutes, for Bartlett to have seen something, heard something?' *'¡Qué va!'* he muttered to himself vexedly. 'Can you think of anything else at all, Walsh, no matter how trivial it struck you at the time, that happened during the whole twenty minutes you were at this place?'

Silence. Walsh was looking nervous and perplexed. 'I don't know what you're after,' he said. 'I just can't think— Well, a couple of the neighbours on each side of the drunks' apartment came out—I think one couple was out when we drove up, I seem to get a picture of them standing there on their front porch under the porch light. That'd be, I guess, Number Four—end apartment . . . What, sir? I think that was the only porch light on except the landlady's. Then when I came back to the car, I saw the people on the other side—that'd be Number Two, in the first building—had come out on their porch. Wanted to see if we were going to take the drunks in, I guess, but there wasn't any need for that . . . I don't remember seeing anybody else out. I guess if it hadn't been raining they would have been—you know, the drunks making such a racket—but the way it was, it was just the people from the closest apartments to them who were outside—though probably everybody else was looking out their windows . . . I don't know what *else* I can . . . Oh, and just before Joe came up, somebody *did* open the door of the apartment next to the landlady's. And that's all I—what, sir? No, they didn't come out on the porch, maybe when they saw it was raining so hard—'

'They,' said Mendoza, excluding any excitement from his tone. 'Two people, three, or what?'

'Oh—well,' said Walsh vaguely, 'I don't know. I said "they" because I couldn't see whether it was a man or woman who opened the door. The porch light wasn't on there. I think there was a light inside but not in the living-room, maybe, not right by the door or behind it—I seem to get that impression. I couldn't see—I don't know if anybody else was there besides who opened the door. I just, you know, sort of registered it in my mind, the door opening . . . This what you want, Lieutenant, about *that*? Well, let's see . . . I remember thinking, they've finally tumbled something's going on, and're looking out to see what—but I didn't *notice* whoever it was—and it was just a minute before the door shut again. Tell you the truth,' said Walsh a little shamefacedly, 'I was looking at the lightning really, I just kind of saw that door open out of the tail of my eye. I get a kick out of electric storms, and we never used to get them out here much, you know, it's only the last ten or twelve years . . . I was waiting for the thunder . . .'

'Yes,' said Mendoza. 'Now, think about this one carefully. Someone was standing in the open door of Number Five—by the way, wide open?'

Walsh thought, shook his head. 'I don't know. I don't think so, but I can't say for sure.'

'O.K. Someone's there, and there's lightning in a flash—big stroke?'

'Pretty close. Lit up the whole sky—it was fine.'

'Yes. And about that time Bartlett was, maybe, on his way to the car from Number Three? Could it be that whoever was standing there saw Bartlett by that big flash, and thought Bartlett might have seen him—or her?' But that was really reaching for it, surely, he added to himself. A flash of lightning. One little moment—to fix in mind the nondescript features of an ordinary cop—and an hour and a bit later, catch up to him and kill him? And Bartlett would probably have had his head down against the rain; whoever was in that doorway would also see that he couldn't be noticing . . .

Walsh's expression took on the glazed look of one trying to recapture a past time in photographic reproduction. He said almost at once, 'No, sir. I got that piece clear, just remembering it by the lightning, now. This is how it went, see: there's the lightning, just *after* the door opened there—and I looked up, and kind of automatically started to count seconds, the way you do, you know—and it was close, it wasn't quite three seconds until the thunder—and *then* that door closed. And right after that—yes, I've got it now, funny how little things come back to you—I heard the *other* apartment door close, and that was Joe and the landlady coming out of Number Three. And almost right away, Joe opened the car door and got in beside me and said, "O.K., let's go."' Walsh looked at Mendoza triumphantly, anxiously. 'Is that the kind of thing you want, sir? I don't see what it has to do with—'

'*¡Oyé, oiga, frene!—¿Qué se yo?*' Mendoza sat up abruptly. 'Wait a minute now, *you* were driving? Bartlett got in beside you, you said—you being behind the wheel.'

'Why, yes, sir,' said Walsh. 'We generally change round like that, you know, if there're two of you on patrol, one drives the first half of the tour, the other the second half. That night, we changed after the coffee break, and Joe took the wheel.'

Mendoza looked at him, but he didn't see Frank Walsh's square, honest, amiable face at all. He saw that ugly courtyard, on that dark rainy night—and a murderer opening a door (all right, no evidence, *nada absolutamente*, to back that up, but it made a picture, it filled in an empty space)—and being confronted with that black-and-white squad car, unexpected and so close; and in that moment, one great flash of lightning lighting the whole scene—pinpointing it in time and space. What picture in a murderer's mind of that one moment? A uniformed cop at the wheel of that car, looking up alertly—apparently towards the open apartment door. And Mrs Bragg's porch light shining full on the front of the squad car *and its L.A. police number*.

That was all. That was enough. Mendoza's patrol days being far behind, that one little fact hadn't occurred to him, that a pair of cops in a squad car changed around at the wheel. The ordinary civilian wouldn't think of it.

So, there was the answer: and say it wasn't backed up by any kind of evidence the D.A. would look at—Mendoza knew surely it must be the right answer. All somebody had known, had been afraid of, was the driver of squad car number such-and-such. It didn't matter *then*—the idea was that Twelvetrees should vanish, that he'd never be found in his makeshift grave down that kitchen trap—it didn't matter if the driver saw and remembered a face. Not if things went the way somebody planned. But just in case Twelvetrees *was* found, in case questions were asked, and the driver of that car was able to identify a face—

Panic? Impulse? And a very damned lucky shot—or a very damned skillful one . . . into the wrong man.

And, after all, Frank Walsh hadn't seen whoever stood in that open door.

CHAPTER EIGHT

'Every other country in the world,' said Alison, clutching Mendoza's arm, 'puts decent lights in night clubs and bars. People go to such places to read newspapers and hold philosophical discussions over their drinks. Or at least so I'm given to understand. Why are Americans condemned to these caves of darkness, like moles?'

'It's the Puritan background,' said Mendoza, stumbling over a pair of outstretched legs and apologising. 'We still suffer from the influence of all those high-minded, earnest people who had the idea that anything a little bit enjoyable, from a glass of wine to a hand of cards—anything that makes life a bit more amusing—is necessarily sinful. It's a holdover—ah, haven,' as the waiter's dim figure stopped and hovered in the gloom ahead, indicating a table or booth, impossible to tell which. On cautious investigation it proved to be a booth, and he slid into it beside the vague slender figure that was Alison—at least, it smelled of the spiced-carnation and faintly aphrodisiac scent that said *Alison*. '—A holdover from the days when those righteous old colonists felt seven kinds of devil if they let the cider get hard, you know . . . Straight rye,' he added to the waiter, 'and I think a glass of sherry for the lady.'

'Yes. It's a great pity, all I can say,' said Alison. 'I expect you're right, and how silly.'

'On the contrary,' said Mendoza, 'very good business. You make people feel there's something a little devilish about a thing, they'll fall over themselves to buy it. Human nature. Prohibition created more drinkers than we'd ever had before. Some principle as banning a novel—everybody reads it to find out why.'

'It's still silly. I can't find my cigarettes, have you got one?'

'Only,' said Mendoza, groping in his pocket, offering her the pack and lighting one for her, 'because you and I were born at par. I got this from Sergeant Farquhar—it's a Scottish proverb, haven't you heard it, and you half Scots? "Some people are born two drinks under. They need the drinks to get up to normal."'

'Certainly I've heard it, and my father used to say that redheads—oh, well, never mind, it wasn't very genteel now I come to think.'

'If it was about redheads,' said Mendoza as the waiter brought their drinks, 'I might guess what it was.'

'I wouldn't put it past you. Well, in polite language it was to the effect that they're born two drinks over. And he *was*, certainly. Did I ever tell you about the time he challenged the governor of Coahuila to a duel? It was over a dam up in the Sierra Mojadas—the governor kept saying if Providence had intended people to have the water, the dam would have been created in the first six days, you know, but as it was the whole thing was immoral and contrary to God's wishes—I've never seen Dad madder—but in the end the governor backed down and they never did get to the duel. I think myself somebody told the governor the *pedazo rojo norteamericano* was a crack shot.'

'These effeminate Latins, all cowards,' said Mendoza. '*¡Salud y pesetas!*' He tasted the rye. 'You and I are the unconventional ones, we don't need this to enjoy life . . . And another thing about these places,' he added over a roll of snare drums, 'if they can persuade you to drink enough they can save a lot of money on what they call entertainment—anything goes if you're sufficiently high.'

A blue spotlight circled a painfully thin girl in silver lamé, on the little low platform at one end of the room, above what was revealed as a five- or six-piece band. On the edges of the light, white blurs of faces, tables crowded close. A tenor sax spoke mournfully, and the girl clasped her hands at her breast and began to moo nasally about missing her naughty baby.

'Oh dear,' said Alison. The spotlight, moving with the

singer, dimly showed them the Voodoo Club: fake handdrums and shrunken heads for wall-décor, zebra-patterned plastic on chairs and banquettes, and the waiters all Negroes in loincloths. There was also a postage-stamp dance floor.

'Yes,' said Mendoza. 'Hardly combining business with pleasure. We'll get to the business as soon as the waiter shows up again.' Which he did as the girl stopped mooing and the spotlight blinked out. The band went into a soft blues and a few couples groped their way onto the dance floor.

'*Re*-peat, suh?'

'No, thanks. Tell me,'—Mendoza flicked his lighter over the blown-up print of Twelvetrees—'have you ever seen this man in here?'

The waiter bent closer and looked at the print. In the little circle of unsteady light, he was very black, very Negroid; out of the dark his hand came up to finger his jaw, a long, slender hand with oddly intellectual-looking narrow fingers. 'Well, I jus' couldn' say offhand, suh. An' we ain' supposed to gossip about customahs, y' know.'

'Just take another look, and be sure.'

'Don' know nuthin' 'bout him, suh. Anythin' else I can do for you, suh?'

Mendoza shook his head. 'So, we'll have to get at it official,' he said when the man had gone, leaving the check behind as a gentle hint. 'See the manager. I don't suppose there's anything in it, or not much, but you never know—he must have had acquaintances in other circles than the Temple. By the little we've got on him so far, I think he looked on that just the way the Kingmans do, as a soft racket, and he'd hardly find the sect members to his social taste. Except for Mona Ferne—and that was for other reasons. I could wish his landlady had been the prying, suspicious kind who took more notice of his callers. Oh, well. Are you finished with that? Let's go.'

They groped their way out to the better-lighted foyer, and Mendoza reclaimed his hat and Alison's coat from the check girl, paid the cashier. As he held out the coat for her, the slab door in the opposite wall opened and there emerged a slender little man who looked exactly like a film gang-boss, from his navy shirt and white tie to his fancy grey punched-pigskin shoes. He had black hair slicked back into a drake's tail, cold black eyes, and a cigarette dangling out of one corner of his mouth. Behind him was a big black Negro wrapped in a white terry robe like a boxer between rounds.

'This them?' snapped the gang-boss.

'Yes, sir,' said the Negro.

'O.K.,' said the gang-boss, walking up to Mendoza, 'what you asking questions for, buddy? Who are you? Got any identification on you? What's this all about?'

'I *told* you, Luis,' said Alison, sliding behind him. 'Every time I go out with you in new stockings—why you drag me to these dens of iniquity—'

'Hey,' said the gang-boss angrily, 'what you talking about, lady, den of iniquity? We don't pay a grand a year for a liquor licence to go foolin' around with that kind of stuff! Just what the hell—'

'You're the manager—good, just the man I want to see,' and Mendoza brought out his credentials.

'Oh, *police*,' said the gang-boss, and his toughness fell away from him like a cloak. 'Gee, I'm sure sorry, Lieutenant, but I didn't know! Anything at all I can do for you—'

'This man,' Mendoza gave him the print. 'Regular in here? Or a casual?'

'Yeah, well—' The manager rubbed his ear and exchanged a glance with the Negro. 'It's him all right, isn't it?'

'I thought so,' said the Negro tranquilly in an accentless, rather amused tone. 'I didn't know you were police either, Lieutenant. Sorry, but one way and another I thought Mr Stuart ought to hear about it.'

'You better come into my office,' said Stuart abruptly. 'You too, Johnny.' He led them into a little square room furnished in excellent modern taste. 'Sit down. Offer you anything to drink?'

'No, thanks.' Mendoza glanced from him to the Negro quizzically.

'I'll apologise,' said the latter, 'for the—er—costume, sir. In the dark in there, it's one thing, but you feel a little naked out here, you know.'

'Customers, they go for the damndest things,' said Stuart. 'Not that that was my idea—I only manage the place. Excuse me, this is Johnny Laidlaw, your waiter.'

'You know how it is,' said the big Negro apologetically, 'we're sort of expected to stay in character on a job like this—'

'Matter of fact,' said Stuart, 'unless the bomb falls or something, this time next year it'll be *Dr* Laidlaw. Right now he's got more schooling than I ever had, which don't necessarily say he's any smarter, but anyway I guess his evidence is as good as mine.'

'A medical degree runs into money these days,' said Laidlaw amiably, 'and you'd be surprised at the size of some of the tips. But this isn't getting to what you want to know. Mr Stuart, I guess your part of it ought to come first.'

'There's your scientific-trained mind,' said Stuart. 'Well, it's like this, Lieutenant. I just took over here about six months ago, see. The guy who'd been managing the joint, Whalen his name was, Andy Whalen, well, Mr Goldstein—he's the owner—he found he wasn't levelling, there was rebates to wholesalers and that kind of thing. So Whalen got the heave-ho and I came in. O.K. Well, I hadn't been here very long—some time in September, wasn't it, Johnny?'

'September the twelfth,' said Laidlaw.

'Yeah, well, Johnny comes in one night and says a customer's kicking up a row—it was about midnight I remember—and so I go out front to settle it. And here's this guy here,' he tapped the print, 'raising hell over his check. He's just leaving, see, he's got this blonde dame with him—Johnny says he'd seen them in here before—and when he gets the check he don't like it. I say, what's the beef, and he says can he talk to me private. Now that I don't like so good, because it usually means the guy's caught short on cash and wants to leave his watch or something—but what can you do, I say O.K. and bring him in here. And first thing he says is, "What's with Whalen?" When he hears Whalen's out, he gets mad all over again. He says Whalen's a pal of his, always made him a cut price, see. I says that's one of the reasons Whalen's out, and I point out to him that I'm no pal, and it's a shame he's stuck for more than he expected, but just one of those things, and what about the thirty-four something he owes? Same time, if you get me, I did think it was kind of funny. I didn't know Whalen, but what the boys here've said, he wasn't no good-time Charlie who'd let his friends in for free.'

'That he wasn't,' said Laidlaw thoughtfully.

'But that wasn't any of my business. The guy didn't like it, but he paid up. I didn't need a blueprint to figure he'd been a regular here on account of the deal with Whalen, and the blonde didn't have a glimmer of that, thought he was just free with his money, and naturally he didn't want to look cheap in front of her. Anyway, he paid up and out he goes, and that was the only time I ever laid eyes on him. And can't say I'm sorry. But I was kind of curious, and so I got Bob Trimming—that's our regular cashier—in and asked him about it. I didn't get an awful lot out of him, to make sense. You see, the boys, well, they'd got kind of used to the manager acting nasty with them, and catching 'em out for little things all the time, see, and *besides*—well, now you tell the gent what you know, Johnny.'

'Now just as it happened,' said Laidlaw leisurely—he sat with arms folded across his chest, at magnificent ease, and spoke serenely—'I'd seen that fellow in here, but I'd never waited on him until that night. When he started to kick up the row, Bob called me in on it because I could back up the check, you see. And later on Mr Stuart asked me to sound Bob out, see if he knew any more about it, as he might talk more openly to me. And I might say I was curious about it too, and I did. Bob's pretty close-mouthed anyway, he doesn't tell all he knows just to be talking, and he'd kept quiet on this, for one reason, because Mr Whalen isn't a man you'd want to get across. But he knows I don't go talking much either, and he told me the whole thing. I realise, Lieutenant, that all this is hearsay and won't do you any good as evidence, but maybe you'll be interested anyway. What Bob said was this. This fellow came in here quite a bit, once a week at least and sometimes a lot oftener, and he never paid out anything but the tips—and he wasn't a very good tipper. The customer doesn't pay the waiters, as you know, but the cashier out there in the lobby. Bob's on duty, eight to closing time, six nights a week, so he was in a position to see what happened every time this customer came in. The first time he saw the fellow, there was a check for eighteen something, and Mr Whalen's name signed across it. The customer just tossed it onto the desk and said, "That's O.K.," or something like that. Well, Bob wasn't going to take a chance that way, and he called Mr Whalen. I might add that the fellow had a blonde with him that night too, whether the same one or not I couldn't say, but she'd stepped into the powder room. Mr Whalen said to Bob, "Oh, yes, that's O.K., on the house"—but he didn't look as if he liked saying it, so Bob says. And later on that night, after we closed, Bob asked him how to cancel out that check for the accounts, and Mr Whalen made up the cash out of his own pocket. Well, I don't want to drag this out too long—'

'You're not boring me,' Mendoza told him.

'—But the point was, every time this customer came in the same thing happened, and it ran into quite a little money Mr Whalen was paying out to make up the tabs for the accounts. Now, about six weeks before Mr Whalen was fired, one night Bob wanted to make a phone call on his break, and he slipped into the phone booth in the lobby, as there wasn't a customer in it at the time. You notice where it is?—well, it's down a little corridor towards the men's room past the check stand—and as he was standing there in the booth, out of sight, you know, sorting out a dime for the call, he heard Mr Whalen talking to this customer. The customer had just come out of the men's room, and maybe Mr Whalen was waiting for him. Anyway, Mr Whalen was mad, and told him he'd got to stop coming in here so often, fun was fun but he couldn't afford it. And the customer just laughed and said Mr Whalen surely didn't mind standing a few drinks to an old pal now and then, it was cheap at the price when it meant Mr Whalen's job, because he didn't figure Mr Whalen would like his boss to know about that taxi he'd done back in Pennsy.'

Mendoza uttered a little exclamation. 'Are you quoting this Bob, or were those the actual words?'

'That's what Bob heard, Lieutenant. Neither of us knew exactly what the fellow might have meant, but it sounded like a threat, which is why it stayed in Bob's mind. In fact, several things that were said sounded like double talk to both of us, and thinking it over I came to the conclusion they must be criminal or professional slang of some sort. The customer told Mr Whalen not to be such a ringtail, for one thing. And Mr Whalen said back at him that two could fill in that game, maybe the customer wouldn't like *his* boss to know he'd done a sleep as a cadet—'

'Ah,' said Mendoza pleasedly. 'Which doesn't surprise me. Yes, go on.'

'—And the customer laughed again and said he didn't give a damn, it'd make no difference to him. There was a little more argument, and finally Mr Whalen got to sounding really desperate, so Bob said, and he said to the customer he'd better not play so deep—meaning, I take it, not to drop in so often for a free ride—if he wasn't looking for a South Gate discharge.'

'*Lindo, muy lindo*, oh, very pretty,' said Mendoza. 'This I like. And?'

'That's about all, Lieutenant. Reason Bob remembered it, you see, was that it sounded a little nasty, threats and so on. Nobody liked Mr Whalen much, and it didn't come as a surprise when he got fired. And so, as you've heard, the next time the customer dropped in, Bob was going to make him pay, and there was this row. Well, when I'd heard all this, I thought Mr Stuart ought to know it—'

'*And* as you can see,' said Stuart, 'what the hell, it was water under the bridge, and I knew damn well the guy'd never come back again—which he didn't. None of my business what he had on Whalen. But just now, when you come in asking questions, Johnny thought I'd better hear about it, because by all this, both Whalen and this other guy, whoever he is, might be mixed up with some funny characters—if you see what I mean. No offence, Lieutenant, I hope—'

'No offence,' said Mendoza. He was looking rather amused. 'I suppose neither of you would know Whalen's whereabouts now? . . . No, I couldn't expect it. But you've been very helpful, thanks. I may want formal statements from both of you and this Bob.'

'Any time, sir,' said Laidlaw. 'Glad to oblige you.'

'Oh, sure,' said Stuart, 'not that I'd like to have to *testify* or anything, don't look so good in this business, snitching on a customer, whatever kind, but I guess it's up to all of us to help the law when we can. I suppose you can't tell us what this is all about.'

'I'm not just a hundred percent sure myself yet,' said Mendoza. They left Mr Stuart brooding over the possibility of occupying the witness stand, and Laidlaw gazing serenely at the office ceiling.

In the car, before he switched on lights or ignition, Mendoza suddenly pulled Alison into his arms and spent several minutes kissing her thoroughly. 'Well, and what prompted that?' she asked breathlessly. 'You always say a car, of all places—'

'Just general exuberance. I got so much more than I expected, and I think there's more to come yet.'

'I see. You seemed to know what those two had been talking about—*was* it criminal slang? And is a translation fit for my ladylike ears?'

Mendoza laughed. 'Yes to both questions. Twelvetrees

said to this Whalen that he didn't think Whalen's boss would like hearing that Whalen had done a five-to-fifteen stretch—that's a taxi—back in Pennsylvania. To which Whalen retorted that maybe Twelvetrees wouldn't like it known he'd done one year—that's a sleep—for enticing minors to enter houses of prostitution—that's what a cadet does. And later on Twelvetrees told him not to be such an old grouch, that's a ringtail. But one of the interesting things is that last reported remark of Whalen's, when he said Twelvetrees had better take it easy unless he was looking for a South Gate discharge. That's what the cons call it when a man dies, in or out of jail.'

'Oh, I see. So maybe this Whalen is the one.'

'Maybe, maybe. No, it doesn't surprise me that Twelvetrees had done time—not much, and he wasn't deep in yet—it's on the cards he was smart enough, after one experience, to intend staying inside the law, in one of the rackets that isn't illegal. But a man's past has a way of catching him up sometimes . . .' He let that tail off, and Alison, knowing his silences, forbore to interrupt his thoughts.

It was two in the morning when he eased the Facel-Vega into the curb just past the entrance to the Voodoo Club's parking lot. The lot was emptying rapidly, the last customers just chased out. He locked the car and walked up through the lot to the narrow space directly behind the buildings which would be reserved for employees' parking.

There were eight cars nosed in there. He peered in the drivers' windows, one by one, with his pencil flash; the fifth one down, a six-year-old Ford two-door, had its registration card wrapped around the steering post, old style, and the name on it was John S. Laidlaw. Mendoza leaned on the fender and lit a cigarette.

He had smoked that and another one—retreating to cover half a dozen times as men came out to their cars—before the rear door, thirty feet away, opened to silhouette briefly a big broad figure he thought was his quarry. The man came down towards the Ford jingling his keys and whistling *The St. Louis Blues* under his breath.

Mendoza had no desire for any violent exercise, and when the man was ten feet off he stepped out of the shadow of the car to show himself. Laidlaw checked for one moment and then laughed very softly.

'You had me scared there a minute, Lieutenant, thinking I'd slipped up on something,' he said just above a whisper. 'So I didn't put it across you.'

'For a few minutes,' said Mendoza. 'Who belongs to the Buick?' It was the only other car left in the lot.

'Stuart. He won't be out for a while, he's working on the books.'

'*Muy bien*, then we can talk here.' They got into the car; in the little flare of the match Laidlaw lit for their cigarettes they looked at each other. 'Fox knows fox,' said Mendoza dryly. 'Though you put up a nice front. But aren't you getting on a bit for a medical student?'

'Yes, that one won't do much longer. Just second cover anyway.'

'I liked the artistic way this nice honest well-brought-up young fellow puzzled over that talk and finally made it out pro slang. It was about then I pinned you down in my own mind—if we stick to the slang—as a gazer, *¿no es verdad?* I suppose you figured to do me a good turn—having spotted me—by handing it to me on a platter. Many thanks.'

'Tell you the truth, I'd be just as happy not to have you city boys sniffing around here too long or too close, which was the main reason. And I've got no credentials on me, on this job.'

'Never mind. I've had enough to do with you Feds that I know lamb from wolf. What is it, dope or illegal liquor?'

'Some of both. I've been sitting on it for a year waiting for the real big boy—this is a drop, and a good safe one. We've left it that way.'

'Whalen in it?'

'As a very minor errand boy. He did that stretch for

armed robbery with violence—that's his style—a small timer.'

'Well, your business doesn't come into mine, I don't think, so I won't ask you any questions about that—'

'Which is just as well,' said Laidlaw imperturbably, 'because I wouldn't answer them.'

'Naturally. The customer who was getting his tabs picked up by Whalen is now dead, and I am, you can appreciate, interested in the fact that Whalen threatened him with a South Gate discharge.'

'Is that a fact?' said Laidlaw. 'Interesting. I see that. Now I'll open up enough to say this, Lieutenant. Obviously the customer didn't know what was going on here—in the way of *my* business—or that Whalen was in it, or he wouldn't have thought telling the tale about Whalen's past could get him fired. But it could have, indeed. Without giving you details, the owner is innocent as day, and so is Stuart. It's quite possible that Whalen was afraid his real bosses wouldn't like it much that someone knew about him, and also there's this aspect: he had a pretty good job a little higher in the organisation than he'd been before, and that was largely due to his ostensible job as manager here. He wanted to protect that. It annoyed the boys operating the drop, just a little, when he got fired. They've sized up Stuart since, and prudently refrained from sounding him out.'

'Yes, I saw some of that—if Whalen's nominal boss wouldn't have cared, Whalen would never have picked up those tabs. Nice genteel way to blackmail somebody, wasn't it? No vulgar cash changing hands.'

'So it was,' agreed Laidlaw. 'You understand that we weren't more than casually interested in Whalen as one of the boys, there wasn't any reason to follow up his private troubles with this fellow, as it was pretty clear that one was outside this particular racket. So you probably know more about your corpse than I do.'

'Not as much as I'd like. What I came back for principally was to ask if you know where Whalen is.'

'Sure I know where he is,' said Laidlaw. 'I read in the

papers the other day, Lieutenant, that you L.A. boys got a pat on the back from some Washington office for being tops among the ten most efficient city forces in the country—but outside that category, we sort of fancy ourselves as pretty hot, you know. We're not much interested in Andy Whalen, but we looked to see where he went. He's driving a truck for Orange State Trucking, on the San Diego-L.A. run, and he lives in room number 312 at the Chester Hotel on Fourth.'

'Thanks very much. Would it discommode you at all if I took him in for questioning?'

'I don't think so,' said Laidlaw. 'His bosses don't rate him any bigger-time than we do.'

'What about the trucking outfit? Can I take it he's still on the payroll of the gang in another capacity?'

'Well, now, I don't think we'll go into that, if you don't mind. I'll just say, it's possible.'

'You boys with your secrets,' said Mendoza. 'Well, I may and I may not, right away. All that rigmarole—your quotes from the cashier—gospel truth?'

'And nothing but.'

'Mmh. Yes, a couple of little things that occur to me aside from Whalen. But I want to look at him closer, of course. Thanks very much, Laidlaw, and good luck on your business.'

'Same to you—happy to oblige, Lieutenant. We like to cooperate with the locals where we can,' said Laidlaw blandly.

'I might,' said Mendoza, sliding out of the car, 'like the polite tone of that better if you didn't somehow sound like a professional race driver assuring his little boy he'll teach him to ride his new bicycle.'

'Why, Loo-tenant, suh, I nevah meant no such thing, suh,' said Laidlaw. Mendoza laughed, shut the door, and dodged back to the shadow of the wall as the building door opened up there. Laidlaw slid the Ford out to the street; Mendoza waited until Stuart had driven out in the Buick before going back to his own car.

CHAPTER NINE

'You want to make it read,' said Hackett, 'that this Whalen got so mad at Twelvetrees—six months after he stopped paying this genteel blackmail—that he killed him?'

'I don't want to make it read any way,' said Mendoza. 'We don't know what dealings they may have had since. All I say is, no harm to look at Whalen.'

'I don't believe it,' said Hackett. 'In the first place, I can't see a rough-and-ready customer like this Whalen taking the trouble to bury him. And there *may* have been a renewed motive, but there's nothing to show they ever laid eyes on each other after last August, when Whalen got fired. I don't—'

'*No seas tan exigente*—don't be so difficult,' said Mendoza. 'If I want a warrant for Whalen, I've got to be able to give *some* logical reason to authority. And it may be that I will. Like—mmh—looking openly pleased to draw a five-spot when I'm already holding a royal flush.'

'Oh!' said Hackett. He laughed. 'So that's what's in your mind. It's a thought. Set somebody's mind at rest so maybe he'll do something silly.'

'Did you spot, in all these inverted quotes I've been giving you, the one really interesting little thing? You remember that Whalen suggested to Twelvetrees that *his* boss might not like hearing about the little stretch Twelvetrees had done—and Twelvetrees just laughed and said it wouldn't matter a damn.'

'Which of course sounds as if these Kingmans knew all about him. Yes. You're laying your blue chips on the Kingmans?'

Mendoza swivelled around in his desk-chair to look out the window at the hazy panorama of the city stretching away to hills invisible this grey morning. 'I've sent out queries to Pennsylvania on Twelvetrees and the Kingmans—we'll see what they can give us, if anything. Unfortunately I didn't have the Kingmans' prints to send, but I sent Twelvetrees', of course. I don't know, Art, there's a couple of things that say this and that to me, on that deal. Look at the way Twelvetrees landed here and slid into such a soft spot—five hundred a month, for what? Woods says, he ingratiated himself. Well, somehow I don't think Mr Dale Carnegie himself would find it very easy to ingratiate that far with Mr Martin Kingman. What it amounted to was muscling in on Mr Kingman's own racket and cutting Mr Kingman's net take by that five hundred.'

'Yes, and you know the thought I had about that? Considering the times. It sounds to me as if just maybe those three had made up a crowd before, and for some reason—maybe because he was inside—Twelvetrees was a little late joining them out here.'

'Also a thought. But I don't like it nearly so well as I like mine—that he might have pulled exactly the same sort of genteel blackmail on the Kingmans that he did on Whalen. Look. The Temple's been a going concern for over a year when Twelvetrees lands here. You never did catch up to this Mona Ferne yesterday but you will today, and I think what she'll tell you is that her original contact with Twelvetrees wasn't through the Temple, but that she met him somewhere in connection with his movie aspirations. And that she was the one who led him to the Temple. Because he took a job when he got here, remember?—not a very good job, clerking in a store—he was broke, or close to it. I get the picture of this fairly canny young fellow, who's taken one rap and means to find some legal racket—where he doesn't have to work too hard. He'd like to get into pictures—he's got all the requirements, so he thinks, but he finds it isn't so easy. Then, by accident, he discovers the Kingmans and their Temple. And almost immediately he becomes "secretary-treasurer" or whatever they call it and starts drawing that nice salary for practically no work. Now that looks to me as if he had something on them. That he took one look at Mr Martin Kingman, maybe, and said, "Ah, my old friend Giovanni Scipio—or Mike O'Connor—or Harold J. Cholmondeley—from good old Philly." *¿Comprende?* And Kingman had to kick in, let him in on the racket, to protect the investment—because, while the people who've fallen for Mystic Truth aren't exactly Einsteins, most of them would think again about dropping folding money into the collection bag if they knew, for instance, that Kingman had done a stretch for fraud or something like that.'

'That's so. It makes a picture, all right. And that'd give the Kingmans a dandy reason to put him out of the way. I'll say this too, it makes it look even more natural, maybe, that they stood it nearly four years before getting fed up. Because con men don't use violence, they like everything nice and easy and smooth, it isn't once in a blue moon you find one of 'em committing actual physical assault. It might be that it wasn't until Twelvetrees got a little too greedy and asked too much blackmail that they got worked up to that. The only thing I don't like about it, Luis, is the spot Twelvetrees landed in—treasurer. The Kingmans wouldn't have handed him anything like that, as blackmail payment. Why, he could have taken off with the whole bank account any day.'

'So he could. But I think we'd find, Arturo, that it was treasurer in name only—that Kingman was damned careful to keep a check on the account. A kind of gentleman's agreement. You know, let me in on your racket and I won't tell—and on Kingman's side, you level with us on the racket or I'll tell what I know about you. Don't forget, Twelvetrees still had dreams of a future as a big star. His agents wouldn't care about keeping him on their books, he wouldn't have a chance of getting anywhere in big-time show business, if it was known he'd served apprenticeship as a pimp and got tagged for it. He got Kingman to give him a job openly—he wanted an excuse to quit the nine-to-five job he had, which he probably didn't enjoy much. But I'll bet you too that the bank will tell us that one of the

Kingmans made some excuse for coming in regularly to check up. It was a fifty-fifty deal, scratch my back and I'll scratch yours.'

'Something in that, sure.'

'I should hate,' said Mendoza, 'to have to arrest Madame Cara. She's a very intelligent woman, she says I have great insight and wisdom. But it would have been so much more convenient, you know, if there'd been two of them on the job, on account of Twelvetrees' car. If just one person did it all, how awkward that part of it would be—driving the Porsche clear down to the Union Station, a good ten miles or more, and then having to get back to pick up the car left at the apartment. If, of course, there was one, and the murderer hadn't been driven there by Twelvetrees. It's a great pity Mrs Bragg minded her own business so assiduously . . . There are a lot of things we don't know yet. But it's very helpful that we can almost pin it down to that Friday night—'

'I don't see that we can,' said Hackett. 'I don't like it much, Walsh's thing, about Bartlett.'

'I do. I think it makes sense.' Mendoza sat up and swivelled around to the desk again. 'I don't say it's certain, no, but I like it enough that I've told the D.A.'s office to get a continuance on bringing those kids up, until we know a little more. Here's what Ballistics says on the gun. It's one of an experimental lot of smooth-bore revolvers made by Winchester about fifty years ago. Not too many like it will be floating around these days, but it's nothing antique in the sense of being rare or valuable—we're not likely to get an identification of ownership on it that way. Now, as the class will remember from yesterday's lecture, I trust, we all know that a firearm with a smooth-bored barrel is never as accurate over distances as one whose barrel is rifled with spiral grooves. However, at fairly short distances a smooth-bore is accurate enough in expert hands. Ballistics had a lot of fun firing different kinds of bullets out of this at different distances, and they tell us that with a cannelured bullet—which, if you will recall, was the type found in

Bartlett *and* on the kids—a reasonably good shot can expect quite fair accuracy out of this at up to about twenty-five feet.'

'You say it's just coincidence the kids were carrying .38 cannelured bullets and Bartlett got killed with the same kind?'

'If you'd just think about these things, that's all I ask—a little rudimentary logic. The kids had a homemade gun, and quite naturally it also has a smooth-bored barrel. Actually a piece of pipe. Anybody who knows anything at all about guns, and is stuck with a smooth-bore, is going to try to make up for the handicap by using cannelured bullets, which are grooved. Has the class any questions?'

'Yes, please, teacher. How does a slick con man—or in fact anybody we've heard of in this case so far—come to be such a Deadeye Dick with an old cannon like this?'

'Now there you do ask an awkward question,' admitted Mendoza. 'I don't know. But it's a fifty-fifty chance that it was just wild luck, you know. And I'll say this. We've been thinking that whoever fired those shots at Bartlett and Walsh did it in the dark—a dark rainy night, along a stretch of road lighted only by high arc lights. I went out there last night, before I waylaid Laidlaw, and roped Gonzales and Farber in on a little game. I'd got Walsh to tell me just where the squad car was sitting in relation to the light at the corner of Cameron and San Dominguez, and I placed Gonzales and Farber there and drove past a couple of times. And you know what? Just the way it had slipped my mind about patrolmen changing round at the wheel, another little thing slipped all our minds when we thought about this before. Go on now, be a detective and tell me what it was.'

'My God,' said Hackett. 'The roof light.'

'That's my boy, you get A-plus. Going on and off almost right over the driver's head, whenever the car's standing still. It's a nice straight road along there, and the shoulder where the squad car was sitting is unobstructed for a hundred yards each way. And thirty isn't really very fast, in relation to an object, say, fifteen feet to the side—you've got time to see it, coming up. I think it must have been a double take—that whoever it was spotted the car by its number, maybe when Bartlett and Walsh had stopped that car for speeding. So X speeded up and doubled back, to try his shot without that additional witness—and so, coming up on them, he knew it was the right car, he didn't have to spot the number *and* get in position to fire, all at once. It's just a question—I tried a dry run on it last night—of taking your right hand off the wheel, your eyes off the road, for about three seconds, and firing at right angles out the driver's window.'

'That's if there was only the driver—even saying it was whoever killed Twelvetrees, that there's any connection.'

'Sure. If there were two, a lot easier. One to drive, one to shoot. But when you come to think, whoever killed Twelvetrees had quite a bit to do that night—'

'I still say there's nothing to show definitely it *was* that night.'

'*Pues mira, chico*—look here—all right, but it was *some* night, because if it had been broad daylight Mrs Bragg, or one of the housewives in the other apartments, would have seen someone arrive and leave. Going to Twelvetrees' place you'd have to walk or drive past all those other front doors. I refuse to believe that human nature has improved so much since I first began to notice it that among the five women who're usually at home most of the day in that court, not one was curious enough about a good-looking bachelor to take at least casual note of his movements and visitors. You grant me that's likely? Then I say it's also likely that whatever happened happened that Friday night, when it was raining and overcast and people were staying inside ignoring the neighbours. And also because on the Saturday and Sunday nobody seems to recall seeing the Porsche in Twelvetrees' carport. True, they wouldn't be looking for it, he was probably out a good deal, and nobody would take special note of it one way or the other, there or not there, so that's negative evidence. But we haven't yet found anybody who remembers seeing him after the Kingmans saw him leave the Temple at four o'clock on Friday. The three or four restaurants he habitually used say he didn't come in that night. The garage where he took the Porsche hadn't seen him for three weeks. No gas station he might hit on his way home sold him any gas. His agents don't remember that he'd come in since several days before. The autopsy says he'd had, probably, beef stew, salad, and some kind of pie about two to six hours before he did. Not helpful unless we find the restaurant where he went, and they remember. All right. Nobody remembers either how long the Porsche had been standing where it was left. We've got no evidence, except negative evidence. But why didn't he show up anywhere on Saturday or Sunday?'

'We don't know he didn't,' said Hackett. 'Maybe somebody just hasn't come forward to say. Maybe this old flame of yours knew where he was those two days. Maybe, for that matter, he never did leave the Temple on Friday and the Kingmans just say he did. Maybe he was killed there and ferried out—'

'*Caray*, let's not make it any more complicated than it is! You're forgetting those suitcases—those carefully packed suitcases. What did we say when we looked at them? He was getting ready to clear out, of his own choice. Now maybe he was just moving to another apartment, maybe he was going to get married, maybe he'd just heard he'd inherited a million dollars and didn't have to stay in the racket any longer—but one of the possibilities is that for some reason his whole private racket was up, here, and he had to get out. Say he was going to clear. Then tell me what he'd have done *too*, just before he left.'

'That's an easy one, he'd have taken some of the Kingmans' money along with him. But it depends on a lot of ifs.'

'Well, I don't know that it does. There are a lot of fishy things about the Kingmans' behaviour, but two things are a little fishier than the rest. In the first place, you'll never get me to believe—no matter whether all this about

Twelvetrees' blackmailing them was so or not—that Mr Martin Kingman is so unworldly and unbusinesslike that he didn't have a home address and a phone number for the treasurer of his Temple. Why didn't he give Woods that information right away, if he was so anxious to catch up with Twelvetrees? And second, he jumped the gun very damned quick, didn't he, on laying a charge? If, as I think we can almost take for granted, the Kingmans and Twelvetrees looked on this Mystic Truth business as nothing *but* a business, there wouldn't be anything very peculiar about dear Brooke missing their Sabbath ceremonies—it must have happened before, his taking a weekend off. He couldn't have gotten into the bank then before ten on Monday morning, either to deposit the month's receipts or close out the accounts. And, *de paso*, that in itself poses a funny little question, you know. If he was planning to run with a big handful of the profit—as much as he could persuade the bank to let him have—why was he packing up and getting ready to leave as early as Friday? It'd be Monday before he could—'

'So there you are, maybe it wasn't Friday.'

'Reason it through,' said Mendoza. 'It wouldn't have been very sensible, if he intended to take off on Monday morning, to start packing on Saturday night. And we *know* it wasn't Sunday night, because Mrs Bragg found the note on Sunday noon, he'd already gone by then. I wonder if that bank—yes, well, file that for thinking about . . . Kingman knew what time the bank opened, after all, *and* closed. When he saw Twelvetrees on Friday afternoon, the banks were still open—if he was afraid Twelvetrees was planning larceny, why didn't he contact the bank then? And bright and early Monday morning we find him "checking with the bank"—evidently because he's leaped to this conclusion over the Saturday when dear Brooke didn't show up—and at a quarter past ten he's up in Theft laying the charge. Which looks—' Mendoza stopped and interrupted himself reflectively, '*Or*, of course—'

'You've argued yourself into a corner there,' said

Hackett. 'If he thought there was any danger Twelvetrees was going to try to clean them out—or already had—then he didn't know Twelvetrees was dead.'

'Or it was a double play,' said Mendoza. 'And also—'

'Oh, the hell with it,' said Hackett. 'We've wasted half the morning talking about it—let's get busy and collect some more facts to fit into the picture.'

'Those we can always use more of,' agreed Mendoza. But when Hackett left he was still sitting there motionless, staring out the window . . . Doubtless still trying to fill in details on his idea about Joe Bartlett, thought Hackett.

And Mendoza knew Hackett didn't go along on that, thought it was a wild one. He also knew it might be, that he must keep an open mind on it himself. His besetting sin was that dislike for ragged edges, wanting everything neat, precisely dovetailed; and criminal cases, like a lot of other things in life, didn't always work out that way. Often there were ragged edges all round the truth—human nature and real life being what it was.

That was a satisfying, dramatic little picture he'd seen, on Walsh's thing—a murderer panicking, killing Bartlett in error. But it might not be the true picture: maybe those kids had killed Bartlett after all, and that had nothing to do with the Twelvetrees case. Maybe it had been Twelvetrees himself who opened the door when the squad car was sitting there and didn't think twice about it when he saw it was the alcoholic Johnstones again.

By the same token, he couldn't let himself get so sold on the Kingmans that he ignored evidence pointing away from them. But he fancied the Kingmans quite highly: if Pennsylvania could offer any suggestions as to what Twelvetrees might have had on them, their stock would go even higher.

He wanted to locate Marian Marner, find out what she'd had to do with Twelvetrees, and he wanted to find out from Twelvetrees' agents anything the man might have said about himself, and possibly contact in that way any friends

Twelvetrees might have made among people in that circle, show business hopefuls. The papers had had this since the late extras on Saturday, and probably everyone who had known him had seen the news: if anyone had any information to volunteer, it should turn up today or tomorrow. And just for the record, they'd have a look at Whalen. But on the whole the Kingmans looked like the obvious bet . . .

He'd see the Kingmans himself.

Before he left his office, however, one of those things happened that a detective had to get used to—some new bit of evidence turning up that made a favoured theory more doubtful.

Sergeant Lake, who was going through the amended list of model agencies looking for Marian Marner, came in and said there was a cab driver outside in answer to the official enquiry sent out to all the companies. 'Oh?' said Mendoza, rather surprised. 'Well, all right, I'd better see him.' Because if it had been the Kingmans working together, there'd have been no need for whoever had disposed of the Porsche taking a cab back to the apartment: one would have driven the Porsche, the other their own car.

The cab driver was tall, thin, elderly, a clerkish-looking fellow with rimless glasses and a diffident manner. He had a funny little story to tell, and Mendoza listened to it in growing annoyance that it couldn't be fitted into any theory he had.

'It was just after midnight that Friday night, the thirtieth,' the driver said when his slight nervousness had been soothed and he was sitting back more at ease with a cigarette. 'I'd just taken a couple to the Union Station, I guess to make the Owl for San Francisco—only passenger I know of leaving about then. Business is always slow that time of night, you know. I hung around waiting for the Lark down from the north, she was late—due in at ten-forty, but she didn't get in until eleven-fifty, some trouble on the line up at Santa Maria, I heard. Well, I guess you aren't interested in all that, it was just—not many came off her and none of 'em wanted a cab—all been met, you see—so I thought I'd go uptown where chances were better for strays. I went up Alameda and through the old Paza, you see, and it was just as I came by the old Mission Church there, this woman hailed me. I guess maybe you'll know it's dark as hell along there, that time of night—all the shops in Olvera Street was shut then, and those old streets are so narrow, and all the trees in the old Plaza square—well, she had to step right off the curb almost into my headlights to hail me. And that was the only real good look I got at her, rest of the time it was all dark—'

'What did she look like?'

'She looked like the Witch of Endor,' said the driver frankly. 'And she acted about as queer. I wasn't surprised one bit to see your official query in our office last night—of course it didn't give any description, but the places nailed it for me, I says right off, that's my girl. This one look I got at her, in the head-beam, you see, well, I couldn't give you a real *description*, I mean how tall she was or what colour eyes or hair or even what sort of age, naturally. But there she was with this Mexican serape over her head like a shawl, see, and kind of wound around her neck, and what made it look so funny was that she'd put it on top of a hat—I guess maybe to protect her hat from the rain. And the hat had a veil, and she'd pulled that right down over her face. But what I *could* see of her face under the veil, well, she'd just plastered the make-up on—looked like a clown, or something—God knows what her natural face looked like under it.'

'Fuera, la drama extravagante,' muttered Mendoza. 'Can it be? Yes, go on, what about the rest of her clothes?'

'She had on a long coat, that's all I could see. It was a lightish colour and it had dark bands, like trimming of some sort, down the front. And when she talked, she had a funny kind of foreign accent. She said "ze" for "the," you know, and "Please to take me," and all that, but I couldn't say what kind of accent it was, French or German or what—and she didn't say much. She was just in the light like that a second, and I stopped, and she hopped around and got in the cab before I knew it, hardly, with her suitcase—'

'A suitcase. What kind?'

'I didn't get a look at that, couldn't say. I've got the impression she was carrying it when she stepped out to hail me, that is, she didn't go back to the curb to get it. And once she was out of the lights I could just see she had some kind of bag. Like she'd just come off a train, but I don't see how she could of. She wasn't on the Lark—I'd have spotted her—and anyway if she had been why didn't she take a cab down at the station, instead of wandering up the hill to the Plaza? Anyway, in she gets, and she says in this funny accent to take her to this address out on Polk Street. Well, it was to-hell-and-gone down towards the beach, fifteen miles easy, and I wanted to be sure she wasn't a nut or something without any money on her, so I said that was quite a ways, it'd cost her four-five bucks, as a kind of hint, if you get me. And right away she says, "That will be all right, my good man," in this crazy accent, and she hands me a five-spot over the back of the seat. So I drove her. It'd mean an empty run back because it wasn't likely I'd pick up another stray way out there, but if she handed over the five so easy I thought maybe there'd be a good tip . . . It's a block of tract houses, one of those new subdivisions—'

'Let's look at a map.' They looked, and Mendoza was more irritated. That block on Polk Street was a short block up and a short block across from Twelvetrees' apartment on 267th.

'—And no streetlights in yet, so I didn't get any better look at her there, and she hadn't done any talking at all on the way. You know, some people want to talk to the driver and some don't, I let them pick. I had a look in the mirror now and then, and she was just sitting kind of huddled up in one corner, holding that serape over her face like she was afraid of breathing germs or something. When we got there, quick as anything she hands me over another five, and before I can get out to open the door, give her her change, she's already out, with her suitcase, and says,

"That's all right, my man, I don't want change," and off she goes. I hadn't even killed the engine yet.'

'So, of course, you didn't,' said Mendoza. 'You made a U-turn and headed back—and you didn't see her go into any of those houses.'

'Well, no, I didn't. She was a funny one, but we see plenty of *them* hacking, you know. But that street's too narrow for a U-turn, I had to go up to the next corner. And by the time I got back past where she'd got out, no sign of her. But I did notice that the house where she said she wanted to go wasn't lighted at all, as if they were expecting somebody. Only way I knew the right address was, the house next to it had the porch light on and I saw that number.'

'Yes. A very funny little story. Thanks very much for coming in. We'll want your name and so on, and a formal statement . . .' And just how did that little piece of melodrama fit in? Why had Cara Kingman (if it had been) have to taxi back to the apartment? And call such obvious notice to herself in the process? Polk Street. Two blocks to 267th. Which in turn was only about a mile from where Bartlett had been killed three hours earlier. The only thing Mendoza liked at all about this was that it had happened on the Friday night; and that was senseless too, just because he was set on *that* theory.

'*¡Ça, vaya historia!* I don't believe it, it's a damned ridiculous coincidence,' he said to himself. But it had to be followed up, of course. He put on his hat and set out on the six-block walk down to the old Plaza and Olvera Street.

CHAPTER TEN

Once, they'd been going to destroy the narrow alley with its uneven old brick paving and the gutter down its middle, the leaning ramshackle old buildings flanking it. Nothing to do, that was, with a progressive and fast-growing city proud of its modernity. Then a few civic-minded organisations got up indignant petitions and committees, and in the end it stayed, to become a landmark, one of the places tourists came to see: the first, the oldest street of that little village whose name was nearly as long as the street—the town of Our Lady, Queen of the Angels, of the little portion.

At ten-thirty on a grey February morning it wasn't much to see: shabby refaced buildings, haphazard stalls cheek-by-jowl in a row down the middle, over the old gutter, and most of the shops shut, boards up in the stall windows. Night was its time, when the lights softened down the shabbiness and the tourists came, the buyers (tourists or not), and the famous old restaurant was open midway down the street, and the women who'd marketed and cooked and chatted all day in their ready-made cotton housedresses got out their shawls and combs. There'd be a couple of men with guitars stationed somewhere, and the man at the mouth of the street with his little bags of hot roasted piñon nuts, and the music and laughter drifting out of La Golondrina, the restaurant, and the buyers drifting along looking at everything (the women stumbling on the uneven bricks, in their high heels)—at the gimcrack cheap jewellery and the beautiful handcrafted real stuff from the little silversmithies here and south of the border, at the handmade baskets, and braided-leather and tooled-leather shoes, at the hand-blown glass and the hand-woven cotton (also at the boxed cheap linens from Belgium, and the good stuff and the bad from Japan, from the Philippines, from everywhere in Europe)—and maybe stopping to have their fortunes told by the old woman at the far end of the street.

And even at ten-thirty in the morning, over the whole street there hung the faint scent of glamour—and that was the combined scents from the little cavelike shop, three breakneck steps down from street level, where the candles were made, the incredible rainbow candles scented with pine, with orange, with jasmine and gardenia, and nameless musky saccharine odours.

Most of the shops were shut, but he knew that behind many of them were living quarters. This was a minor little errand, he needn't have come himself, but—he also knew—he might have a better chance of getting whatever there was to get than the most fluent of his Spanish-speaking sergeants.

He could have wished that the article in question had been something other than a serape. That inimitable object of Mexicana, the long strip of rough cactus cloth or cotton, garishly striped and fringed, was to be had at all but a few specialty shops: but maybe that fact was balanced by another, that it had been raining that night.

He started at the mouth of the street and took one side at a time. Not every shop had quarters attached; not everyone was at home. Everyone who was was anxious to be helpful but remembered nothing of any use to him . . . To be sure, most places had remained open that rainy evening. When one was under shelter, and it was the regular time for business, why not? There was always a chance that the rain would slacken, that a few people who had decided to come to the street would not be put off by the weather. And so it had been: business had been very poor, of course, but a few buyers had come—chiefly people who had reservations at the restaurant and visited the shops afterwards. But many places had closed earlier than usual, ten to ten-thirty. Not all, no.

Wine was pressed on him. In one place a very old woman looked on him in contempt and called him a police spy. In the place next door a pretty high-school-age girl asked him please would he talk to her brother and tell him he was crazy: 'See, Joe keeps saying he's got nine counts on him to start, being Mexican—what's the use of trying to get educated and so on, he'd never get anywhere, might as well get things however you can. He's in with some real bad fellows, Mama and I get worried—and if you'd just *show* him—' He took the name and address for Taylor in Juvenile; Taylor would see one of the youth counsellors contacted Joe and did what he could . . . By the time he got to the mouth of the street again, having worked his way right up one side and down the other, Mendoza, who was not a wine drinker, was feeling slightly bilious and disgruntled at this waste of time.

But there, in the end shop—scarcely more than an alcove, now, shut off from the street by a large board, with a single room behind it—he found Manuel Perez, improving the out-of-business hour by making up his accounts. Mr Perez removed his horn-rimmed glasses, listened gravely to Mendoza's questions, and said at once that he remembered the occasion very well indeed.

'At last I arrive,' said Mendoza. 'Now why didn't I start here? Tell me.'

It seemed that Mr Perez had kept his shop open later than any other that rainy night, not in the hope of customers but because he was waiting for his son, who had borrowed the family car to take his girl to a school dance. *La familia* Perez lived a couple of miles away from the street, and especially on a cold wet night Mr Perez had not fancied the walk home. The dance was to be over at midnight, and Diego, who was a good reliable boy, would then deliver his girl home and come to pick up his father at the shop: which in fact he had done, somewhere around twelve-thirty.

Meanwhile Mr Perez had spent a quiet evening sitting in his shop, waiting on the few customers who came. 'And you comprehend, later on it's pleasant sitting there alone—a few other shopkeepers who don't live here, they called out goodnight as they left—the Garcias two doors up stayed open late, and Mrs Sanchez across the way too, it's anything to make a dollar with that one—but the lights go out, one by one, and presently I'm the only one left open, and all is quiet but for the rain, splat-splat-splat, outside . . . I took the opportunity to write a letter to my brother in Fresno, and later on I read my book—I always keep a book here for the slow times, I'm a great reader and at home with the children it's noisy . . .' And just about midnight, as Mr Perez sat reading in his little lonely circle of light, a woman's voice spoke to him from the street.

Startled, he had looked up, and there she was outside the perimeter of light, no more than a dark figure. His glasses were for reading distance and in his surprise he hadn't taken them off, so he could give only a vague description. She spoke hurriedly and with a strange foreign accent on her English; she said she wanted something to protect her hat from the rain; one of his serapes would do, how much were they? The whole queer little transaction happened so quickly that it was not until she was gone that Mr Perez told himself it was surely odd, when she wanted to save her hat from the rain, that she had not naturally stepped over the threshold into the shop . . . 'But no, she stays outside, she is really only a hand and arm reaching into the light, you understand?' On hearing the price, two dollars, she held out the money, said any one would do, and he took it over to her. But she had forgotten the tax, the eight cents for the state, and when he reminded her she had impatiently handed him another dollar bill, said, 'That's all right, don't bother about change,' and walked away rapidly. This Mr Perez had not liked, because he was an honest man and also had his pride, and he did not like to accept tips like a waiter; however, she was gone—'and money is money.'

'That is very true. Was she carrying anything?'

Yes, she had had a suitcase; this she had set down a little in front of her to open her purse, and Mr Perez had seen it a trifle more clearly than the lady. It had been an old brown leather suitcase. And the purse she was carrying, it had glistened as she opened it, catching the reflection of light from the shop—he thought it might have been of that shiny plastic, or perhaps patent leather, a dark colour.

'And her hand—you saw her sleeve and hand?' Mendoza thought of Cara Kingman's silver-enamelled fingernails.

Yes, so Mr Perez had. A light-coloured sleeve, of a coat he thought, but could not say whether a long or short coat—and it had a dark cuff, like velvet. As for the hand, the lady had been wearing gloves.

'Of what sort?' asked Mendoza.

'One small thing I can tell you about that,' said Mr Perez. 'You comprehend, her hand is closer to me, and partly in the light, so I have a better look—for just that one small moment. She handed the money to me between her fingers, and then when I spoke of the tax, she reached into her purse again—impatient, you know—and held the third bill out on her palm, like so. Her gloves were a very light tan colour, like raw leather—I don't know if they were leather or cloth—but they had buttons on the inside of the wrist, and when she held her hand out so, I saw that on that glove—her left hand it would be—the little button was missing.'

A small amber-coloured button in the loose earth raked over the corpse. *'¡Diez millón demonios negros desde infierno!'* said Mendoza.

'This does not, I fear,' said Mr Perez sympathetically, 'please you to hear for some reason.'

'On the contrary, it is very helpful indeed. But at the moment I don't know what it means—except that I have been wrong somewhere—or exactly what to do with it . . .'

Hackett's older sister had a couple of kids, and when they were smaller, a few years ago, once in a while he'd got roped in to sit with them, read to them. There was a thing the little girl had been crazy about, *The Wizard of Oz*; he'd read out of that one a good deal, and right now something in it came back to him. The way one of the wicked witches had just disappeared when she died—nothing left at all, because all there'd been to her was a kind of shell of malice.

He wouldn't, some odd superstitious way, be at all surprised if the same thing happened to Mona Ferne before his eyes. Maybe Mr Horwitz took a jaundiced general view, but he'd been so right about this one. The front, and that was absolutely all . . .

'Such a terrible thing, I can't bear to think of it,' she said in her light, sweet voice. 'Poor darling Brooke. He *did* have talent, you know, he'd have done *great* things, I'm convinced—it's a tragedy for *that* reason as well as for all his friends.'

'Yes, of course,' said Hackett. 'When did you see Mr Twelvetrees last, Miss Ferne?'

She sat in the same chair her daughter had slouched in yesterday, but easily upright, graceful: everything about her was finished to a high gloss, from the lacquered flaxen coiffure to the fragile patent leather sandals with their stilt heels. Ten feet away, she looked an attractive thirty-five; any closer, no. All artificial: the smallest gesture, the tinkling laugh, the expression, the whole woman a planned thing into which God knew what minute calculations had gone. He didn't know much about such things, but he could guess at all the desperate, tedious, grim effort put forth—over the years more and more—on the front: the important thing. The massage, the cosmetics, the diets, the plastic surgery, the money spent and the time used, so much time that she'd had none left over for anything else at all, and so everything else about her had shrivelled and died, and she was an empty shell posturing and talking there. All to preserve the illusion that was no illusion, closer than across a room. Any nearer, you saw the lines and the hollows, the little scars at the temples and in front of the ears, the depth of the skilful cosmetic mask, the little loose fold of skin at the throat, and the veins standing up on the backs of the narrow hands with their long enamelled nails, their flashing rings, and the expensively capped front teeth, and the faint blistering round the eyelids from strain because she ought to wear glasses.

Those carefully made-up brown eyes widened on him. 'Heavens, Sergeant, you can't think *I* had anything to do with—? No, no, I see you must ask *everyone*, mustn't you? Well, now, let me see—I believe it must have been that Thursday, the twenty-ninth it would be. Yes. Brooke dropped by and asked me to go to dinner with him, but I had an engagement already . . . I never could bring myself to believe it was so, what dear Martin thought—Brooke would never—I've been quite upset about it, but then all of us who *knew* him—and now to have this terrible thing happen! I've hardly taken it in yet, but I'll try to help you however I can—'

'Yes, thank you.' This house, Hackett thought—something haunted about this house, with that great tree brooding over it, the rooms like caves until you turned on a light. But this wasn't the ghost who haunted it: the ghost was the other one . . . She had let him in—looking like hell again, today in an old-womanish grey cotton dress, ugly clumping shoes, her sullen face naked without cosmetics in the daylight from the door. Yet that clear pale skin—looking at her there, he suddenly saw that her eyes were beautiful, her good hazel-brown eyes clear as brook water, framed in heavy lashes. It was an oddly disturbing discovery, and almost immediately he'd made another which disturbed him even more.

And that wasn't his kind of thing, either—the intuitive understanding of emotional secrcts. He was a cop, not a psychologist; his business, and one he was pretty good at, was collecting facts and fitting them together to make a picture. Mendoza was the one with the crystal ball . . .

It was the way she did it, the tone of her flat voice—turning to call up the stairs, 'Mother!' All of a sudden he knew about this Angel Carstairs . . . You'd think she could do *something*, Mr. Horwitz said. *I'm twenty-six years old and* . . . But she was doing something: the same thing she'd been doing, probably, most of her life. She was punishing Mona—for being her mother, for being what she was. And so anything Mona was or did or said, she had to go the opposite way—just to annoy. It was the negative approach, and also a trap she'd got caught in; because now for such a long while this had been the one reason for Angel Carstairs' existence, she couldn't stop and turn another way and go out to find life away from Mona. Maybe she understood that, maybe she didn't; either way, she lived in a little hell she'd made herself, because every way she tormented Mona (reminding her with every mocking *Mother* of their ages, making herself the graceless ugly duckling in mute rebellion against the creed that beauty was the sole importance), she was tormenting herself too.

Yesterday he'd felt sorry for her; today, she made him mad. At the deliberate waste, the senseless negation.

And at the same time, facing this empty shell of a woman, he understood it.

He didn't want to stay in this house any longer than necessary, but he had questions to ask; he went on asking them. Mendoza had guessed right on one thing: it had been Mona Ferne who introduced Twelvetrees to the Kingmans and their Temple. She had met him through a small theatrical group—very careful to emphasise, not amateurs, but studio extras, bit players, that sort—'These *brave* young people, so ambitious and hard-working! I was one myself at one time, you know, and I realise how much it means, any little encouragement and support.' Now and then they put on shows, in a community theatre they could rent cheap, near Exposition Park; it was at one of those she'd met Twelvetrees. He'd been a new member of the group then; this was four years ago, he'd have been here only a few months. 'I saw at once he had talent—oh, he needed training and experience, but the essential thing was there. The work this splendid little group was doing was excellent for him, though the poor boy was impatient at the lack of recognition.'

Did she (he didn't expect much on this one) remember any comments Twelvetrees had made about the Temple or the Kingmans, after his first visit there? Well, nothing *specific*; he had, of course, been tremendously impressed, as anyone would be. Such a spiritual atmosphere, and dear Martin so impressive in his robes.

'Yes. Do you happen to know whether Twelvetrees owned a revolver?'

'A *revolver*—heavens, I don't think so, did you *find* one, I mean in his apartment? Oh, I mustn't ask questions, of course, I'm so sorry! I don't think I ever saw him with— But *there*,' she said with a coquettish little *moue*, 'I'm telling a lie. I *did*. But I don't think it was his. It was when he was in a play they were doing, oh, all of a year ago it must have been—and he only had it on the stage, of course, it would have been a prop.' She angled her new cigarette in its jewelled holder at him, in expectation; perversely he bent over his notebook, pretending not to notice, and let her light it herself.

'And if you don't mind, just for the record, Miss Ferne—were you at home on that Friday and Saturday night?—the thirtieth and thirty-first, that was.'

She didn't answer immediately, and then she said, 'Oooh, I *will* begin to think you suspect me! Was that when he was—? Do you *know*, I mean? I thought—the papers said—but you police are so clever, I expect you have ways of finding out things.' And by now Hackett was unwillingly fascinated, at the apparent extent of the woman's faith in her private illusion. A pretty sixteen-year-old innocent on her first date might get by with such provocative glances and giggles, such arch wriggling girlishness; from this woman it should have been absurd, and instead was somehow horrible. 'Well, let me *see*. Of course I know you have to ask, it doesn't mean you think I— As if I'd have any reason, my dear Brooke—but I mustn't make a parade of feeling, one has to bear these things . . . Let me see. That was a week ago last Friday and Saturday? Oh, of course, on the Friday night I went to see Miss Kent. Janet Kent—do you want the address? She's an old servant actually, she was Angel's nurse, such a reliable woman, but she was quite old then and now she can't work any more, and hasn't much to live on, poor thing. She's very proud, she won't take money, but I *do* give her clothes and things like that, you know, and—not to sound as if I'm praising myself or anything—I do go in as often as I can, if it's just for a minute or two, to cheer her up a little, you see. It's rather tedious sometimes—old people can be *such* bores, can't they?—but I try to do what I can.'

'Yes. What time did you get there and when did you leave?'

'Well, it *felt* like eternity, I couldn't get away from her that night, she wanted to talk—she gets lonely, poor thing—and she does so love to play cards, I had to sit down and play with her. I couldn't tell you exactly when I got there, but I think it must have been about seven-thirty, because I left right after dinner here—and when I did get away, I felt so exhausted—*such* a bore—I thought it must be midnight, but it was only a quarter to eleven. I came straight home . . . And the *next* night, of course, I was at the Temple for the service, as I am every Saturday night.'

'Thank you,' said Hackett, and stood up.

'Is that all you want to ask me? I do hope I've been of some help, though I don't see how *I* could tell you anything important.'

'One more thing,' said Hackett, and made himself smile at her, sound sympathetic, 'I hope you don't mind a personal question, Miss Ferne, but—well, you'd been out with Mr Twelvetrees socially quite a bit, and—er—well, was there anything like a formal engagement, or—er—?' He thought he'd done that quite well, the insensitive cop trying to be delicate.

'Ah,' she said, clasping one hand to her cheek, lowering her eyes. 'I—I shouldn't like to feel that such a *private* matter would go into your records, to be pawed over by anyone—' An appealing glance. He produced a very obviously admiring smile and murmured something about off-the-record. 'I—I can't say what *might* . . . But there were difficulties, you see? Dear Brooke was so proud, and of course I do have more money than he did. And there was a *little* difference in our ages, nothing to matter, but he—I'm sure you understand. But mostly, it was—Angel. I'm afraid the poor girl was quite foolishly in love with him—oh, quite *understandable*, of course, but utterly hopeless, naturally. Brooke *never*— She never *said* anything to show she was jealous, or—but I knew, and so did Brooke, of course. The way she behaved. I've seen her look quite—quite *wild*, sometimes, when we were going out somewhere together. These young girls . . . But it

would have made difficulties. Brooke was so understanding, he hadn't said a word to me, yet, but we both knew—you *do* see what I mean?'

Hackett said he did. She added suddenly, a little nervously, 'I do hope you won't have to question her, Sergeant—she's so *odd*, she never shows what she feels. Now *I* simply can't help it, a bundle of emotions, but then most women *are*, aren't we? But she hasn't been herself at all the last—well, since we knew, I expect it's been, though she's been very quiet and strange for a week or so. I really wouldn't like her upset further—'

'I don't think it's necessary.' Hackett didn't know when he'd been more anxious to get out of place; it was an unhealthy house, as if a miasma hung over it like that damned tree, darkening the spirit as the tree darkened the rooms. He went out to the entry hall, her high heels clacking sharp and light on the parquet floor there, behind him. And there was the girl again, swinging the door open for him, mocking, metallic . . .

'What, isn't he arresting you, Mother dear? What a disappointment!'

He felt the hate like an invisible sword poised.

'Darling, you mustn't joke to the police, they might take you seriously. And I hoped you were lying down, you've not been at all yourself lately, you know.'

'What d'you mean? I'm all right! What on *earth*—oh, I see, showing how *solicitous* you are of me! How ridiculous, I—' And she caught his glance, that held anger and pity because he couldn't help it, and suddenly, astonishingly, shamed colour flooded her face. She flung around furiously and ran away from both of them, up the stairs.

'*So* difficult—young girls,' murmured the woman. '*So unpredictable*. Quite wild, sometimes—she has always been— But I mustn't bore you with my troubles. I do hope you'll find whatever wicked person did this dreadful thing, soon. You've been so kind and understanding, Sergeant—'

CHAPTER ELEVEN

There was, of course, one obvious thing to do with this new information, and Mendoza did it; he came back to headquarters and set about getting a search warrant for the Temple and the Kingmans' apartment. As that would take a little time, he deferred his visit there until after lunch and meanwhile did some looking at various other odd bits of news that had come in, and some thinking about them.

They didn't have much on Twelvetrees' close associates aside from the Temple crowd; but barring the emergence of a girl friend with a grudge, or a rival ditto—something like that, maybe from among his theatrical acquaintances—the Kingmans still looked like the best bet, because when it came to motives for murder, money was always high on the list. That Miss Katherine Webster, the old lady, had been about the only one of that crowd who hadn't liked Twelvetrees, but it scarcely looked like anything that would have led to murder. She was one of the Kingmans' prize pigeons, a very wealthy old lady indeed; it was a little confirmation of his idea about Twelvetrees blackmailing the Kingmans, that in the face of old Miss Webster's dislike and openly voiced distrust, they hadn't obliged her by getting rid of him.

Miss Webster employed a chauffeur and had a four-year-old black Cadillac. It had curved-up fins.

The Kingmans had a three-year-old dark grey Buick with curved-up fins.

Mrs Bragg, urged to remember, said she had at various times seen cars belonging to Twelvetrees' visitors standing in front of his place but, beyond the fact that one she'd noticed once was dark-coloured and big, could give no details. He hadn't had many people come to see him; he wasn't there much, and had never given parties, anything like that. She herself had a two-year-old dark red Olds, and (depressingly) it too had curved-up fins.

But there was nothing to guarantee, of course, that Walsh had been right about that, his brief glimpse of that car.

At least, if this rather curious story of the exotic lady who'd bought the serape from Mr Perez and taken that cab ride out to Polk Street, had come unexpectedly, still it served a useful purpose: it pinned down the night pretty definitely. Again, not exactly solid evidence, but suggestive. Coincidences did occur, but that missing glove button, the scuffed brown leather suitcase, the obvious attempt to evade recognition, and the areas in question—near where the Porsche had been found, near the apartment—all pointed to the fact that she had something to do with this business. Even more eloquently was that indicated by what he'd got from a phone call to that address on Polk Street: people named Fawcett, sounded like a young housewife he'd talked to, baby crying in the background: no, they had not expected any out-of-town visitor that weekend, no one had come to the house all that Friday evening.

And about that time Mendoza remembered Dr Graas on Fairfax Avenue, and the allergy: not much in it, he'd thought, but you never knew. He called Dr Graas; and what he learned then sent him calling elsewhere . . . When Sergeant Lake came in with the search warrant about noon, he was brooding over a half page of notes. He tucked the warrant into his pocket, told the sergeant to have Piggott and Landers meet him at the Temple at one o'clock, and went out for lunch, meeting Hackett in the corridor.

'Let's catch each other up over a sandwich. You're looking gloomy about something, what's gone wrong?'

'Just human nature generally,' said Hackett. When they were settled in a booth in the hole-in-the-wall café, he described the Mona Ferne set-up.

Mendoza listened in thoughtful silence, and at the conclusion said irrelevantly, 'It'd be a help if we could get that gun identified. I do wonder if it's the same one Twelvetrees used in that play. No, no particular reason it should be, but you know those amateur groups—make-shift arrangements—they need something as a prop, somebody says, "Oh, I think I know where I can get one." . . . It might have been his own. Quite a few honest people don't bother about a licence, and I doubt if Twelvetrees would have . . . Bainbridge thinks, by the way, that it may have been the weapon. The wrong end of it, that is. Failing anything else there—we know the man wasn't knocked down against the bedpost or something, the way it's always happening in books—I'm inclined to agree . . . Yes, nasty—those women—just as you say. And a kind of culmination of everything else between them, if the girl was in love with Twelvetrees too—'

'Not *too*,' said Hackett. 'That woman's never been in love with anybody but herself.'

'*Es claro*. And neither of them, probably, meant anything to dear Brooke. He'd have taken up with La Ferne to begin with thinking she could do him some good in the way of theatrical contacts, but he must have found out by now she doesn't have a pull there any more. It was her money kept him dangling—an ace up his sleeve, *tal vez*. I'll bet you she'd given him other little presents than that fancy cigarette case—maybe those expensive shirts and ties, the flame-of-love bottles. Nuances in these things, sure—nothing crude about it, pay for services rendered—he'd make the graceful protests on the ground of his pride and so on, he'd have been good at that. And in case worst came to worst, and all his other rackets played out on him, and he'd got nothing in prospect better, he might have married her. She'd have jumped at that?'

'Oh, very definitely, I'd say.'

'Mmh. But it'd have been a last resort for him. I'll bet you something else, that the services rendered wouldn't, shall we say, call for overtime pay. That kind of woman is always cold as a fish, and Twelvetrees could have picked up something a damn sight more bedworthy . . . We ought to get something from Pennsylvania some time today. Meanwhile, I'll tell you what I've got . . .'

Hackett listened, said, 'Well, maybe it's a good thing I didn't lay any bets on Walsh's business. Though I still think— But anyway, it begins to look as if it *was* that Friday night. You don't really think you're going to find that light coat with dark trimming, or a glove with a missing button, or the serape, at the Kingmans' apartment, do you? Neither of them is that stupid.'

'You never know. One thing to remember here, somebody got one hell of a shock on Saturday night or Sunday when it first came out in the papers that the body had been found. That hadn't been the idea at all, and it's quite possible that until then whoever it was hadn't thought it necessary to get rid of those things. Maybe there hasn't been a chance since. We can hope, can't we? And I've had another idea—to start with, you remember what I said about a laundry bag? Well, I've got some idea of what went into it.'

'How?'

'I called this doctor Twelvetrees had been going to. And he said among other things that he'd prescribed this and that, and,'—Mendoza sat back over his coffee and lit a cigarette—'I got to thinking. You know, it's like the roof light on the squad car, and patrolmen changing round—we're so apt to overlook the little, familiar things. I called some pharmacies in the general areas where Twelvetrees might have gone—hit the right one fourth try, place near the doctor's office. And then I thought some more, and what I came up with was this.' He handed over a slip of paper.

'Atomiser, bottles, tie—' read Hackett. 'What's this?'

'It's a list of things we didn't find anywhere that ought to have been there. *Ya lo creo*, I'm not sure about all of them, but a couple of things we've got for sure. Dr Graas had prescribed a solution for spraying up his sinuses, and for that he had to have one of those atomiser things. And some antihistamine capsules. *And* the pharmacy says, and the doctor says, that on Friday afternoon, a little after four o'clock, Twelvetrees came into the pharmacy to have both prescriptions refilled, though he had some of each left, and he asked for a double amount because he was leaving on a trip.'

'You don't tell me,' said Hackett. 'More confirmation. That's very nice.'

'I thought so. The pharmacist called the doctor to check, and the doctor spoke with Twelvetrees over the phone and gave his O.K. Well, as I say, having my attention called to these little items that hadn't been there—in the apartment, the suitcases, or on Twelvetrees—I began to think of other things we hadn't found. First of all, there's the atomiser bottle, and the spray solution in a bottle about five inches high—holding sixteen fluid ounces, so the pharmacist says—and the little plastic bottle of antihistamine capsules. Both those bottles with his name and the doctor's on them, the name of the pharmacy and the prescription numbers. Those we know were missing. Then, you know, the corpse wasn't wearing a tie. He was all dressed except for that, and all the ties we found had been neatly packed. I think we can say almost for certain he was going to leave for somewhere that night, and he'd have put on a tie before he left. While he was busy packing, he'd have taken it off, or more likely he'd changed his clothes when he came in—hadn't put on jacket or tie while he packed. I can see that, can't you? But he'd leave a tie out, ready to put on. What else? He had on a shirt with button cuffs, so, no cuff links. But he had quite a collection of jewellery, didn't he? I think he'd always wear a tie clasp, or one of those new tie tacks. There'd be that left out ready. And—'

'Well, maybe. He might not have intended to wear a tie.'

'Sure, I said some of this is maybe, but keep it in mind. He was a snappy dresser, and it's not hot weather, when a lot of men aren't wearing ties. But here's something that *must* have been there—his watch. You're not going to tell me he didn't have one—how many men you know don't have some kind of watch, if it's only a five-dollar one from the drugstore? The odds are it was a wrist watch, because only older men or very conservative types carry a pocket watch these days.'

'That I'll give you. Funny we missed it before—one of us should have spotted that.'

'I see him, you know—thinking of what we've got so far—coming home to pack and clear out. Changing his clothes, maybe, and leaving off a few last-minute things that'll hamper him a bit in the process of packing and so on. The tie. The jacket—'

'He had a jacket on. Have you ever seen anybody put a jacket on first and *then* his tie?'

'I'm telling you about this little vision,' said Mendoza. 'Wait for it. He's packing. He leaves a few little things out, ready, for when he's finished. A tie and tie clasp. His watch. His jacket, probably hung over a chair, with a fair supply of handkerchiefs in it—or maybe a couple of clean ones waiting there on the bureau with these other odds and ends. The atomiser and the prescription bottles—maybe he meant to carry those on him, but I think more likely to put them in last, on top of everything else, to be handy. It's possible he had one of those plastic or leather cases for medicine bottles, to put them in. And possibly a hat. Quite a few young men don't wear hats any more, out here, but he hadn't been in California long, maybe he'd kept his Eastern habits. And another thing we can say for sure about—the bankbooks. He'd have carried those on him, but I think because he'd changed his clothes they were lying there on the bureau with the other things. And the twenty-three hundred bucks, in cash—not a little item to be overlooked, *¿no es verdad?* And something else that's a maybe—documentary evidence on what he had on the Kingmans. I don't say he'd *need* a document to show the faithful congregation, because—always assuming that he was blackmailing them—it was probably something fairly concrete, like a prison term, that anyone could verify with a little trouble. But the kind of people who go for Mystic Truths are usually pretty hard to unconvince, and

Kingman's a very smooth and plausible fellow. I don't think Twelvetrees could have stayed the pace this long without some tangible threat to hold over them, something that would have convinced even Miss Webster.'

'Very much maybe.'

'O.K., so it is. Then, did you ever know a male from the age of ten up who didn't carry some kind of pocket knife? Whether it was one of those genteel little flat silver things, or a horn-handled sheath knife? *That* was there on the bureau. And while he doesn't seem to have been a heavy drinker, I think almost certainly he'd have kept a bottle at home, for the odd occasion when he wanted a drink before going to bed, or if somebody dropped in. I don't know what'd it be, Scotch or gin or vodka, but I think it was sitting there too. He wouldn't care about leaving the odds and ends of stuff in the kitchen, and there wasn't much—a half bottle of milk, a few strips of bacon, a couple of eggs, a little coffee. But he'd take the bottle along. And I also think there was another package or so of cigarettes, maybe a whole carton—because there were only ten or eleven in his case, and a smoker doesn't let himself get down so low.'

'I'll give you that one too.'

'So there he is, almost finished packing—we still don't know why he was getting out, or whether he was in a hurry or just leisurely. Anyway, there he is, almost finished, except for a few little things *and* his soiled laundry, for which he has this bag laid out ready—I'm not guessing whether it was a paper bag or an ordinary cotton laundry bag. And at that point he has a visitor. Say two—the Kingmans. Skip the cross-talk, if there was any, and come to the murder. Now, here's my new idea. I see them in a little dither, as we've agreed confidence operators aren't given to violence. They're in a hurry to get away, also to protect themselves, and I see them snatching up this hypothetical documentary evidence, having a last look around to be sure they've left nothing incriminating—wiped off all prints and so on—and starting to leave—only to find that squad car sitting out there. So?

They aren't sure they haven't been seen—it doesn't matter then, nobody knows yet there's been a murder, but it will matter, later on. By the time they decide that patrolman, who has apparently seen them there, had better be put out of the way, the car's gone. And they spend a while chasing after it, cruising around looking—and getting in more and more of a dither—before they find it. I'm supposing, by the way, that the gun was Twelvetrees', and was lying there on the bureau, all convenient. Well, after they've found the car and had a try at the driver, they've got no way to be sure the man's dead and no danger to them—and so back they come, with another idea, to get rid of the corpse and try to pass his disappearance off as voluntary.'

Hackett said, 'This is a fine story, I can see Hitchcock making a dandy movie of it. But you're building it without much evidence.'

'I know, I know. But go on listening. I think that note to Mrs Bragg was either already written—by Twelvetrees, just to save time and trouble—and sitting there on the bureau, or he'd mentioned to them that he hadn't yet told her he was leaving, or they'd have had no other way to know that and consequently know the necessity for the note. Anyway, they make the whole plan hastily. Casting around for what to do with the body, they find that trap—and what better place? They can work at leisure, and no need to go trundling the body around in the car. They get the body buried, and they finish his packing for him and dump those suitcases down the trap. By this time they're worked up some more, they've had quite an evening, and there's still his car to dispose of. And then, just as they think they can relax a little, all of a sudden they spot these miscellaneous odds and ends on the bureau. Easy to overlook, you know, the state they were probably in. They'd remembered to put his jacket on him—easier than to cram it into a suitcase already full—but they hadn't bothered to put a tie on—what did it matter?—so they hadn't looked for one. And the idea of going down that trap again to jam all this stuff in a suitcase, or even just dump it—well, can't you see them just sticking it all into that bag handy there, and taking it away for disposal later?'

Slowly Hackett nodded. 'I can. Yes. But where does this woman down at Olvera Street come in? Why did Mrs Kingman have to do all that alone? And why was it the woman who drove the Porsche down there instead of him, anyway?'

'That part I don't know,' said Mendoza. 'Some reason may show up. But so far, I like all that, don't you?'

'It hangs together, after a fashion,' agreed Hackett grudgingly. 'And one thing, a couple of those items wouldn't be so easy to destroy or get rid of. They could soak the labels off the bottles. But if it's a modern apartment there'll be no open fire, to burn anything. Nothing identifiable about a tie, or the cash—but a watch, even the knife—'

'Especially as dear Brooke was given to having things monogrammed. Me, in that position I'd take the whole collection down to a lonely stretch of beach and consign it to the Pacific, but they haven't had much time, as I say. And speaking of that, I'd better not sit here detailing theories any longer—I'll see them and we'll have a look. What's your program?'

'I'm going out to Eagle Rock,' said Hackett rather morosely, 'to see this fellow Dave Morris who's some leading light in that theatrical club. See what he can give us on Twelvetrees.'

'Then, *¡pues vamos!*—let's go, and see what turns up.'

Hackett hadn't sounded very enthusiastic about all that, but on his way out to Eagle Rock he found himself hoping Mendoza was right, that it was those Kingmans. Because he'd started having a little vision of his own, and he didn't like it. Which was absurd on two counts: the first being, of course, that an efficient police officer should look at a case, and the people in it, objectively. You began feeling sorry for them, or mad at them, or contemptuous of them, and you couldn't look at the evidence fair and square.

And the second count was that the Kingmans were the obvious answer, that a thing like that in his mind was out of a paperback detective thriller; you just didn't run across such things every day.

But they happened, oh, yes. Now and then. Maybe this was one of the times.

And he wasn't happy to think it might be. No reason for it; what the hell were these people to Art Hackett?

Just because she had nice eyes, and he'd felt sorry . . . The things people did to each other. A lot of talk about active, deliberate evil, and it did harm, no question; but he sometimes thought more mischief was made by the plain stupidity, by the passive, self-centered uncaringness.

A culmination, Mendoza had said. And Hackett could see that happening. The last straw, you might say, for that girl Angel (my God, what a name!). That after Mona had, in a sense, turned her into what she was, the graceless ugly duckling—when she fell in love with a man, knowing he'd never look twice at her, it was Mona who *had* him. Never mind in what way. Making everything boil up in her all at once.

And how the hell any woman—a man like Twelvetrees, another one all front, the too-handsome collar ad—But look at it objectively: people didn't show much common sense about these things. Ever. When it came to feelings. How many men had fallen for a beautiful face and found that's all there was? And he was, wasn't he, just the type a girl like that *would* have fallen for—a girl without experience, younger than her age in some ways.

A girl not in a very sound psychological state to begin with. Whether she knew it or not . . . All right, he told himself almost angrily: build it; how might it have happened?

Mona Ferne would have had his address: the girl would have known where to go. Did she drive, have a car of her own? Find out. What would it be in her mind? Please look at me, *I* could give you more than she ever could! And him laughing at her? Or, If I can't have you, *she* never will!

The gun. His own? Or had she planned it, come prepared?

All that business afterwards—no, she couldn't— How could he say for sure? A streak there of deliberate planning, yes; the ways she devised for punishing Mona. She wasn't a mental defective by any means.

'Hell,' he said aloud to himself. The law said motive wasn't very important. You needn't go hunting up a plausible motive to match the nice solid tangible facts the law liked—ownership of weapon, presence on the scene, witnesses, fingerprints, and so on and so on. But in practice, that was one of the first things you had to look for. A lot of murders were done for very little reason, a moment's loss of temper, the ten bucks or thirty cents in the victim's pocket, a mere suspicion of wife or husband, things like that; but as a general rule, nobody got worked up to murder without some hell's brew of emotion churning inside them—whether it was what you might call rational emotion or not, lasting a minute or a year.

He didn't like the idea, but he could see it happening, since he knew the girl had been in love with Twelvetrees.

And it was, of course, a really wild one, no evidence there at all—something like one of Mendoza's hunches. He thought he'd keep it to himself for a while, see how things piled up—or didn't—on the Kingmans. If and when there was nowhere else to look, then look.

Meanwhile, he found the address Mona Ferne had given him; Dave Morris was at home and unsurprised to see him.

'I wondered if I ought to come in, when I saw the papers—but I hadn't seen him for a day or so before he supposedly left, I don't know anything really to tell you. Everybody's been calling me up, shall we go to the police or not—you know—' He shrugged. He was a stocky dark young man with an ugly, attractive face, and vitality exhaled from him with every breath; he was a restless talker, gesturing, changing position every ten seconds.

'Well, maybe you can help fill in some of the background, but first, when did you see him last?'

'On Wednesday the twenty-eighth,' said Morris promptly. 'I've got all this pat in my mind, ready for you, see. Some of us met here to talk over a new show we're thinking of doing, and for what it's worth I'll tell you that it was the first time Twelvetrees didn't jump at a part. He was—oh, what the British call very cock-a-hoop that night—kept hinting we might get a surprise soon, that sort of thing . . . No, nothing definite. He was just—on air, as if he'd just heard he'd inherited a fortune or something. Tell the truth, I wasn't very curious, and when he didn't show at our next meeting, I didn't do any crying over it . . .

Morris liked to talk, and Hackett was used to listening. Some more background emerged. Most of the people in this group had got on the lowest rung of the show-business ladder at least; Twelvetrees had been one of only three amateurs, without any experience, among them. 'And he was an awful ham, but the girls fell for his looks, you know.' It hadn't been for quite a while they'd found out how he'd earned a living—'if you can call it earned'—he'd apparently tried to keep his different lives in separate compartments; and when they did, they'd kidded him about it some. If Hackett wanted Morris's opinion, Twelvetrees didn't take the Mystic Truth very seriously, except of course as an easy living. Which was understandable. Morris himself wouldn't look down his nose at anything like that; eking out subsistence with on-call TV work as an extra was pretty precarious. No, Twelvetrees had never said much about his background, specifically where he came from, except just Pennsylvania. He wouldn't say that Twelvetrees had been bosom pals with anybody in the group, though he was faithful in attendance at their meetings and always eager to take a part in one of their plays.

'Which kind of cancelled out, if you get me, because while some of us aren't always able to take on a part—on account of prior commitments we'll get paid for—we do like to have competent actors in our little productions. We get a certain number of producers and so on keeping an eye on what we're doing, you see, which is why we go to the trouble and expense of putting shows on, besides giving ourselves experience. Stop me, by the way, if I get irrelevant, maybe you're not interested in all this. Well, for one thing, he was a bit older than most of us, you know, and the men didn't like him—including yours truly—because, well, we don't usually care much for the too-too-handsome boys who go round preening themselves in mirrors, do we? Yes, he was rather like that. And the girls, a couple of them are faithful devoted wives, and a couple more have enough common sense to see through that kind. And as for the couple left who'd have been thrilled-to-pieces-darling if the divine creature had asked them for a date, he did a lot of arm patting and general showing off, but beyond that, not a tumble.'

'You trying to say he was on the nance side?'

'Oh, Lord, no, don't think so. A bit la-de-da, but I put that down to his having deliberately taught himself, you know—not to be snobbish about it—upper-class manners. I think he may have come from somewhat lower down, which is nothing against him, and acquired the polished veneer, and people like that usually overdo it a little. He never acted casual, if you get me. About the girls, I figured myself he had a steady, and for some reason never brought her round or mentioned her. Just conjecture, but maybe when it came to females he preferred the kind he knew in the lower ranks, and didn't care to exhibit one of 'em to us.'

'Possible,' said Hackett. 'Any of these girls in your bunch named Marian Marner?'

'Never heard of her. Not even a Marian in the lot.'

'Well,' said Hackett. 'Of course, he was going around with Miss Mona Ferne—'

Morris let out a bellow of laughter and started to tell him just what *that* amounted to. They'd all got a hell of a kick out of that—not, of course, in front of Twelvetrees. Like all that kind, he didn't have much sense of humour about himself. The first time he'd met her he'd been all over her, putting out the full wattage of boyish charm. Maybe it'd been a dirty trick, but the rest of them hadn't said a word to him—seeing what was going on—about her being a dead one so far as the profession went, *kaput*, washed up long ago, and no use as a patroness. Which was obviously the idea in his mind. And of course she was all too pleased to have him dancing attendance . . . 'that *woman*, that damned awful woman.' They put up with her because she was a regular at their shows, one admission ticket to count on, and you couldn't offend people who might talk, good or bad, about you in public; one thing you could bet on, they never had got and never would get any cash support from Mona, however much she talked about her sympathy for these brave struggling young people. Had Hackett met her? Wasn't it the damnedest thing how she still saw herself as the glamour queen? All the same, not that she needed convincing about it, one reason she'd been a soft mark for Twelvetrees; it wouldn't be every day she picked up a handsome young man so anxious to oblige. And mind you, she wasn't—Morris would say—a fool, when it came to money and so on, either; a shrewd streak there, but by all accounts she never had seen through Twelvetrees, because she was so anxious to believe it was, so to speak, her *beaux yeux* alone that held him.

'Another little reason none of us cared much for him—I mean, hell, I'm no moralising prude, but there are limits. He found out for himself soon enough she couldn't wave the fairy wand and waft him in front of a big producer who'd fall on his neck with the glad cry, "My boy, you're just what I've been looking for!" But by then he'd also found out she was loaded, and so damn pleased to have him hanging around there was graft to be had—you know, the little present for a good boy.'

'We'd figured that one,' said Hackett. 'Off the record, you think it went any further than taking her around night clubs and so on?'

'Who knows?' said Morris. 'All I can say is, I doubt it very strongly. For all I've been saying about him, he was fastidious as a cat—me, I'm not, exactly, but *I* wouldn't have wanted to go any further, in his position, if you take me. Would you? No matter how much you liked the gold cigarette case and the fancy clothes?'

Hackett laughed and said you never knew what you could do until you got really strapped, but it didn't seem Twelvetrees had been down so low. Morris agreed. 'Why didn't we get rid of him? Not so easy. And maybe it's a case of the pot calling the kettle black, because he had more money to spend than most of us, and he was always glad to fork over—props, theatre rent, costumes and so on—so long as he was one of the boys and girls all chummy together, *and* got a chance to tread the boards once in a while.'

'Speaking of props, about a year ago you people did a show that called for a gun. Where did it come from and where did it go afterwards?'

Morris cocked his head. 'A gun? He wasn't shot, was he? I know you can't answer any questions, but I'm being a good boy and not asking any because I know that, I'm not disinterested. We're all seething with curiosity—our glamour boy murdered! *Was* he shot? The papers didn't say.'

'No, he wasn't. There's no reason you shouldn't know. We found a gun there and just wonder if it was his. This gun you used in the play—'

'*Bitter Harvest,*' said Morris. 'I remember. Twelvetrees supplied the gun, all right, but I don't know whether it was his or he'd borrowed it somewhere. He never said. I don't know much about guns, it was a pistol of some sort—' He measured with his hands. 'Longish barrel—looked fairly old, but I don't know. When we went over the list of props for that show he said he'd contract to get the gun, and he showed up with it at the first rehearsal—that's about all I know. Don't think any of the others could tell you any more, but you could ask . . . Loaded? My God, no, at least I don't think so, he wasn't *that* big a fool. Well, actually it doesn't get fired during the play, and Twelvetrees had it all the time on stage. We ran that show for seven nights, our usual, and then packed it up, and that's the last I saw of the gun—he took it away again.'

'Would you recognise it?'

Morris thought so. Hackett said they'd have him take a look; but when he'd thanked him and started back downtown, it didn't seem Morris had added much useful. Except the cocky mood Twelvetrees had been in on Wednesday night. Not likely to be much in that—or was there? Be nice to know why. Be nice to know a lot more than they did.

Suppose it was the same gun; that didn't say it was Twelvetrees' own, or where he'd borrowed it . . . Question the whole lot of these people who'd known him, about seeing him with a gun, hearing him mention one. And probably come up with nothing.

A little routine to take care of. Not that it mattered much, but send somebody to check with that Kent woman Mona Ferne had visited on Friday night: (yes, and it might matter, for consequently Mona wouldn't have known if the girl was out). See if anything had come in from Pennsylvania. Also, now they knew that Twelvetrees had been at that pharmacy on Fairfax after four o'clock, it might not be a bad idea to have a look round the places adjacent, see if he'd stopped anywhere else in the vicinity.

He thought again, unwillingly, about that ridiculously unwelcome hunch of his about the girl . . . He wondered how Mendoza was getting on.

CHAPTER TWELVE

Mendoza was in a very bad mood with himself. It seemed that from the beginning in this thing he had, like some thickheaded ex-patrolman working his first case in plain clothes, been overlooking little niggling details that were, on analysis, of the first importance. The only thing he could figure, and it was a depressing thought, was that he must be getting old.

Mendoza, who had made a little reputation for himself as one of the bright boys at headquarters! Maybe he needed glasses; maybe he needed to take one of those memory courses.

He'd stood outside his damned Temple, on Saturday night, and read the sign, and among other things it had said in black and white, *Ceremony of the Inner Chamber* (whatever in God's name that was), 8 P.M. Fridays. So? So he'd gone along building up this beautiful story about how the Kingmans had committed the murder beginning at about seven-thirty and ending after midnight on a Friday night. When, by their never-enough-to-be-cursed schedule, they were expected to be at the Temple. And it appeared that was just exactly where they had been on Friday the thirtieth. Because Mr Martin Kingman wasn't the hypnotist to get twelve members of his flock to swear to a lie on his behalf.

'. . . *And* Mr Lester J. Derwent,' concluded Kingman, and looked up from the list in his mind. 'I hope that's satisfactory, Lieutenant? I cannot help feeling you are wasting time here, on ourselves—but I repeat, of *course* we are willing and eager to help you however we can, we have no secrets, indeed your search warrant was quite unnecessary. I'm sure I speak for my wife too in saying that you would have been welcome to search anywhere without it.'

'Oh, of *course*,' she agreed immediately, using her eye-widening trick on him. 'Anything that will help in this dreadful thing, though I *do* agree that it's a waste of time to suspect *us*. We thought the world of Brooke—'

Of course, of course. One of these twelve people (those who had progressed to some higher Temple rank and were admitted to that particular ritual) was a respected stockbroker—another was a wealthy art patron whose name appeared frequently on the social pages. And there were, in any case, definitely no flies on Kingman, when he sat there so confidently welcoming the cops to pry into his cupboards, the cupboards would be bare.

Mendoza looked at them with a dislike he concealed with difficulty. At paunchy, respectable, plum-voiced Kingman, bald head shining with honesty, as it were; at Madame Cara gracefully arranged on her couch, draperies trailing, silver-nailed hands gesturing, looking rather like an earnest horse. Damn the pair of them.

And he was going senile. Now he was wishing they didn't have all that suggestive evidence to say it had been that Friday night. Not that it would make any difference; the Kingmans couldn't have done it on Saturday night either, on account of their damned Sabbath ritual.

They sat there beaming innocence and integrity at him, this pair of slick fraud artists, and he shut his teeth on some impolite remarks. 'Thanks very much,' he said. 'It's more or less a formality, you know—we have to look everywhere.'

'Oh, yes, I see that,' said Kingman. 'You can't be sure, of course, until you do. Yours must be an interesting job, Lieutenant. Of course you can regard these sad affairs—um—impersonally. I fear we who are involved in them cannot. I still find it quite incredible that the poor boy—ah, well, we must not take up your time with irrelevancies.'

'By the way, another little matter, while I'm here. Do both of you have drivers' licences?'

'Dear *me*, how mysterious,' exclaimed Madame Cara. 'What can that possibly have to do with—? As a matter of *fact*, no, Lieutenant, we don't. Poor Martin has some visual defect, they never would—'

'Er—technically I believe it is called "tunnel vision,"' said Kingman seriously, adjusting his glasses. 'In our home state, it prevented me from obtaining a licence, and I have never, consequently, learned to operate a car.'

'I see.' That could be checked; but it would without a doubt prove true. And there was the answer, the reason the woman had had to dispose of the Porsche alone. And what the hell good was it to him when they had an alibi for that night?

'I'm *afraid* I'm not a very good driver,' said Madame Cara with a sudden nervous giggle. 'The traffic quite terrifies me. But one must have faith to *accept*—it's a little exercise I practise *every* time I get into the car—whatsoever the great All-Parent *intends*, I say to myself, I must not fear or rebel against. It's really a great pity that Martin can't drive, I'm sure he would be *much* more competent than I am—being an Earth person, you know—he is a Virgoan—of course it's *not* to be wondered at that an Air person like myself isn't good at dealing with these *mechanical* things. I expect you find that true yourself as a Piscean, Lieutenant—a Water sign, of course you are governed by Neptune—'

'My dear,' said her husband gently, 'we must not—um—proselytise at the lieutenant. I fear he is not much in sympathy with our views.'

'Oh, do forgive me,'—she picked up the cue at once. 'Nothing must be forced—understanding must come of *itself*, when the spirit is open to receive.'

Mendoza eyed her with exasperation and asked (in the rather vague hope of frightening them a little with how much he knew) whether she had ever possessed a light-coloured coat with dark trimming down the front and dark cuffs. He did not, of course, have any hope at all that his men had found such a thing in her wardrobe.

No, she could not remember ever having a coat like that and certainly had none now; it sounded *quite* attractive, very smart.

Mendoza thanked them, listened again to reassurances that they were *eager* to help however possible, and came away. Downstairs, Piggott and Landers were just finishing an expert going-over of the Temple; nothing of any interest had showed up. No weapons, no incriminating documents, nothing unusual among personal possessions or down here: that is, said Piggott disapprovingly, if you didn't count all the funny-looking robes and them heathen statues standing around. Looking downright wicked to him—Piggott was a pillar of the Free Methodist Church—would it be, he asked (dropping his tone discreetly) one of these *cults*, like, where they had *orgies*?

Mendoza said he doubted it, unfortunately, or they might be able to turn the damned pair over to Vice. He sent the men back to headquarters, and most unusual for him sought out a bar and had a drink before going back downtown himself.

There he met Hackett, and confessed his sins with bad grace. Hackett looked gloomier than ever, and passed on the gist of what Morris had said. He was going to take a couple of men and set out on a hunt for all these show people, in the hope that one of them would remember something more about the gun; Morris had said he had to come into town late this afternoon, he'd stop by and take a look at it.

Nothing had come in from Pennsylvania. 'What the hell are they doing back there,' said Mendoza irritably, 'pawing through all their records by hand? Damn it, and what good will it be if they hand us our motive? You know, I do wonder why Twelvetrees was so set up that Wednesday night?'

'Does it matter?' asked Hackett.

'It might. It might tie in somewhere.' He wondered harder about it an hour later. Hackett took off on his hunt, and Mendoza annoyed Sergeant Lake by wandering around the sergeants' office and the anteroom, asking every three minutes whether Pennsylvania had communicated. The patient recheck with all those agencies hadn't turned up a smell of Marian Marner. Then, about four o'clock, a trio of nervous men came in together and said they had something to say about this guy who'd been buried under a house, and who should they say it to?

They were, it appeared, respectively the owner, cashier, and waiter of a small restaurant on La Brea Avenue, and what they had to say was that Brooke Twelvetrees had been in the place about five o'clock on that Friday afternoon. It wasn't the first time he'd been in; he wasn't a regular, but every now and then he came in early like that, and once when he'd been talking with Charlie here—that was the waiter—he'd happened to mention that it wasn't far from his doctor's office, so maybe it was the days he saw this doctor he stopped in at the restaurant.

And, deduced Mendoza, the times he wasn't going out with anyone later; by these men, the restaurant would be the kind of place without much tone, a cheap place Twelvetrees would go to alone to pick up a casual meal.

Well, early like that, there weren't many other customers, and this guy did a little talking to the waiter and cashier. They'd gathered he was hoping to get in the movies, and he sure had the looks for it, didn't he? That Friday, he'd come in (some confused, anxious calculations of time here) about ten to five, and left about half past. Charlie, specifically asked about his order, came up with nothing more definite than that it *might* have been beef stew and so on. They could try to pin it down by the waiter's checks, but of course the name wouldn't be there, it would be a question of the time the check was filed, and not definite. Anyway, both the waiter and cashier got the impression the guy wasn't feeling so hot—like he'd, oh, just lost his job or got slapped down by his girl or something. He was usually kind of friendly and cheerful, but that time he hadn't much to say. And when the cashier had remarked it sure was good to see all this rain, they needed it bad and he'd bet the farmers were celebrating today, well, the guy had said —with various profane adjectives—that it was nice *somebody* was happy. And he'd paid his check and walked out.

And it was always nice to have additional information, but Mendoza wished he had some idea of what this meant. It might be quite unimportant as far as the murder was concerned. But it looked as if something had happened to spoil some hopeful plan the man had had. On Wednesday night he was on top of the world, hinting mysteriously at surprises; on Friday he was in a bad temper, and packing up to clear out.

Mendoza swore to himself, called the Kingmans, and put the question. After fractional hesitation, he thought, Kingman said, really, the exchange he'd had with Twelvetrees that Friday afternoon had been so casual, he couldn't say what mood the boy had been in. Mendoza was slightly encouraged to detect this as a lie; but what did *that* mean, why should Kingman lie about it?

About then, Dwyer, who'd been out seeing various people, came in and said that if it meant anything, it looked like those Kingmans had been on the hunt for Twelvetrees as early as that Saturday morning. Four people so far, Miss Webster among them, had said that Mr Kingman had phoned them that morning asking if they'd seen Twelvetrees or knew where he was. Giving as excuse some unspecified business suddenly arisen.

'*¿Oyé, para qué?*' said Mendoza vexedly. 'What's the use—this I don't see head or tail of! I'm getting old, Bert. Old and decrepit.'

Dwyer said sympathetically that sometimes a thing got stuck, that was all, until all of a sudden you got hold of something that explained the whole thing. Mendoza said morosely that when and if it came along probably somebody would have to point it out to him, the elementary mistakes he'd been making—premature senility, without a doubt. He told Dwyer about Morris coming in to see the gun, left a note on the sergeant's desk of a few places where he might be between now and midnight, added an injunction to call him *immediatamente* if anything came in from Pennsylvania, took up his hat, and left the office.

He walked into Alison's apartment at seven o'clock and found her contemplating a small canvas propped on an easel in front of the window. She operated a moderately successful charm school through the week, in her spare time was a painter—and a ruthlessly self-critical one. She said now despondently, 'I've missed it—it's no good at all, is it? Looks like a postcard.'

Mendoza looked briefly at a pleasant, if undistinguished,

painted view over the immediate rooftops, and said it looked all right to him. 'All *right*!' said Alison crossly. 'I don't know what you mean by that! It's hopeless, that's all.'

'*Claro qué si*, it's hopeless. *Ambos tu y yo mismo*, you and me both. Stop worrying over that, come and soothe me. I need soothing like the very devil. I need to have my hand held by a sympathetic female and be told what a big strong smart masterful fellow I really am. I might even find it helpful to lie down quiet with my head in your lap, of all ridiculous conventional poses, and listen to the same theme at infinite length.'

'*¿Pobrecito, qué paso?*' asked Alison, sufficiently alarmed by this unprecedented behaviour to forget her art. 'Come and sit down, tell Mother who's been mean to you.'

He pulled her down beside him on the couch. 'That's the damned awful thing, *mi vida*, it's nobody else but me—I've been a stupid, thickheaded, imbecilic dunce. I don't know any more of importance about this thing than I did before we found the corpse—and because I *am*—tell me, tell me!—because I *am* a brilliant and gifted detective, quite unused to failure, I'm out of sorts with myself.'

'You are,' said Alison obediently, 'a brilliant and gifted detective, *un macho muy valoroso, un hombre inteligente, y agraciado, y amiable, y de aspecto bravo y bello, y atractivo, y importante, y—y encantador, y concienzudo, y—y elegante, y honorable, y un jefe muy justamente, y—y—y magnánimo, y absolutamente un caballero muy satisfactorio y maravilloso*. Do you feel any better now?'

'A little, a little. This I like to hear. So I am, I know—'

'*¡Y un egotiste!*' said Alison.

'That I know too.' The kitten Sheba, who resembled her mother in being brown, sleek, and affectionate, leaped up beside him, walked onto his stomach, and settled down to purr as he stroked her. 'Ah, I do begin to feel better—I am being duly appreciated . . . Even, I think, my mind begins to work with its usual acuteness . . . Damn it, I can still be right! Friday night—Friday night. That ritual or whatever it is, it was over at nine. All right. Say they got away by a quarter or twenty past, they *could* be out at 267th by ten o'clock. I'd give myself an hour at least, that drive, but they could have done it.'

'Undoubtedly,' said Alison.

'You know nothing about it, *silencio*.'

'I'm only soothing you. Whatever you say is so must be so, *naturalmente*.'

'*Muy bien*, soothe me in silence.' He slid down comfortably, cradling the kitten, stretched out and put his head in her lap. 'They could have. Now, Bainbridge says two to six hours before death for that beef stew and so on. Seven to eleven. That's all right, that can fit. Say he's raised his demands, and—of course, *¡claro está!*—because whatever plan he was counting on that Wednesday had fallen through. Yes. They want to see him. They chase right out there after their damned service, and get there about ten, say even ten-thirty. And—and there's an argument. But, a fight? This namby-pamby blackmailer and a smooth con man? Why? Can we say maybe Twelvetrees insulted Mrs Kingman, and Kingman was protecting her honour?'

'*¡Oyé, la drama magnífico!*' said Alison. 'Next week *East Lynne*.'

'*¡Chiton*, I'm thinking! Well, anyway, there's a struggle, Kingman snatches up the gun lying there on the bureau—Twelvetrees' gun—and hits him a little too hard. O.K. Then, just as I built it up before—the dither, the inspiration of the trap, etcetera. Only Bartlett had nothing to do with it, it all happened at least an hour after he'd been killed—that was the kids after all. And because Kingman doesn't drive, the woman went off to do that part of it while he buried the body and so on. It'd have taken that long easily, the time it took her to drive in with the Porsche—after they'd made the plan, too—that took some time—to put her on the spot to be the lady in the serape.'

The kitten got up, stretched, yawned to show him a pink mouth and needle-sharp white teeth, turned around and settled down again. '*¡Perfecto!*' said Alison. '*Obvio*, that's how it was.'

'You are no help whatever,' said Mendoza. 'And this is a most uncomfortable position, regardless of all the movies and the award-winning photographs of couples in parks. If it wasn't for disturbing the cat, I'd move . . . Obviously it is *not* how it was—not exactly, anyway. I can see them finding the trap by accident, or just possibly Twelvetrees had called their attention to it on some former visit. As confidence workers, they're used to making slick plans on the spur of the moment. But how the hell did they know where to find that trowel? They—' He stopped abruptly.

'These are the people from that Temple? Well, she's psychic, isn't she? She divined it.'

'*¡Aguarda, un momento! Si, como no? Yo caigo en ello!*—yes, of course, of course!' He swung his legs off the couch and stood up abruptly, holding the kitten. 'Why didn't I see that before? I tell you, I'm going senile!'

'But you get it now, or so you just said. Better late than never. You've solved the whole case—*and* under my helpful feminine soothing.'

'Well, not exactly. But look. Is it likely—I ask you—that this brash young fellow with his movie ambitions, his record as a pimp's apprentice—a city man, an apartment liver—is it likely that he was remotely interested in gardening? Not by any stretch of the imagination! Then why did he go to the trouble of convincing Mrs Bragg he was, buying that plant food for her damned Tree of Heaven and so forth? Why else?—because it gave him an excuse for fooling around it, and probably when he undertook the care of the thing she wouldn't bother with it any more. I'll bet on any odds you name that was his safety deposit box. I'll swear it, he had something concrete on them—and he wouldn't leave it tucked in the toe of a shoe or in a drawer, he wouldn't carry it on him—not that cautious, canny, ladylike boy—to be stolen so easy or maybe involve him in a roughhouse, not that one! He found a safe place to stash it away, where nobody would think of looking—buried with that Tree of Heaven—and he'd just brought the trowel from Mrs Bragg's carport to dig it up with, to take with him, and that's why the trowel was there in his kitchen. And—'

The phone rang and Alison went to answer it. The kitten scrambled up on his shoulder and began to lick his ear thoughtfully. 'For you,' said Alison.

Mendoza took the receiver, listened, began to smile, and finally fired rapid orders. 'Get hold of Hackett—oh, beautiful, beautiful, just how I'd figured it!—who's in the office? O.K., I want Boyce, one man'll be enough, and a blank warrant—jump to it! I'll be there in twenty minutes, I want it waiting! I felt all along that was the answer— Tell Hackett to step on it, I'll meet him at the Temple in forty-five minutes . . . O.K., thanks, get busy!' He slammed the phone down, handed the kitten to Alison, kissed her, and snatched up his hat. 'I'm vindicated—not so senile after all! Pennsylvania has come through and I think we'll tie up this case tonight—*se buena, hasta más ver*,' and he was gone.

'Well!' said Alison, and returned to dissatisfied inspection of the canvas.

What Pennsylvania—specifically, the Chief of Police of Philadelphia—said was that the prints of the corpse identified him in their records as one Robert Trask, particulars as follows—etcetera. Nothing of Trask's antecedents were known beyond the fact that he had come from some place in New England, to the detriment of Philadelphia, some twelve years back. He had been mixed up in various unsavoury businesses, but had been charged and convicted only once, seven years ago—contributing to delinquency of minors, a year's sentence.

After he got out, he had been on the scene for a couple of years, and twice private citizens had lodged complaints of attempted extortion on him, but he had managed to wriggle out of the legal net. He had then disappeared, and Philadelphia was interested to learn what had subsequently happened to him.

As for the description appended of a middle-aged couple

calling themselves Kingman, it was of course impossible to say definitely without fingerprints to check, but it was likely that they were the same pair known to Philadelphia as Martin and Caroline Sellers. The Sellers had been charged with fraud on a private complaint in the same year that Robert Trask had been put inside, but had got off on some technicality with the aid of a smart lawyer; the case had attracted some local publicity. They had held private séances with all the trappings, Mrs Sellers being the medium, and been detected in fraud by a local officer of the Society for Psychical Research. Investigation of their background at the time (by the Society, not the police) had turned up the fact that they had at one time been in show business with a mind-reading act, billed as The Telepathic Turners. Turner appeared to be the legal name. Two years previously they had been charged and convicted of fraud—on the same count as the Philadelphia arrest, fake séances—in Chicago, were fined, and had served a year apiece inside. If Los Angeles could oblige with prints of these Kingmans, Philadelphia could say definitely whether they were the Sellers-Turners; but as the latter had disappeared from the scene so far as the police knew about five years back, it was a matter of small doubt.

'We'll send prints,' said Mendoza to Hackett happily, 'but it does look like a foregone conclusion. So there's our motive—and I wonder, considering that they were tried the same year Twelvetrees-Trask was, I wonder if that's where he met them. Or saw and remembered them. In a courtroom corridor, somewhere like that. And it's also nice to know that he'd apparently settled on gentlemanly blackmail as an easier racket than what he'd been in—you see how the pattern worked out with Whalen.'

'Yes, he couldn't leave it alone.' They had just joined forces outside the Temple. 'You're going to spring it on them straight?'

'Might just give them enough of a jolt to come out with something damaging, yes.'

Boyce asked if there was likely to be a roughhouse about

the arrest. '*Nada*, they're con artists, grifters—never any trouble with that kind.'

The entrance to the place was dark, only the discreet sign lighted, and the door locked; but there was a bell push. They waited, and presently a light went on and beyond the glass-panelled double doors Kingman could be seen approaching unhurriedly, neat and respectable in his navy suit and immaculate white shirt, the light shining on his rimless glasses. He looked like a verger about to welcome the congregation. He swung back the right-hand door, and there they were, close, crowding in; he took a couple of steps back, but his genial expression didn't alter. 'Why, Lieutenant Mendoza—good evening, sir—'

'Good evening, Mr Turner,' said Mendoza, grinning amiably at him. 'Let's go upstairs and include Mrs Turner in this little get-together, shall we? And no fair communicating telepathically on the way! My friends and I think it's about time for you to start telling us the truth—about various things, but mainly about your dealings with the late Mr Robert Trask, and just how you came to murder the poor fellow.'

Kingman took another step back. His round ruddy face lost some of its colour. He said dispiritedly, 'Oh, hell. Hell *and* damnation.'

CHAPTER THIRTEEN

'Oh, *dear*,' said Cara Kingman. 'Well, I suppose you'd better come in. I was afraid they would find out, Martin, you know I said at the time, let it go and be thankful it was only the twenty-three hundred. You see what's come of it, not that I'd dream of reproaching you, dear, you only did what you thought best.' She looked at Mendoza resignedly.

Kingman put an arm around her. 'Now don't you be

frightened, Cara, but it's a bit more than that, they think we *did* it, you see. I—'

'*Murdered* him? Oh, Martin! Well—well, we'd just better tell them the *truth*—'

'I'd advise it,' said Mendoza, sitting down. 'And not the kind of truth you've seen in a crystal ball, Mrs Turner. Of course there's quite a lot you don't have to tell us. I know that Trask was blackmailing you, and what he had—that last business in Philadelphia. Your present little flock wouldn't like hearing about that, and how well you knew it. A spotless reputation is the chief thing in your business, and it annoyed you considerably when Trask showed up. You had to play ball with him, but that five hundred a month was quite a bite out of your take—'

Kingman said gloomily, 'You couldn't speak a truer word.'

'It was *wicked*,' said his wife. 'After all the bad luck we'd had, it's not a very steady living after all—those awful night clubs and so on—horrible places most of them, but I shouldn't be uncharitable, perhaps all this liquor does serve some purpose of *destiny*. But when everything was going so *well*, and we'd quite settled down— We're neither of us getting any younger, you know, Lieutenant, and we must try to save towards our old age, and besides it's been so *nice* here, so peaceful, we'd quite felt we were *settled for good* until that *wicked* young man came. He was, truly. Going to all that trouble of sending back East for that copy of the *Telegraph*—the one where the trial was reported, you know, and our pictures in it too, *quite* good ones, I'm sorry to say—and he had it, what do I mean, Martin, photo—?'

'Photostated,' sighed Kingman. They sat side by side on the couch, holding hands, looking at the police solemnly; a little of Kingman's precise manner dropped away, but not much—he'd played his part for so many years, he'd grown into it. 'Oh, it was awkward, I can't deny it. In a way, the most annoying thing about it was that, well, it wasn't as if we'd been convicted of any wrong-doing—'

'However, you had been before—in Chicago,' said Mendoza, and mentioned the year.

'That *terrible* jail,' said Madame Cara, and closed her eyes.

'Now wait just a minute here,' said Kingman fussily, adjusting his glasses. '*Wait* a minute. (Don't fret, my dear.) I do *not* think of myself as a—a confidence man, Lieutenant, *nor* do I hold any sort of grudge against the police for doing their duty. That unfortunate affair in Chicago was due to a misunderstanding on my part regarding Illinois law. We have always made an earnest effort to see that we conform to the law—it's only common sense, after all. When you come down to it, Lieutenant, we are only selling a service the public wants and is eager to buy. And I confess I do not see the difference between presenting an—ah—act to amuse an audience, and doing essentially the same thing without the footlights.'

'I always *hated* all the travelling about,' said his wife. She looked about the room sadly. 'That is such a nice place, and I did think we were settled down at last. But—but it doesn't matter, Martin dear, we'll get along as well somewhere else, I daresay, the main thing is to explain to them that *of course* we didn't *kill* him. Why, I'm sure such an idea never entered our heads, even when he was being *horridest*. Really, Lieutenant Mendoza, we're *not* that kind of people.'

'Boyce, close your mouth,' said Mendoza *sotto voce*, 'and try to look more dignified. Now to go on a step further—we'll hear your side of it in a moment—the annoying Mr Trask had recently increased his demands, hadn't he? He was asking too much, and it decided you not to be bullied any longer. You had had a few words with him that Friday afternoon, and far from not being sure what mood he was in, you knew he was feeling ugly. A little side racket he'd been planning had fallen through—' He paused, ostensibly to light a cigarette, watching Kingman: did he know what the side racket had been?—but the other man only nodded glumly. 'You had a show to put on here at eight, you couldn't chase after him then, but as soon as you could get away, you drove out to his apartment. You got there about a quarter past ten—'

'I remember noticing,' said the woman, 'it was *exactly* a quarter past by my watch as we drove into that—that court. Oh, please don't hesitate to use that ashtray, Lieutenant, that's what it's *for*. Really, for the time of night and the traffic—so nerve-wracking—we made excellent time. You see, Martin, how very clever they are to find all this out.'

'My dear, you needn't say *I told you so*.'

'But I never *would*. I do believe in destiny, so it's no use. Do you know, Lieutenant, we'll have been married thirty-one years on the twentieth of this month, and never *any* serious disagreement between us. I put it down chiefly to the fact that we *do* always remember to be polite to each other, although it is true that Martin is a very even-tempered man.'

Mendoza grasped grimly at the tail of his last remark. 'There was a quarrel, and you hit Trask—with the butt of a pistol which—'

'Now wait *just* a minute, please, sir,' said Kingman. He leaned forward with a kind of desperate earnestness. 'I don't know exactly how we're going to prove it to you, because naturally there were no witnesses present. And I must say I do understand how you came to pick on us, though how you found out we were there that night I don't know. But I do assure you that you have—um—leaped to a wrong conclusion when you accuse me of killing that—that *most* unpleasant young man. I hope to *God* I can convince you, sir, that we hadn't any hand in the murder. Never had such a shock in my life as when you turned up and told us—' He whisked out a handkerchief and polished his bald head. 'Now suppose I just tell you the whole business straight, so to speak, and if I miss out anything you want to know, you ask, because I don't know all the ins and outs of the—um—circumstances of the murder. You've got it right up to that night, sir. Trask . . . Perhaps I had better explain that that time in Philadelphia he was being held for trial, on a very nasty low charge too, at the same time I was, and that's how he knew me, and knew to send back for that newspaper report. And it wasn't only the money that made the situation awkward and annoying—it was having him around. Any day we'd both have preferred to pay over the money as straight extortion, and never seen him between, but you see, he wanted an open job, as an excuse for not working. I didn't like it, I never liked it, but what could I do? And besides keeping an eye on him, you know, I had what you might call a handle, too. You'll never know how both of us hoped he would make the grade and get into the profession—though he'd nothing to offer but looks, as an old trouper myself I knew *that*, but still, *Hollywood* . . . If he only had, perhaps he'd have gone to looking on us as very small stuff, you see, and left us alone—'

'And also you could then turn the tables and threaten him with his past,' said Mendoza. 'If he acquired a public reputation to be put in danger.'

'Good God, no,' said Kingman, genuinely shocked. 'God forbid that we should stoop so low as *that*. I tell you, we'd have gone on our knees to give thanks if he'd just left us alone! Well, you're not interested in all this background, I'd better—ah—cut the cackle as our English friends say, and come to that Friday. You said a minute ago that he'd had some plan go wrong, well, I couldn't tell you what that was, but I *did* deduce that for myself, from his manner. Now it's quite true, what I told you, that we exchanged only a few words as I met him leaving. But—um—what actually passed was not exactly casual. He—'

'Demanded that you raise the ante.'

'Well, no,' said Kingman. 'Actually, no. He was simply in a vicious temper. He put on a good front, you know—that charming boyish manner—but only with people who mattered, people he thought could do him some good. He never troubled with us. But that day he—er—lashed out at me, at the Temple—sneeringly, you know—more viciously than he'd ever done before. However, it wasn't until just before the—the ceremony that night that I became seriously disturbed. I must explain that I—oh dear, and possibly I should have mentioned it to you when you searched this afternoon, I do apologise—I have a small wall safe built into the robing room downstairs, where the—um—receipts are kept. Now, Trask did *not* have the combination of this safe, and I can only assume that he must have visited the apartment when we were out, perhaps several times, and hunted until he found the notation in my address book. I should have carried it on me—I have such a bad memory for figures—it was careless—'

'Now you mustn't blame yourself, dear, it might have happened to *anyone*.'

'I do not very often have occasion to go to the safe, that is to take *out* cash, over a weekend. Naturally, after the service on Saturday night I put the collection into the safe, but I seldom look at what's there or count it. But *as* it happened, I did have occasion to do so on that Friday night—Cara was going shopping the next morning, and I went to get out some money for her, just before the service. There is no collection for that Friday night service, you see. And I knew there should have been twenty-three hundred dollars in one of the velvet collection bags. You know,'—he took off his glasses, began to polish them slowly with his handkerchief—'on thinking it over since, I can see that he took a gamble on that. In the ordinary way, on Saturday evening I should have simply dropped the collection into that bag and locked it away again—a bag isn't like an envelope, I wouldn't see that it was nearly empty beforehand. He had left some one-dollar bills and a lot of silver, enough to look to the casual glance as if the bag hadn't been touched. You see? If all had gone as he planned, the deficit wouldn't have been discovered, probably, until some time on Monday—when I'd be going to the bank to deposit the month's receipts. But I discovered it then, at seven-thirty that Friday night.'

'Yes, I've grasped that,' said Mendoza in a bored tone. 'So you went out after the service to ask him how come.'

'Now I'll tell you,' said Kingman, 'I may be a fool this way and that way, Lieutenant, but I was not fool enough to think that Trask would walk off with a month's receipts like that if he intended to carry on in the current situation. The moment I made that discovery, I knew he was clearing out for some reason. And I was *thankful*—I tell you!—and if it had been *merely* the twenty-three hundred, I'd have said good riddance, cheap at the price.'

'*Which* was what I said, dear, though I *did* follow the thought in your mind. He really had *no* scruples at all.'

'But, well, just put yourself in my position, if you can, Lieutenant. Knowing Trask, I thought it very likely indeed that he would not be satisfied with that amount, but would attempt to withdraw more from the bank on Monday morning—before I had discovered what he'd already done, you see. I don't know why he should have stolen that cash on Friday when—if he did intend to withdraw more—he couldn't very well have planned his—his flight until Monday. When I came to reason it out, it occurred to me that *possibly* someone was in a position to blackmail *him*, and he *had* to have that cash on Friday. That he meant to abandon his—ah—racket here, in the face of that blackmail, and stole the cash to satisfy his enemy over the weekend, trusting to luck that I shouldn't discover it—and then on the Monday meant to take what he could from the bank, you see. However, there it was, and the reason I was anxious to contact him was to inform him in no uncertain terms that I knew of the theft, and would take steps immediately to warn the bank not to allow him to make any withdrawals. *That* I didn't want—well, naturally not—but it wasn't only the money—I couldn't very well prosecute him for it, could I? Everything coming out in the open then. I tried at once to telephone him, but got no answer—of course it was early. I tried again after the service, with the same result. So—'

'So you drove out. Very well. And when you got there, you found him packing—'

'It was quite *mysterious*,' said the woman plaintively,

'and I *hated* it—I felt there was something queer about it then. There was no one there at all, Lieutenant. I do hope,' her voice quivered a little, 'you will *believe* the truth, I do see as Martin says it's only our *word*. But it *is* the truth. The front door to his apartment was unlocked, after we'd knocked and knocked. Martin tried it and the door opened. We knew he was there because there was a light—not in the living room, but the bedroom—you could see it from that silly little front porch. So we went in, and *no one* was there at all. Yes, you're quite right, he had *been* packing—there were two suitcases all packed and locked, and another on the bed half full of things—and things standing on the bureau, all untidy, he'd never have left it like that, he was almost *too* finicky for a man, you know. And the light on. The kitchen light too. We couldn't see that until we'd gone in, of course. And *no one* there.'

'That's gospel truth, gentlemen,' said Kingman earnestly. 'I can't lie to you that I'm a religious man, but I swear by—by everything that's dear to me, that's the *gospel* truth.'

Mendoza had been leaning back in a bored way, smoking, impassive; Boyce sitting stolid and foursquare, just waiting; Hackett listening and looking intently. Their noncommittal silence worried Kingman, who had grown progressively more ruddy and earnest. Now suddenly Mendoza sat up and fixed him with a frowning stare.

'The kitchen light was on?' he said. 'Was that trap open?'

'*God*, no,' said Kingman with a shudder. 'And if I didn't have the cold grues about *that*, when I read in the paper how he'd been—disposed of! It occurred to me then that, my God, whoever it was might have—must have—been down there *with him*—when we walked in.' Now he lost all of his ruddiness, and mopped his bald head. 'He—they—whoever it was, would have had warning—we knocked and waited, you know. If—if there was a way to close that trap from below . . . well, you take me. Must have been down there in the dark—with *him*—waiting for us to leave. God. No, of course we didn't dream, at the time

. . . There were all his things, you could see he was getting ready to clear out, and—I don't know—it looked queer, but as if he might have just run out to get something, you know—some errand. I—'

'Did you go into the kitchen? . . . Where was the table?'

'I remember that, dear. It was an impossible kitchen—but of course a man wouldn't care—far too small, and there was only *one* little place for a table, at the very end—but it wasn't there. It was pushed right up against the stove, a very awkward position.'

'Did you see a trowel?' asked Mendoza softly. Hackett turned and looked at him. Nothing about the trowel had been released to the press.

They both stared at him. 'A *trowel*?' said Kingman; and then he lost what remained of his colour. 'Oh, my God, is that what he was—what they used—? No—no, I don't remember anything like that. We—well, you know, we didn't know quite what to do. It looked as if he'd be back any minute, and we waited around a little.' He mopped his brow.

'You have so much imagination, Martin—not that *I* wasn't a little upset about it too, when we *knew*. But it's all over now, dear, we must simply try to tell them how it was—the *facts*.'

'How long did you wait?'

'Oh, it was quite some time before we decided that he wasn't—and of course then we did think it even *odder*, that he should just walk out like that—and then we thought of looking to see whether his *car* was there. And it was. In the carport. And there was another one too, that is I don't know if it had anything to do with all this, but you see, I opened the back door and looked out—I don't know why, it was the silly sort of thing you *do* when you're looking for someone. And there was a car there. There's quite a wide alley behind that building, you know, and an empty lot behind *that*—and this car was just standing in the alley. There wasn't anyone in it, its lights weren't on or anything. I thought at the time it might be someone visiting the next apartment, maybe there hadn't been parking space in front when— Well, and *then* Martin said—'

'Now I'll tell you,' said Kingman, 'I didn't especially want to *see* him. I was *thankful* he was clearing out, I simply wanted to make it clear to him that it was—um—quits between us. And I'll be honest and say too that it seemed a good opportunity to have a look around for that photostat—not that that would exactly take away his hold, because I daresay he could have replaced it, and of course the mere information—that is, anyone could have checked up, once they knew where to check, so to speak. Nevertheless, we should feel much safer—you get me . . . I hadn't tried to do anything in that line, no, sir, not up to then. I won't say I hadn't thought about it, but it didn't seem that it'd be much use—for all I knew he had a safety deposit box or something—'

'So he did,' said Mendoza. 'In a manner of speaking. I know where it was—'

'So do I, now,' said Kingman unexpectedly. 'I make no apology for saying that we had a look round. And we didn't have to look far. It was right there on the bed. I expect you found it with his things, later on. One of those quilted plastic laundry bags—green—and he'd just emptied it out on the bed, it looked like, to get at what was in the bottom. I don't want to—ah—sound as if I'm trying to do your job for you, Lieutenant, but it occurs to me that perhaps when you first saw the place, things weren't just the way they were then, and it may be you'll be interested. First of all, there was a big brown manila envelope lying there with that photostat in it—the newspaper report about us, you know—and of course I took that. But I think there'd been something else in that bag—I took it that's where the envelope had been, you see, there it was among all his dirty clothes, as if he'd just dumped out everything—because there was another manila envelope, empty, and he—or someone—had burned something in a big glass ashtray on the bureau. Something fairly bulky, like—well, maybe another photostat. There was quite a little pile of ashes.'

'What was on the bureau besides?'

'Oh, dear,' said Kingman, and thought. 'I'll try to recall—you understand, I wasn't noticing things to *be* noticing, as it were—I'll do my best. Let's see, there was a bottle of Scotch, I think it was—I don't know if it was empty or full—and his wrist watch, and a folded necktie—and, oh, yes, his hat, a grey felt hat—and a clean handkerchief—and a couple of little medicine bottles, I think. Well, to go on, as I say I took that photostat, and we had a look for the money but it wasn't there, not unless it was in one of the locked suitcases. He must have had it on him, though you haven't *said*—' He looked at them doubtfully.

Mendoza shook his head. 'You find crooks everywhere, true, but we do pride ourselves on higher standards these days.'

'Oh, I *never* meant to imply—! But, odd as it seemed, you know—the place standing empty that way, as if he'd just dropped everything and walked out—we weren't much interested in what was behind it. Not then. There wasn't any reason to wait about. I wrote a note to him, on a page torn out of my address book—I don't know what happened to that, perhaps that's how you know about us being there—telling him, you know, not to try any tricks, and so on—and we came away.' He got out his handkerchief again. 'I hope to *God* you believe all this, all I can do is tell you everything. I don't know if it means anything, if it'll be a help in clearing us, but we got a traffic ticket on the way home—maybe that would confirm the time, but I don't suppose—'

'Where and what for?' asked Mendoza.

'The officer was *perfectly* right,' said Madame Cara. 'I do find it one of the most *awkward* things in traffic, changing lanes. But it's like everything else in life—one must seize the opportunity. And while the road was *quite* clear (I *never* take chances, for one must think of other people, you know, if not oneself) it seems it wasn't allowed right there. The officer was really very nice about it, and it was a small fine. I went right down to the traffic court next morning. It was six dollars, five for the ticket and one for education—this new system you know and a *splendid* idea, we can't grudge anything for the children.'

'My dear, the place—I don't recall—'

'Oh, of course, it was on Avalon Boulevard, Lieutenant, not very long after we'd left the apartment, I don't know *exactly* where.'

'We'll find it,' said Mendoza. He looked at them in exasperation, in doubt. 'I've got a warrant in my pocket for your arrest on a charge of murder—'

'Oh, *dear* God,' said Kingman, 'I swear to you—'

'But I'm not going to use it, until we've checked that ticket anyway. I'll be frank to say that it looks to me as if you had the best motive to do away with him, and I thought I had it worked out how you'd done it. But there are just a couple of little things . . . I'll go along with this awhile, and take you at your word. But I'd like to know why you didn't leave matters there. What took you to the bank on Monday morning?'

'Don't think we're not grateful,' said Kingman almost tearfully. 'Thanks very much, sir, for listening with an open mind . . . It's a sobering thought that if I hadn't—I should have let the whole thing go, I know that now. But the more I thought about it, the odder it seemed—his being gone, like that—and I thought quite possibly he might not have found my note. Even if he came back. Well, of course I expected he *had* come back, for all his things. But in the event that he didn't see the note—I felt I'd been a coward in a way, I should have seen him and made sure. I tried to locate him that Saturday morning, but nobody had seen him, and there was no answer at his apartment. In one way that relieved my mind, I thought he'd come back, finished packing and left—but we didn't *know*, you see. I was still worrying that he might try to get something out of the bank—'

'He had absolutely *no* scruples,' said the woman. Her large plaintive eyes swerved unblinking to Mendoza. 'We *are* grateful, Lieutenant, for your kindness . . . After *so* much trouble and upset and worry, it didn't seem fair. Such an unpleasant young man. But, you know, it really is very strange, they say there is *some* good in everyone, and there was, I daresay, a *very* little, in him . . . I was so surprised—do you know, he liked flowers. He liked to grow things. Perhaps he came of a long line of farmers, or something. He was quite enthusiastic over the landscaping around the Temple, just that little bit of fern or whatever it is, in built-up boxes, I expect you noticed it—he even brought a little garden fork one day and poked around at them because the earth was too dry, he said. Really very odd. But then people *are*.'

'—*And,'* said Kingman, 'more especially I worried about it, because he'd have discovered by then that I had been at his place and taken the photostat—he might try to clear out the bank account in revenge, you see. Well, we worried around it all that weekend, and on Monday morning when I knew there'd be someone at the bank—before opening time, that is—I called. All I meant to do was to ask them not to let him make any withdrawals, because he had um—severed connections with us. I was very stupid about the whole thing, Heaven knows I should have known better, but what with worrying and not being able to sleep—you see, I got hold of the assistant manager, and I had to give *some* reason for calling to warn them—after all, just because a man resigns or is fired from his job, it isn't any reason to suspect him of larceny—and before I knew it, he'd got out of me that Trask had gone off with that cash. And as soon as he heard that—Mr Rowell, I mean—he got excited and said of course I'd be seeing the police to lay an official charge, and perhaps he'd better go with me because it would save time if he could give the police the man's official signature and the recent records and so on—'

'I see,' Mendoza said amusedly. 'You couldn't get out of it?'

'It was like a nightmare from start to finish. I never intended to do such a thing, but of course it would have looked queer after that if I hadn't. What I was afraid of, you know, was that Trask *would* be caught up with—or even if he'd seen it in the papers, that I'd accused him—why, he might have told all he knew about us just to get even. It was a terrible position. I had to seem as if I was giving the police all the help I could, and at the same time I held back what I felt was *possible* to, because, my God, I wasn't anxious for them to find him, wherever he'd gone and why. I said I wasn't sure where he lived because, you know, he might have mentioned to someone there where he was going—and no one could prove we did know, I tore that page out of my address-book—and I was sure no one had seen us there on Friday night. And then, as soon as we'd—er—got that on record, so to speak, I wondered if the police would somehow find out anyway, and look for fingerprints there—and whether we'd left any—'

'I was wearing gloves. I always do when I drive and it was cold that night, I didn't take them off at all. And as I told you at the time, Martin, I don't believe you would have left any either, because we just *looked* mostly, didn't we?—not touching anything. You see, there wasn't any need to open drawers and so on, Lieutenant, there *was* this photo-thing right on the bed—we burned that as soon as we got home—and when it came to looking for the money, well, all the drawers were wide open and empty, because he'd been taking things out to pack, you know. We just felt all through the things in the open suitcase, and they were clothes, they wouldn't take prints, would they? Martin *did* try the other cases to see if they were locked, and they were. So—'

'And then,' said Kingman with a strong shudder, 'when you came and told us he'd been *murdered*—! And in such a way . . . I did some more worrying about it then, I can tell you—'

Mendoza got up, looking at them thoughtfully. 'Yes, well, we'll leave it this way for the time being. I needn't caution you not to leave town and so on—you'll be familiar with the—mmh—ritual, shall I say?'

'Believe me, Lieutenant, we're grateful—that you believe, I mean—'

'Oh, I never said I believed you,' said Mendoza gently, smiling at them. 'Just that I'm not quite ready to use that warrant—yet. We'll see. We like to be sure about these things—I'll do a little more thinking on it.'

CHAPTER FOURTEEN

'I have not been brilliant in this thing,' he said. He lit a cigarette and in the cold clear night air the little column of smoke was frost-white.

'They're not cleared,' said Hackett. They stood there on the curb in front of the Temple, between the tail of the Facel-Vega and the bumper of Hackett's humbler black sedan. Hackett had his hands in his pockets, shoulders hunched, staring down at the sidewalk.

'By implication you might say they are,' said Mendoza. 'That traffic ticket. I can't see a third person unknown mixed up in this with them, and we can't get away from the fact that that woman who bought the serape and took that cab ride had something to do with the murder. If she didn't kill him, she disposed of the car. And if Mrs Kingman-Sellers-Turner *and* her husband were on Avalon Boulevard about eleven o'clock or a bit after, getting a traffic ticket, then she wasn't that woman. Without using a siren, would you guarantee to get from 267th to the old Plaza or thereabouts inside an hour—even at that time of night? Most of the signals would still be working.'

Hackett didn't look up, but rocked meditatively back and forth a little. 'I might. She came down kind of heavy on playing the scatterbrained woman driver, I thought.'

Boyce said, 'I can't say I'd like to ride very far with her, Sergeant—I mean, after just listening to her dither.'

'*De veras,*' said Mendoza. 'Nor me. Babes in the woods.

No way to prove they'd known where Trask lived because Kingman tore that page out of his address book.' He laughed. '*¡Ça!* No, I haven't been bright here . . . Do I believe them? It's a story, you might say, too full of double takes and dither not to be true. This gentlemanly old trouper and his amiable scatterbrained wife . . .'

'Would you think I was crazy, Lieutenant,' asked Boyce diffidently, 'if I said I felt kind of sorry for them? It must be an awful hard way to earn a living.'

'Yes, but look at the living!' said Hackett sardonically.

Another frosty little cloud rose around Mendoza's head. 'Well, this is probably the first really big money they've made . . . There are points in that story. Oh, yes.'

'What the *hell*,' said Hackett savagely, 'they're slick actors, they pick up cues from each other and build a scene out of thin air, and you swallow it whole! You swallow this—this concoction as meek as be damned—like any new ranker on his first case—'

Mendoza smoked in impassive silence for a full half minute, looking at him; Hackett moved restlessly, got out his keys to play with. '*¿Que paso, chico?*' asked Mendoza softly.

'Damn it, nothing's the matter except that I'm fed up with this whole slippery business. We haven't got anywhere at it, and we ought to have *some* idea by this time! I—'

'*Tómelo con calma*, early days—we found him on Saturday, this is only Monday. We'll get there. Something on your mind?'

'Yes,' said Hackett, 'yes, there's something on my mind, but I'll turn it over once or twice and tell you about it in the morning. Nothing we can do tonight anyway. I'll see you at eight.' He turned away abruptly and got into his car.

'What d'you suppose is eating the sergeant?' wondered Boyce.

Mendoza dropped his cigarette, put a foot on it, and pushed it carefully into the gutter. 'That I couldn't say . . . I'll drive you back to headquarters. You might get on to Traffic and locate that ticket.'

* * *

He did a little wondering about the usually even-tempered Hackett on his way home, but more about the case. There were indeed a few interesting points in that story—which he was inclined to believe. Irritating, of course; but some new piece of truth—or what looked very much like it—came up and you had to change your mind, look at things another way . . . Something else in Trask's safety deposit box. (And didn't it point up one of the elementary pitfalls for detectives, that! Rudimentary deduction according to types of people—the man couldn't have been a gardener. You couldn't know. People, they just didn't come in standardised patterns. And not a bad hiding place, either: shades of *The Purloined Letter*.) Something else of the same species as the document held over the Kingmans? Something burned in an ashtray.

He slid the car gently into the garage, let himself into the apartment, switched on all the lights. All three cats came to welcome him, and because El Señor was usually stand-offish, Mendoza made a little fuss over him, encouragingly . . . A note from Mrs Carter, the cats last fed at four o'clock. Another note from Mrs Bryson, which announced simply, *He's learned to open cupboards*.

'Now have you?' he said to El Señor, who had both paws round his neck and was sampling his necktie. '*¡Basta, ya!*—not good for cats, leave it alone! Sometimes you act like a very smart boy indeed, too smart for your own good.' It was apparently true: the low cupboard doors of the record cabinet stood open, and so—uncannily—did one of the cupboards over the kitchen drainboard.

'This,' said Mendoza, 'is too much of a good thing altogether. Must I put locks on all the cupboard doors? Or keep all the things not intended for curious cats on the very top shelves?' He put El Señor down on a kitchen chair, went to get their evening meal from the refrigerator.

Somebody else in the same position *in re* Trask as the Kingmans. Not surprising. Somebody refusing to pay—did that account for his ugly temper that day?—but surely not a reason for him to clear out. Somebody a good deal more determined than Kingman, walking in on him and killing him . . .

As he put down the three dishes, the phone rang. 'Oh, Lieutenant Mendoza, I thought I heard you come in,' said Mrs Bryson in his ear from the other end of the building. 'Did you find my note? . . . Yes, the *oddest* thing—really, you know, it sounds silly but sometimes I'm almost afraid of that absurd kitten!' Mrs Bryson was large, buxom, fiftyish, and blonde; she had no children, and perhaps consequently a deplorable habit of cooing baby talk to her beloved cats—but one must overlook these faults in otherwise nice people. 'When I came to let them out for a little run, about two o'clock, he had your record cabinet open and an L.P. record out on the floor—Bach's *Suite No. 2 in B Minor*, it was—and was sitting *looking* at it. Really quite uncanny.'

'Well, at least he has good taste,' said Mendoza.

'What I called about, I forgot to put down that your grandmother phoned, and you're to be reminded that her goddaughter, I think it is, is getting married on Saturday, and you're expected to come and—'

'And bring a gift,' he supplied as she hesitated. 'This autocratic old wretch, I know how she put it! Thanks very much, Mrs Bryson . . .' He had no intention of doing either. In the first place, he had not set foot inside a church for twenty-two years and had no desire to break the record; in the second, the goddaughter was an unpleasantly smug and pudding-faced girl whom he disliked.

He let the cats out and got undressed.

Somebody—somebody—from that theatre crowd? Senseless to blackmail someone who hadn't any money . . . But there were other things of value than money: someone, perhaps, who could do him a favour—introduce him to a producer, cast him in TV?

Mendoza took a bath. He let the cats in. He sat up in bed smoking, and El Señor sat on his lap and tried to catch the smoke wisps, batting at them with his large blond paws. 'Señor Rídiculo,' said Mendoza.

Someone—

He put out his cigarette and switched off the light. A few more facts, and maybe it would suddenly come unravelled.

One small fact came in the next morning, from the routine gathering of miscellany. About that bank: that it kept old-fashioned banking hours. And that helped quite a lot in reconstructing Trask's plans. And then Hackett came in, and abruptly handed Mendoza a wholly new idea . . .

'And where did that idea come from?' asked Mendoza. 'It's definitely a thought, but a little offbeat . . . that girl Angel. Mmh, yes. Motives, motives . . .' He looked at Hackett's back in mild curiosity. Hackett, terse and noncommittal, had put forward this theory walking around the office as he talked, and stood now looking out the window.

'I know it's one of those things that doesn't happen often—'

'It's not as odd as all that—kind of thing that has happened. But what's reached you about it? You're acting as if you were telling the tale on your sister.'

'Sister be damned,' said Hackett. 'I know it's senseless, Luis, but I'm sorry for the girl. She hasn't had much of a break from life. That damned woman . . .' He shrugged and turned around.

Mendoza was leaning back looking cynically amused; he shot Hackett a glance from half-shut eyes. 'What heresy is this, Arturo—my big dumb sergeant smitten? *¡Cuidado, amigo!* That's one of the beaten paths to the trap, feeling sorry for them.'

'Don't be a fool—and you can keep your opinions to yourself. Just because *you* make a hobby of collecting the free samples without any intention of buying—'

'*¡Ay qué risa!* Where've you been hibernating, friend—since when is it free? This one I don't believe, *de veras absolutamente*—Hackett the impervious, and old enough to look after himself, God knows—Hackett the stolid—Hackett who never so far as I know, the ten years I know him, takes out the same girl three times running—and not because he's looking for free samples but because he's got a wide streak of caution, having some common sense if not quite as much as me! You don't tell me—'

'No, I don't tell you, damn it! I said I felt sorry for her and that's exactly what I meant, no more and no less. For which reason I'd also be sorry to prove that she killed a man. I'm well aware that you keep your emotions all carefully locked away in a secret compartment somewhere to take out and look at once in a long while—but if you think real hard, you may remember one or two occasions, maybe when you were a tender young rookie answering traffic calls and manhandling drunks, when you had a kind of feeling of sympathy for somebody who'd got knocked around a little through no fault of their own. I don't,' said Hackett, 'say you ever *did*, because about you I wouldn't be sure, but maybe there was just once you felt a little something along that line for a second, hah?'

'*Esto queda entre los dos*, only for your ear—because I wouldn't want it to get around that this thinking machine Mendoza is a real live human being—if I sat here quiet and concentrated a while I might remember a couple of those times. But I won't tell you about them, to set a bad example. I've got a reputation to maintain, you know. Everybody thinks Mendoza's always been what he is now, you drop a little problem in one slot and his month's pay in another, and click-click-click, out comes the right answer—*¿no es verdad?*'

'*Es verdad. Lo siento muchísimo*—sorry, boy,' said Hackett tiredly. 'I just—I can *see* it happening, that's all. The way she is, that girl—all tied up in knots, poor little devil, and that woman hardly knowing she's alive. I don't know, but I'd bet you she's got nobody on the face of the earth to talk it out to, to give her any little sympathy, and you know as well as I do that's damned important. If you can blow off steam to somebody, even a stranger on a bus, it's a safety valve. You talk enough, you don't do anything about it. A hate, a grievance, a—desire. And she's not the kind who'd ever have made friends, at school or later on—ever had *anybody*. All this eating at her inside, keeping her—all to herself. If you get me. She'd put people off, she'd never have reached for it . . . She's just a—a mess, to look at. And prickly, because she's been hurt. Another thing I thought of, it's on the cards she got started acting standoffish because when she was just a youngster and that woman was still in the big-time, more or less, a lot of the kids she knew'd have pretended to like her because of who her mother was. And kids know these things. Just stiffened her up all the more, suspicious, you know, so she couldn't *trust* anybody enough to be friends. So it's all got magnified inside her, because it's stayed inside—and nobody to sympathise a little—'

'That's all very true,' said Mendoza. He swivelled his desk-chair around and looked out the window himself, and for about five seconds he thought about the time when he was graduating from sixth grade into junior high. Nobody down there that side of Main Street had much money, but every other boy in the class had some sort of new suit for that occasion, even the Los Reyes kid and Johnny Li-Chong; and his grandmother had tried to get a few dollars out of the old man; she'd gone on asking a long time after he had, himself. The old man, with all those bankbooks tucked away then (if they'd only known it), sitting on a fortune out of canny investments of his gambling takes, and grudging her the five bucks a week for groceries, the twenty a month for rent of the cold-water flat . . . He'd been ashamed, getting up there with the rest of them in the same shabby old pants and mended shirt he'd been wearing all year. But she'd said to him afterwards, how proud she'd been that he was the tallest boy there, and how Mr Jackson the principal had told her he was a good smart boy and a credit to her . . . And somehow the clothes hadn't mattered quite so much. Little things like that, they weren't always so little in the long run. Somebody to listen to you, somebody to share a feeling. Even if there was nothing to do about it.

He swivelled around again, absently straightening his tie, brushing a small fluff of cat hair from his sleeve. He was still of two minds about this suit—he should have looked at the bolt by daylight first, he reflected: you couldn't exactly call it loud, but the faint pattern was a good deal less discreet than he had thought. A nuisance; he'd call Harrington down for it too, the fellow ought to know better with a good customer. He said, 'Well, we can kick this around a little, and I'd like to see those two; you've aroused my curiosity. But I'm wondering if and how that might fit in with a couple of suggestive little things in that story of Kingman's. Something burned in an ashtray. That laundry bag. Something else there besides the stuff on the Kingmans, and it looks as if whoever killed him was interested in it. Maybe . . . Sure, sure, *if* you take the Kingmans' story as gospel. *But—*'

'There wouldn't be anything like that with her,' said Hackett doubtfully. 'I don't know if I do take that story or not—it hangs together, sure. And on the face of it, it's more likely that it was somebody with that kind of motive.'

Mendoza agreed. 'Let's see what we've got on these people.' They looked, and besides Hackett's character analysis as gleaned from Mr Horwitz and his own observation, there wasn't much and it didn't look remotely interesting. Higgins, sent out routinely to see the old Miss Kent that Mona Ferne had visited that evening, reported everything in order: the old lady confirmed that Miss Ferne had been with her that night from about a quarter to eight until half past ten or so. Where the girl Angel had been, that they'd find out.

'It's just—bits and pieces, and it could be I'm crazy. But that first time I met her, she didn't seem interested at first in who'd been murdered, and when she heard it was Twelvetrees, she was very casual about it, who'd want to kill him and so on. And then two minutes later she was ready to go into hysterics. Keeping up a front, it could be, and not quite managing it. And then yesterday the Ferne says to me—*and* not realising what she said, because she couldn't be less interested in the girl, you know—that "Angel's been odd" for a week or so. It just added up in my mind, the way I say—'

Mendoza said, 'Yes? Yes . . . Girl have a car?'

'I don't know. Probably.'

'She'd have money of her own. There was something said about a trust fund from the father. Not really big money, maybe, but substantial.'

'I'd think so,' said Hackett heavily.

'I don't know that you sell me on this, quite. But we'll have a look. No harm. Suppose we go and see them if they're home.' Mendoza got up and reached for his hat.

They were home. When the sour-faced maid opened the door to Hackett and Mendoza, letting a little light into the dingy entrance hall, the first thing they heard was the girl's shaking voice, loud, from the living room: 'That's a *lie*—you know it's a lie!'

Mendoza handed his hat to the maid and walked past her, ignoring her protesting query, to the doorway of that room. He looked at the pair of them interestedly, and added a few mental comments of his own to Hackett's.

Mona Ferne was elegantly slim in honey-beige and dark brown today. Evidently she'd been about to leave the house: her alligator bag, gloves, a chic little brown felt hat with a veil waited on the arm of the couch. He paid academic tribute to the finished article, while guessing far more accurately than Hackett how much time and effort had gone into it. The gleaming perfect flaxen coiffure, the figure, the face—a very expert piece of work, all of it; and from fifteen feet away, before he heard her speak or saw her move, he knew it was all just about as emotionally affective as a combustion engine . . . The girl. Could be pretty. Alison would say, and be right, built to wear clothes—the height and the figure. Not one of the types he admired himself.

'Darling,' said the woman, 'I'm only saying—' And she saw them then in the doorway, and for the fraction of a

second her eyes held an expression which surprised Mendoza very much indeed.

¿Vaya, qué demonio—? he said to himself.

And the girl turned to follow her glance, and looked startled—looked confused, and took a step back to bring up against the white brick hearth, and leaned there.

'Why, it's the nice police sergeant back again—*do* tell me, Sergeant Hackett, have you found whoever it was did this awful thing? Is there something else I can do for you now?—I'm only *too* anxious—' But her eyes were busy on Mendoza, recognising him as worthier quarry. She came forward gracefully.

Mendoza glanced at Hackett, who was looking at the girl. Incredulities came at him from two directions, he thought. That girl. And—

'You may indeed help us, if you will, Miss Ferne—it *is* Miss Ferne, I take it?' He knew instinctively just the sort of thing this one would like, would respond to: essentially it was the small-town Main Street mind—a veneer of sophistication very thin; and he smoothed his moustache thoughtfully in the approved man-about-town manner, gave her a faintly sardonic smile nicely blended of veiled admiration and cynicism. 'Lieutenant Mendoza, madam. I apologise for intruding at such an early hour.'

'But not at *all*, Lieutenant! Anything I can do, of *course*—' She gushed at him a little, and he let his eyelids drop and put more cynicism in his expression, to conform to type. He knew exactly the kind of girl she had been, all giggles, curls, and inconsequence; the tiresome kind, not a thought beyond the conventionalities; and the kind too who wouldn't grow out of it to any extent. 'Do sit down.'

'Thanks very much. You can oblige me first of all by telling me something I'd very much like to know. Who owns this coat here?' He nodded at it, getting out a cigarette.

It was the first thing he'd noticed in the room. It was flung carelessly over the back of the couch, a woman's long wool coat, full-cut and voluminous: it was creamy beige and its sleeves had wide dark brown velvet cuffs.

Before the woman could answer the girl spoke. 'It's *not* mine,' she said. 'I never saw it before. I f-found it in my—I thought *she*—it's not mine!'

'Darling, I don't understand you lately. How absurd, you're not going forgetful so young, are you?—of course it's your coat, Angel, I've seen you in it a dozen times. One of the few halfway *smart* things you have. But why should you be interested, Lieutenant?' She wasn't much concerned with the coat or the girl; she sank into a chair, carefully arranging the display just right, and preened herself under his gaze.

'That's your coat, Miss Carstairs? Well, well.' He went over and picked it up. It was a costume coat, with a narrow rolled shawl collar, no buttons: its only decoration the dark velvet cuffs and a dark panel of velvet down each side of its front. 'That's very interesting,' and he divided a smile between them.

'I never saw it before! I—I—I— What's it got to do with *you*?'

Hackett came into the room, stood looking at the coat as Mendoza turned it in his hands, examining it. 'We're asking the questions here, Miss Carstairs,' he said harshly.

'Oh, now I don't see any reason to be mysterious about it,' said Mendoza gently. The coat bore a label inside the collar with the name *Jay-X, Fine Fashions*. Not a name he was familiar with, but any department store buyer could supply information, and he had an idea what the information would be. Hardly a brand name you'd find at Magnin's or Saks': third-rate-quality wool, inferior cut. About thirty-nine-fifty retail, he judged. 'We have reliable evidence that a woman wearing a very similar coat to this one is intimately concerned in the murder of Mr Twelvetrees. Naturally I'm interested in knowing'—he cocked his head at them—'whether it was, in fact, this coat.'

'In the *murder*!' exclaimed Mona Ferne. She sat bolt

upright, graceful, horrified. 'What *are* you saying? That *Angel*—? But that's ridiculous! Why, I expect there are hundreds of coats like that—'

'Oh, I don't know,' said Mendoza. He sat down, with the coat over his lap, in the chair nearest hers, where he could direct leers as broad as he could manage with more effect; he noticed that she'd automatically chosen a seat which put her back to the light. 'It's not a fashionable line this year, is it, the very full cut, and the velvet—more of a spring coat, too, by the weight.'

'I think she got it last spring,' said Mona Ferne vaguely. 'I can see *you're* one to watch, Lieutenant Mendoza!'—and she actually giggled at him, looking up under her lashes coyly. 'You know too much about feminine styles to sound quite respectable!'

Caray, but with this one you could lay it on with a trowel, he thought. With a trowel. Appropriate . . . What was this, what the hell was this? Motives. He remembered saying to Alison, sometimes you have to find out about the people first. 'You're flattering me, lady,' he said, and let a little more interested admiration show in his eyes. She giggled again and smoothed her hair, to show off long garnet-coloured nails.

'I never—' said the girl Angel. She came to the middle of the room, looking from him to Hackett; she twisted her hands together, tight and nervous. 'You mean—whoever killed him had—? I don't underst—I never saw that coat before in my life! It's not—it's not—it's not—'

'Do control yourself, Angel, you sound quite hysterical, dear. I'm sure the lieutenant doesn't mean he thinks an innocent young girl like you had anything to do with such a horrible thing.' It was a vague murmur: most of her attention was on Mendoza, a new man to gauge, to angle for, to play to.

The girl Angel stared at her; suddenly she raised her clenched fists to her mouth. 'No,' she said against them. 'No, I didn't—why would I—I didn't—*him*! I never—'

'No one's accused you of anything, Miss Carstairs,' said

Hackett in a colourless tone. 'We'd just like to ask a few questions, if you don't mind. Do you have a car of your own and what make is it?'

She nodded mutely at him; she whispered, 'The s-same as—hers—it's a '58 two-d-door Cad— I don't like it m-much, I don't—I don't drive much, *she* made me—Listen to me, please listen, I know by the way you look you think—but why, *why*, *why*? No reason—*him*—He wasn't *anything*—and I tell you I never saw—'

'Do you mind telling us where you were on the evening of Friday the thirtieth?'

'I—was—here,' she said dully. She was looking at her mother again, not Hackett. 'All that evening. Like every night. Like always and forever and eternity. I was here—and nobody else was.'

'Really, Sergeant,' said Mona Ferne, absent and sweet, 'you can't think *Angel*—' And now her eyes were busy gauging Mendoza's suit, the Sulka tie, the custom-made shoes. Gauging his prestige value as something in pants to be seen with. He read them (fascinated, curious, passionately interested in this woman, now) as he would read a page of print. *Money*, they said—*more than presentable, if not exactly handsome—charming—knows the score*.

'The maid—?' said Hackett.

'She isn't here—at night,' said the girl. 'Nobody— I went to bed, I think, about—about midnight—I—' But that was absently said too; she was still looking at her mother. 'The coat,' and that came out in a whisper. 'Somebody with a coat like that—? D'you mean—the one did it, k-killed—' Slowly she turned back to Hackett. *Could be* and *was*, different things: she looked plain, dowdy, in a shapeless grey dress, flat brown shoes; hair pinned back carelessly to fall lank and lifeless, and no make-up. 'Please,' she said, 'how can you think—you *do* think so, I see you do, but I don't understand! I didn't—he was *nothing*! The coat. The—I never saw it before, why d'you think it's *here*, because I f-found it there in my wardr—just a while ago, I thought— It's a hideous coat, I'd never have—I brought it down to ask—*It's not mine*! I—'

'When did you buy it, Miss Carstairs, how long have you had it?' asked Hackett woodenly.

'Oh, my God,' she muttered. 'No. I don't—not—*oh, my God*!' And she moved from her rigid stance; her eyes went blank and she ran, as a child or an animal ran from inexplicable wrath. They heard her on the stairs, stumbling.

'So clumsy, poor child,' murmured Mona Ferne, and crossed her legs the opposite way, with nice attention to arranging the skirt at just the proper place to show off the ankle and not the ugly swell of the calf with its blue-mottled veins.

Mendoza nodded at Hackett to go after the girl. And he knew: now he knew: and it was a psychic knowledge, the D.A.'s office would laugh at it—so, look for solid tangible evidence to back it up, sure. But the thing inside him, that was worried by ragged edges, by the picture hanging crooked, by the answer to the problem that he didn't know (and that offending his essential egotism, too), settled back with a satisfied sigh and said, *So, that's the answer*. He felt better; he felt good.

Much of the reason Mendoza had this little reputation as one of the bright boys (maybe a head doctor would say) was that he had to prove it, over and over again: anything he didn't know, it was a kind of insult to the essential Mendoza; he had to find out. So finding out the answer, the truth—it affected him like a good stiff drink, and he felt fine.

Now he knew. But he didn't know why, or exactly how.

He gave Hackett a glance and nod, to go after the girl; and he gave Mona Ferne a look that was almost a leer and hitched his chair a little closer to hers . . .

CHAPTER FIFTEEN

Hackett caught up with the girl at the top of the stairs. She was leaning on the bannister there, crouched and shaking, silent. The maid stood in an open bedroom door nearby, staring curiously.

'What's the matter with her *now*?'

The girl straightened abruptly. 'Oh, go away!' she said wildly to both of them. And then, 'No—wait—Winter, please, *you* can say, you can tell them! That coat I brought down, just now—you've never seen me in it, have you?'

The maid sniffed. 'I dunno, couldn't say. I don't take no notice what *you* wear much. It ain't Miss Ferne's, that I do know.'

Angel shut her eyes, leaned on the bannister again. 'You wouldn't say—if you could. I know. People never—like me, want to help—and no wonder. No wonder . . .'

Hackett said angrily to the maid, 'Go away, for God's sake! Go downstairs or somewhere. I'm—questioning Miss Carstairs officially and that means privately.'

A spark of interest showed in the maid's eyes. 'Questioning? About the murder? Did she do it? For the Lord's *sake*—all right, all right, I'm going . . .' But she lingered on the way, looking back avidly.

'I didn't,' said Angel. 'Really I didn't.'

Hackett surprised himself by saying, 'I know you didn't. And damn it, it *isn't* any wonder you haven't any friends and stay around alone, when you look like this, when you don't go to meet people halfway! Why the hell don't you cut your hair and comb it once in a while?—put on some make-up—get some decent clothes—my God, you've got the money! Make a little *effort* at it, for God's sake! It doesn't mean you're acting like her, going to turn into one like that, you know. There's a—a middle course to these things, after all! You can't expect anything out of life if you don't put something in—hanging around here feeling sorry for yourself like a spoiled kid—'

She looked up at him through a straggling lock of hair that had come unpinned, fallen across her cheek; she brushed it back, and her mountain-pool eyes were blurred by tears. 'Oh, God, I know,' she said. 'I know. How did *you* know? I—I—got off on the wrong track, it was *her*, but I—but it's too late, I don't know *how*, I don't know *anything*, how to do—how to—be nice, make people—I want to, I *want* to, but I don't know where to start, or *how*. She—'

'You listen, you just listen,' said Hackett. He was mad; he didn't know exactly what he was going to say or how they'd got onto this, but at the same time he thought this was about the oddest examining of a witness he'd ever done. He made her sit down on the top step and sat down beside her—like a pair of kids, he thought. 'Listen, you've got to get out of this house, this damned haunted house. That tree—my God, it's like living in a cave. Don't be silly, it's never too late to *do* something. Only you've got to put a little effort into it.'

She blew her nose and looked at him solemnly over the wadded handkerchief. 'I j-just hate my name,' she said. 'It's such a *silly* name. She—thought it was cute. A baby named Angel. Only I g-grew up, and it's *silly*. A great big lummox like me—she said that. D'you think I could change it?'

'You can do anything you want to, damn it. It doesn't matter what your name is, it's what you are yourself! Listen, you know what you ought to do? You ought to go to one of these charm schools. Sure it sounds silly but they'd teach you all those things, see? You could be a pretty girl, Angel, just take a little trouble.'

'C-could I?'

'Well, sure. I know someone runs one of those places too, she'd help you a lot—Miss Alison Weir, she's in the phone book. You remember that, now, and do something about it.'

She mopped at her eyes again. 'Is she your g-girl friend or something?'

'No,' said Hackett. 'Not mine, she doesn't—belong to me.' Suddenly (this was the strangest little interval he ever remembered experiencing) he was filled with inexpressible sadness for all the lonely, cheated, needing people. Because, once or twice, he'd seen Alison Weir looking at Mendoza when she didn't know anyone was watching her. At cynical, marriage-shy, self-sufficient Mendoza, who ranked women along with poker as off-hours recreation and that was all . . . 'Listen, stop crying, can't you?'

'I'm n-not, really. I'm—it was just—yes,' she said with a little gasp, 'I've got to get out of this house. *Her* house. I knew she hated me—I've always known that—ever since I stopped being a baby and began to grow. To let people know she was getting older *too*. And to be a—a person, not just like a—pet she had, other people taking care of it. But I didn't think—it was so much that she wouldn't mind if I was arrested—for—'

'Nobody's going to arrest you,' said Hackett. He thought, damn it, it's got to be the Kingmans—logical thing; that story was a slick bunch of lies, that's all. They were on the spot at the right time, they had a motive; what the hell else did you need? Look around and the solid evidence would show up. But, he thought, *but* . . . That coat. Oh, hell, coincidence. And she was easily rattled, of course she'd deny it in panic. He took a breath to begin talking calm and sensible to her, persuade her to tell him all about the coat; and Mendoza came out to the entry hall down there, shot a glance up the stairs, and beckoned him down.

'Now don't you be scared,' and he got up reluctantly. So Mendoza wanted to question her himself. 'You just—'

But Mendoza was taking up his hat, thanking the Ferne suavely for her help. He looked at the girl with narrowed eyes, a little grim, and Hackett cursed himself for ever saying anything about . . . And what the *hell* had got into him, anyway, feeling like that?

When the door was shut and they started down the sunken steppingstones to the street, he said irritably, 'And what the hell got into you? You looked like the villain in an 1890 melodrama, twirling your moustache and ogling that—that—'

Mendoza grinned, getting out his keys. '*Vaya*, I always like to oblige a lady. She expected it of me.' He looked at Hackett curiously. 'Very odd,' he murmured to himself. 'You, of all people, too. I won't say you have quite as good a brain as me, but I've always found you reasonably quick on the uptake, and you've worried through more complicated cases than this on your own.' He shook his head and slid under the wheel.

'What are you talking about? Look, Luis, that coat—it looks funny, but she'd naturally deny it when she knew why we were interested. She got rattled—'

'Oh, the coat,' said Mendoza. He had brought it with him, presumably with the Ferne's gracious permission. 'It's not the one that figured in that little adventure, so don't worry about it . . . Every once in a while I'm surprised to find all over again that some cliché is true. But it does astonish me to find this one operating on you. At least I hope it's just that—the one without love causing temporary derangement—and not that you're losing your grip on the job.'

'I'm *not*—will you lay off that? What d'you mean, you've got an idea—'

'*Nada de eso*, nothing doing,' said Mendoza. 'I shouldn't have to explain anything to you, so I'm not going to. But when I think how close I came to— An idea? I have a very good idea, now, of what happened, but there are still a lot of little things to fill in. Work it out for yourself if you can—meanwhile, be quiet, I've got some serious thinking to do.'

They were greeted in the anteroom of Mendoza's office by an unusually excited Sergeant Lake. 'Lieutenant, I've found that Marner woman for you—'

'Oh, good,' said Mendoza. He didn't sound very interested. 'One of the agencies?'

'No, it was the damndest thing, it looked hopeless, you know—not a smell anywhere—and then I go out for coffee and buy a paper and there she is on the front page! Look.'

They looked, and Mendoza laughed. 'Well, I will be damned! And I wonder now if maybe that ties into this . . .' It was a good-sized cut, of a pretty brunette and a middle-aged man; and the story took up two short columns. *Pickering to Wed Second Wife* was the head. *'Revealed yesterday was the forthcoming marriage of Thomas ("Toby") Pickering, the famous producer and vice-president of Capital Films, Inc. A widower for eleven years, Pickering, 47, confirmed that he is shortly to wed Miss Marian Marner, 38, model. Miss Marner—'*

'Producer,' said Hackett. 'I don't see quite how, but it might— Anyway she knew Twelvetrees-Trask, we'd better see her—'

'Pronto,' agreed Mendoza. 'You get hold of this Pickering on the phone, Art, and find out where she is. I've got some routine jobs for, let's see, about three men, Jimmy—who's available? I'll brief them . . .'

After a good deal of trouble with a succession of receptionists and secretaries, Hackett got hold of Pickering in his *sanctum sanctorum*. (Easier to get on the direct wire to the President than to any Hollywood film official.) Pickering, curiously enough, seemed to know more about it than Hackett did. His voice on the phone was incisive, crisp. He said, 'Hell. We were hoping it wouldn't be necessary. And I hope to God we can keep the whole damned mess away from the press. But if you've got hold of it, of course, that's that. Yes, well, look, Sergeant—sorry, what did you say the name was?—Sergeant Hackett, suppose I call Miss Marner and we arrange to meet in your office. O.K.? Say eleven-thirty . . . Right. I don't know if you have any control over that part of it, the press, but I hope— Oh, you do. Yes, but there'll be the legal end, if there's a trial and so on. Well, we can say the hell with it, if people want to gossip let them—it's one of the hazards in my business—but that isn't to say we wouldn't prefer the whole damned thing was kept under cover. If you see what I mean. At the same time, I'm aware that you'd like to know what we have to contribute, and while I'm not at all happy you've connected us with it,'—a short laugh—'maybe I shouldn't be surprised, I understand from that recent magazine article we've got a police force to be proud of . . . O.K., I'll contact Miss Marner and we'll be in your office at eleven-thirty.'

Hackett relayed this information to Mendoza when he came in with Higgins, Dwyer, and Landers. 'Good, good. I have a fair idea what they're going to tell us, but it'll be nice to know the details.'

'I'd like to know what's in your mind. You act like it's about all over, barring an arrest. I tell you, that girl . . . I still think you swallowed that tale of the Kingmans' too easy. We know they had a motive, we know they were there at the right time, or thereabouts—what more—'

'*¡Atrás, atrás*, out of the way!' said Mendoza briskly. 'Before we get to the arrest, there are all these niggling little details I have to find out, to satisfy the D.A., and no time like the present to start. You're getting paid to be a detective too, I'm not going to explain it in one-syllable words—you go off somewhere and think, maybe it'll come to you.'

Hackett said a rude word and went away. Mendoza sat down at his desk and called the Temple. He asked Madame Cara a couple of questions, and the answers were just what he expected to hear. Then he went through the phone book, made a list of the clothing wholesalers and divided it up with the three men, and they started on that tiresome routine.

By the time Sergeant Lake looked in and said Miss Marner and Mr Pickering had arrived, among the four of them they had accumulated a dismaying list of retail stores. Mendoza shooed the others out to go on checking, and

Hackett came in, still looking disgruntled, behind the two new witnesses.

Mendoza looked at Marian Marner with interest. Twelve years hadn't changed her a great deal; she didn't look much younger than she was, but she was still pretty, her figure was still very good, she was smartly dressed. She checked a little when she saw him standing there at his desk, and then said, 'Oh—well, hello, Luis. I didn't know we were coming to see you. And I don't suppose it's Sergeant Mendoza now, is it?'

'Lieutenant.'

'Yes, you were always one to get on. I used to know this one, Toby.' She sat down in the chair Hackett held.

'Really, well, that makes things a little easier maybe,' said Pickering, looking slightly amused. He was handsomer than the newspaper cut had suggested: a biggish man with thick greying hair, erect carriage, and his voice and eyes said he was aggressively capable. He took the chair Hackett indicated and planted it firmly closer to hers, sat down, and looked at Mendoza consideringly.

'We can trust him,' she said, 'that I'll say.' She smiled a little tautly. 'He's sharp enough to cut himself, but he'll be honest.'

'I don't know that reassures me,' said Pickering. 'We've been compounding felonies and maybe acting as accessories before the fact all over the place. This is going to make the hell of a stink if it has to come out.'

'Well, suppose you tell us about it, and we'll see if it has to come out,' said Mendoza. 'Things don't, always. You'd be surprised how many little things—and sometimes big—come into a case that don't get aired in court. I've got some idea of what you're going to tell me, I think, and it's possible that it needn't come into the legal end. I'd say even probable, barring one or two little bits that may serve to confirm times and so on. I can't say for sure, and of course I can't guarantee that a smart lawyer wouldn't get hold of it and bring it up to confuse the issue—but if it's what I deduce, to do with the late Mr Twelvetrees' blackmailing operations, well, that's got nothing to do with the murder—I don't think, anyway.'

They all looked at him. 'I see,' said Pickering interestedly. 'You know who it was, and you think it was—another reason? I see . . . But all the same, I suppose you want the loose ends tied up.' He got out cigarettes, gave her one, lit both with an angry little snap of the lighter. 'I can't say I feel vindictive towards whoever killed the bastard.'

'Vindictive, possibly, no,' said Mendoza, 'but it's a funny one, an offbeat one, Mr Pickering—if it's what I'm beginning to think. Let's save a little time. I think Miss Marner was being blackmailed by our late friend?'

'Attempted,' said Pickering. 'Just attempted, Lieutenant. I saw to that. I don't think there's any necessity to go into details—'

'I think maybe we'd better,' she said quietly. 'Maybe not in a formal statement, if we've got to make one, but you'll want to know enough to—add it up, won't you, Luis? I don't mind. I mean, it was—in a way—the sort of thing that might happen to anybody, though I don't excuse myself. It was—oh, well.' She shrugged; her tone was even but her hand shook as she raised the cigarette to her mouth. 'And a legal charge too—I wouldn't like to go to jail for it now—I don't know how that kind of thing works, if you could—'

'I think it would be a question of a fine, that's all,' said Pickering, 'but if the press get hold of it there'd be a little mess, and while it wouldn't make any difference to my position, anything like that—and the hell with it if it would—we'd just as soon that didn't happen. But if you think we'd better come out with the whole thing, hon, O.K., we're in this together.'

'I do, Toby. Well, I don't want to bore you, Luis, but I guess you'd better have a little background—not that I'm trying to excuse myself, as I say. I got married a while after we knew each other, and it didn't turn out so well. To make a long story short, he was a drinker and I got to drinking too, and by the time I'd got the divorce, well, I wasn't much good for anything. I'd lost a lot of jobs, and the agencies got to know I wasn't—very reliable, and finally I couldn't get *any* jobs. It's all right, I don't mind talking about it now—I pulled myself up and used some common sense, got back on an even keel. But it was while I was—down—that way, and pretty desperate—I hadn't any money and I had to do *something*—I ran into this Shorter. He had a photography shop, a little hole in the wall, but it seemed he did a nice side business in—in feelthy peectures, if you see what I mean. Well, he offered me good money and I took it. I did two series for him—six shots apiece—and maybe you can say the whole business was what—pulled me up, because I loathed it, and I got to thinking, how low can you get? I used that money to live on while I got myself back in some kind of physical shape, and after a while I got a decent job, in a department store. As a clerk really, but when they found I'd had modelling experience they used me for that too, sometimes, at the fashion shows. I just quit there last week, because Toby and I are going to be married.

'Well, every once in a while I'd think about those pictures, and I didn't like the idea of them floating around. Shorter had the negatives, of course. A-about two years later, when I'd saved some money, I sent and saw him and asked if he'd sell the negs to me, and he just laughed and said for five hundred apiece. I didn't have that kind of money. Well, about a year ago I was introduced to this Brooke Twelvetrees at a party. A couple of girls I know do extra work, bits in TV mostly, and it was in that crowd I met him, he was a hanger-on, I gathered. I didn't think much of him one way or another, you know—I saw him maybe three or four times in this crowd, at parties, that's all—it just came out of the blue when he—approached me.' She took a breath, leaned forward to put out her cigarette.

'You take it easy now,' said Pickering, and she smiled at him.

'It's O.K., Toby, I don't mind really . . . You see, I—I got to know Toby, and we'd been going around some together, and of course there'd been a little smart talk—you know—gossip. And when I read in the paper one morning, about three weeks back it was, that Shorter had been arrested and all his—stuff—confiscated, I nearly died of fright. I mean, there'd have been those things I posed for in with the others, and identifiable as me, if the c—the police—'

'I thought the name Shorter rang a bell,' nodded Mendoza. 'I remember.'

'I figured out,' Pickering broke in, 'from a couple of things that bastard, Twelvetrees I mean, said, that he was responsible for that. D'you know whether that was a—so to speak—routine investigation, or if they had anonymous information? Do the police act on that kind of thing?'

'Not my department, but I can find out about the arrest from Vice. Yes, certainly, Vice and Narcotics especially, the anonymous tip often sets the ball rolling. Sometimes it turns out a dud, sometimes not.'

'Well, what I think happened was this,' she went on. 'Twelvetrees knew Shorter, that came out when he approached me with these negs. He said—because naturally I asked how he got them—he *said*, in a jeering sort of way, not as if he expected to be believed, you know, that Shorter'd had a premonition about being arrested and had handed over some stuff for safekeeping. But later on he started to say something else, about how he and Shorter had been together inside—and caught himself up. I think he might have been in prison, and met Shorter there. And it's just a guess, but I think Shorter showed him some of his—things—and Twelvetrees recognised me in those pictures, either then or later. He didn't do anything about it because *I* couldn't do anything for him then, you see? I mean, he wasn't interested in me any other way but—for money. It's a funny thing to say, but when it came to girls to—go around with, well, I gathered from what Netta said—she's in the crowd that knew him best—he was a little nervous of anything from the right side of the tracks. You know? He didn't feel at home with the kind who—oh, likes ballet and cocktails instead of the amusement arcade and beer.'

'Very much in character.'

'That I believe,' agreed Pickering. 'You let me carry on, hon. The way I figure it, Lieutenant, when he heard on the grapevine that it was a serious thing with Marian and me, then he saw how he could do himself some good. Maybe you know he had—time out to laugh—movie ambitions. That—! Well, I think he stole those negs from Shorter and then "shopped" him, as our British friends say, before he could find out or retaliate.'

'Quite possible.'

'Anyway, he showed up at Marian's place—'

'On that Tuesday evening, maybe?' said Mendoza. 'Evening, because you'd be at work all day, he couldn't have a private talk with you. And it wasn't Wednesday because he was elsewhere that night. Or was it Thursday? On Wednesday night he was hinting joyously that some good fortune was coming his way.'

'He *told* someone? My God, he—? Is that how you—?'

'No, he was too canny for that. And while we're clearing up details, how we got onto you was that he had a snapshot of you in his wallet. Why?'

'So that's what happened to it,' she said slowly. She sat back, looking angry. 'May I have another cigarette, Toby, please . . . Netta told me he'd asked her for one. She was looking through some she'd just had finished, and he was there and asked if he could have the one of me. She refused, but he must have taken it anyway when her back was turned, she said. I think—maybe he wanted it to check against—those others, to be sure. She said it wasn't a very good one, but it was full-length, and you know people photograph differently sometimes from the way they really—though with *those*—well, I don't know. And maybe he just stuck it away and forgot it—or more likely kept it as window dressing, he was the kind who liked to have you think he had a raft of girl friends . . . It was Tuesday he came, Tuesday the twenty-seventh. He had one of the negatives with him, and—and prints of the rest. He—' She broke off, trying to control her shaking voice.

'You take it easy, hon, I'll tell the rest.' Pickering lit a fresh cigarette; he looked very angry. 'The bastard. I'll tell you how the lyrics went, Lieutenant, if you haven't already guessed. He didn't know quite how it was with us, if you get me. He had it figured that Marian was the hell of a lot more interested in my bank account than in me, *and* that I could be scared off if I heard all this. As a matter of fact, I knew—she'd told me. He didn't want money—'

'He wanted the nice send-off with a big producer,' said Mendoza. 'That figures. A heaven-sent opportunity for him, our stage-struck glamour boy! No wonder he went to all the trouble—which, I agree, is likely—of stealing those negatives and getting Shorter put away. And he was thinking ahead too, probably. If you weren't impressed enough to whisk out a contract right away, after you were married he could always do it the hard way, bring pressure to bear on the grounds that you couldn't stand the publicity.'

'*Ah*, that damned little—! Yes, I suppose. Well, anyway, Marian had sense enough to call me, after putting him off on a plea of making up her mind, and I took over from there. He thought he had her scared, had us just where he wanted us.' Pickering laughed, short and ugly. 'Money isn't everything, but it sure as hell helps. I hired a couple of the best private detectives in town'—he named the agency—'and we wired Marian's place but good. We really set up the trap—me and two other witnesses in the bedroom, *and* the tape recorder. He came over swell.' He grinned. 'One qualification he had for the business, nice clear-cut voice and good diction. We'd coached Marian, of course, and she slipped him enough leading questions that we got the whole layout, his whole plan, in detail. Beautiful. And then she did a little acting and gave in, said she'd do whatever he wanted—only of course we didn't tape that. My God, I'm giving myself away—but you can see the spot we were in, only way to handle it—and besides he'd made me damn mad. I wanted to cuff him down good, so he'd stay that way.'

'Very nice, very nice,' purred Mendoza. 'It's deplorable of me, Mr Pickering, but I don't think I'll be vindictive enough—or honest enough—to turn you in for all these little legal misdemeanours. I'd probably have done much the same thing myself. I suppose you saw him on Friday, the next day. It was, I assume, on Thursday when you sprung the trap.'

'That's right. I saw him Friday morning, as soon as we had legal statements drawn up by the witnesses and so on. We'd set it up—she'd told him to come by about eleven and she'd introduce us, give him a good send-off. And, brother, we did. Marian wasn't there. I told him what we had on him and just how I felt about it, and that, by God, I enjoyed. I told him first, as far as his damn fool ambition for the movies was concerned, he was dead before he started, right now, because in the inconceivable case that anybody ever hired him to sweep a stage I could and would see he got fired—I could blacklist him in this town, in that line, and he knew it. I told him I wouldn't lose one damn thing but a little of my upright reputation if he gave those negs to the *Examiner* tomorrow, and that sacrifice I wouldn't mind, it was just on Marian's account I'd prefer the whole thing kept private. I always had a kind of admiration for that old bird—was it the Duke of Wellington?—who said *Publish and be damned*. And I told him I'd take great pleasure in charging him publicly with attempted extortion, and putting in all this nice clear evidence to prove it. And, let's face it, money talks—even to the law. I could have arranged for a trial like that to be held *in camera*, and protected ourselves that way while he got it in the neck. At that point he began to back down fast, said he'd never dream of doing anything with those negs to embarrass Marian. O.K., fine, says I, and just to guarantee that, we're going with you right now to get them, and if you get out of town within twenty-four hours, I'll keep still, I won't lay the charge. But I'll check, and if you're still here, brother, you get everything the law can hand you—and if some damn fool jury lets you off, I've got the money to put you behind a dozen eight-balls, other ways. I don't need to tell you he didn't like it—that's an understatement. When he saw I wasn't going to back up a sixteenth of an inch from that stand, he called me every name in the book. But he had to go along, he couldn't do anything else—unless he wanted to get slapped in jail besides losing out everywhere else.'

She gave a little half-tearful laugh. 'He didn't know much about Toby, you see, or he'd never have started all this.'

'That I believe,' grinned Mendoza. 'So you all took a ride out to 267th Street.'

'We did. I went with him in his Porsche, and the detectives trailed us. And the hell of a squalid little hole it was, wasn't it? We didn't waste any time—he got the negs and gave them to me, and I identified them as the ones we were after *and* the whole dozen of them, and burned them right there—'

'In a big glass ashtray. Mmh. He had them in a brown manila envelope in the bottom of his laundry bag, and he emptied the whole bag out on the bed to get them for you.'

'He did,' said Pickering. 'What's more, there was—'

'Yes, I know, a second envelope. I know all about that one. But not a third?'

'Not that I saw, no.'

Mendoza leaned back, looking thoughtful. 'Motives. Yes, I wonder. Well, and so now we know why Mr Twelvetrees was clearing out in a hurry.'

'That was bluff,' admitted Pickering. 'I'd got no way of checking to see if he really left town. But I would—and he knew it—have come back to see if he'd left that place, and I knew where he worked, this damn fool cult, that Temple—and I'd have gone there to check. Hounded him a little, anyway.'

'Sure, sure. That he knew too, and I see how his mind worked on it. He had to cut his losses. What time was all this?'

'We got there about a quarter to one, and it couldn't

have been much after one when we left, we didn't linger at it, as I say. No, I didn't give a damn where he went or what he did, once those negs were burned. Matter of fact, I didn't try to do any checking, but he might have thought I would—like all that kind he was a coward when you backed him against a wall. He was so mad at me he'd've liked to kill me, but he didn't have the guts, even with a gun there to his hand. And what the hell he wanted with that—I mean, that wasn't his line, the direct action. Maybe it made him feel big and dangerous . . . I couldn't tell you the make and model, a pistol of some kind, it was in one of the drawers of the bureau. I saw it when he yanked the drawer open to get a handkerchief—he had a sneezing-spell . . . Yes, I think I'd know it again.' Pickering laughed contemptuously. 'Oh, he'd've liked to see me drawn and quartered, and he had about fifteen years on me too, if I had a better reach—but he never lifted a hand. You know what he did? It was the damndest thing. He came out of that apartment with us when we left, and went over to the carport on the other side of the building. And just as we were pulling out of that court, he came out with a trowel or a fork or something and started to dig around that funny-looking shrub planted in a tub there. Going at it in a kind of blind fury—as if he had to dig at *something*, if it was only a shrub.'

Mendoza laughed. 'Yes—and so that answers another little question. I've heard it said that gardening's a very relaxing occupation in cases of nervous tension. Maybe his doctor had recommended it.'

CHAPTER SIXTEEN

'Answers,' he went on to Hackett dreamily, after they had gone. 'We're getting them in, finally. *Va aclarando*—it's clearing up. And very nice too. So now we know almost all that happened to dear Brooke that Friday. His unlucky day, all right. He was finished here, after that business with Pickering . . . It looks as if Marian's got herself a man, *absolutamente* . . . He'd have no chance at all to get anywhere in show business, and he was also finished taking an easy living out of the Kingmans, because Pickering knew his connection with the Temple: he'd promised to hound him and he would. Everything had turned sour on Brooke Twelvetrees. First of all, he had to get away from 267th Street, in case Pickering did come back to check after the twenty-four hours' grace . . . There he is, hacking away at that Tree of Heaven in his blind fury at the way everything's turned out. I can see him, when that thought takes shape in his mind, stalking back into the apartment, throwing down that trowel anywhere—he's forgotten he had it—and starting to pack. He—yes. Yes.' Mendoza was sitting on the end of his spine, eyes shut, looking peaceful, hands clasped across his lean middle. '*Eso es*, of course. He got here with just that old brown leather suitcase, he's had no occasion for luggage since, and he's accumulated too much to go into it. So he leaves his packing, he gets out the Porsche and goes off to buy a couple of new suitcases.'

'I follow you,' said Hackett. 'That's nice deducing, but is it very important?'

'It might be. I think on the way he started thinking a little more clear and shrewd, and his first idea would be, What can I salvage out of this? He *could* try to go on blackmailing the Kingmans from a distance, but that's always a little more difficult. And I think he must have been very tired of the Kingmans and their Temple. Also, I think he needed some cash right then—he was the kind who spent everything as it came in, maybe he hadn't even enough for those suitcases on him. So he thought of the Kingmans' safe—and then he thought of the Temple bank accounts . . . Cut his losses, sure, and take everything along he could lay hands on. Now we don't know how long he worked at his gardening, how long he spent starting to pack. But we've got a kind of *terminus ad quem*, because the bank shuts at three. This just came in this morning. If it hadn't been that particular bank, this would be a different story, because a lot of banks now stay open later on Fridays and don't open on Saturday at all. But that one sticks to the old rule. So we deduce that by the time it came to him how he could salvage something out of the wreck, it'd be too late to get into the bank when he got there—it'd be quite a drive, you know. *De paso*, it's maybe a little confirmation of how our friend Kingman could get into the dither he did, you know, apparently he didn't know that, wasn't familiar with the banking hours. Because if he'd known the bank was open from nine to twelve on Saturdays, he'd have been down there to lay his warning then, and all this would have started two days before it did. Are you with me?'

'*Yo seguir*, right behind. Twelvetrees figured to take the cash and let the credit go, clear out the bank account and vanish into the wild blue yonder, probably under the name of Eustace J. Humperdink. O.K. He took a little chance clearing out the safe in the Temple—being too greedy. That he should have left alone.'

'I think it was more economy than pure greed. He'd gone to a little trouble to get hold of the combination, silly not to use it now. And it wasn't a long chance at all. Not when it was a matter of hours. He knew Kingman probably wouldn't open that safe until Saturday night. And he fully expected to be at the bank when its doors opened Saturday morning, primed with a glib story for the manager of sudden unexpected expenses that had to be paid in cash—I wonder what he'd have said. I wouldn't put it past him to have intended forging some notes of instructions from the other officers. Yes. Clear out of 267th, he'd think, and get settled for the night in some quiet hotel, and maybe he meant to sit up over those forged notes, to have them ready. He wouldn't have closed out the bank accounts, that'd call for more red tape—just stripped them down to a hundred or so. No, it wasn't too much of a chance . . . Well, he went to the Temple and took the month's receipts. He went and got his prescriptions refilled, and he bought those suitcases somewhere—probably a big cheap department store where the clerks are always in a rush, don't notice individual customers usually. And he had an early dinner, and he drove back to 267th Street—he'd get there about six-thirty, a quarter to seven, if he left that restaurant at five-thirty. It had started to rain, you remember, it was coming down steadily, that would slow him on the drive. And he started to finish his packing.'

'Yes. And?'

Mendoza's long nose twitched. 'I'm doing all the work. Can't you fill in a bit? Come on, think hard.'

'Well—I think he wrote that note to Mrs Bragg, to have it ready. He didn't want any backchat, or delay in getting away either. *And* it's nice to know he had the gun—it was his . . . Can we say he had a visitor, then? Before he got away, when he was nearly finished packing . . .' Hackett fingered his jaw, looking troubled. 'I don't know—'

'There are a lot of little things I don't know, but I know who the visitor was. Thanks to you.'

'Now look—she—'

'*Eso basta*, you stop right there, I'm tired of listening. I think, though there are jobs you could do, you'd better take the rest of the day off. I'm worried about you—you're going to pieces. I could take time and explain, but I think it'll be salutary for you not to be told—force you to do a little thinking of your own.'

'Are you ordering me—?' began Hackett stiffly.

'*Es mas listo de lo que parece*,' said Mendoza to himself with a sigh. 'Smarter than he looks—I hope. You go and have a nice quiet drink somewhere, Arturo, and maybe take in a movie. And don't worry, trust your uncle Luis, everything will be O.K. with a litte luck.'

'Oh,' said Hackett, staring at him. 'You *don't* think—And what are you going to be doing, if I'm allowed to ask?'

'I have dispatched minions—that's a nice word, no question but English has certain advantages—to discover, if possible, where that coat was purchased, by whom, and when. I think we'll get it, because it was only yesterday, you see, it'll be fresh in the salesclerk's mind. And for other reasons too. *De veras*, this love of melodrama . . . I am presently going to call on a new witness, or at least one we haven't thought very important, and meanwhile I am going to sit here and do some serious thinking, along the same line the famous idiot boy took with the lost horse. Goodbye, Arturo. Shut the door when you leave.'

Hackett looked at him, opened his mouth, thought better of that and shut it, and stalked out.

Oddly enough, he did more or less what Mendoza had told him to do, though without conscious plan. He went and had a drink, and then he walked up Main Street for a little way, thinking—not to much purpose—and dropped into a newsreel theatre.

He didn't take in much of the news; when he came out he went back for his car and drove up to Fairfax Avenue in Hollywood. He located the doctor's office and the pharmacy, and drove slowly on from there, watching the right side of the street. He stopped and parked twice, to go into large shops where luggage was sold, and drew blank. It was at the third place he got somewhere, a big department store branch; one of the clerks thought he remembered a man who looked like Twelvetrees' picture coming in to buy some luggage: he couldn't say exactly when, a couple of weeks back he thought, and he couldn't remember exactly what the man had bought.

Still, it all helped a little. Though the suitcases didn't matter, weren't important. But at least it gave him an illusion of working at it.

It was nearly four o'clock, and he remembered he hadn't had any lunch. He had a sandwich in a drugstore, and started back downtown, aimlessly.

He was on North Broadway, stopped at a light and looking around idly, when he saw the sign. It was an old movie house, newly refurbished in the desperate hope of better business, and for the same reason running a new gimmick to compete with TV. Like the fad for foreign films, there was a little boom these days in silent movies; maybe it made the middle-aged feel young again, and the kids superior; a lot of people seemed to get a kick out of saying, *Did we ever think that was good?* This house featured them once a week, so the sign said, and the one running now was called *The Girlhood of Laura Kent*—the name leaped at him from below the title—*with Mona Ferne*.

He turned into the next parking lot and walked back. On the way he suddenly found himself thinking about that gun. It had been lying on top of the bureau, Kingman said; so Twelvetrees had taken it out of the drawer, where Pickering had seen it, to pack. His visitor presumably had not (was that a fair deduction?) come with the idea of killing him, or he or she would have been prepared with a weapon. It was surprising how tough the human body was: you couldn't be sure of killing someone with a bang on the head—when it happened like that it was usually the sudden violent impulse and the blow landing just right at random. But if a suddenly enraged visitor snatched up that gun, why in hell hadn't he or she used the other end of it? A much surer way. The noise, yes: but that was the last thing anyone in a sudden violent rage would remember . . . So, the gun hadn't been loaded.

Yes, it was, he thought the next second. Or the cartridges for it were there. Because a while later it was used on Bartlett.

He stopped under the theatre marquee, and in absent surprise he thought, Well, well: so he had come round to Mendoza's viewpoint on that, Walsh's thing.

He went up to the ticket window, past the resurrected posters where Mona Ferne's young, insipidly pretty face smiled. 'This *Laura Kent* thing, when does it go on?'

'You're lucky, just starting now.'

Hackett gave up his ticket stub to the door attendant and groped his way down the aisle. Even in the dark there was an empty feel to the house, and when his eyes were adjusted and he looked around, he saw that there were only about twenty people in the place. Wouldn't think it'd pay them to stay open . . .

As he watched the opening scenes of what could never have been a good picture (even allowing for changes in style) he thought of what Stanley Horwitz had said. *Couldn't act—just took direction*. Too true. And the kind of thing she had done: this was probably a fair sample.

It must have been one of the earliest pictures she'd starred in, by the date: it was thirty-four years old. A year older than he was: but when his memory started, a few years later—well, it was hard to say, you remembered childhood backgrounds distorted, sometimes, but he'd have said that even then audiences would have been a trifle too sophisticated to go for this. But they must have: she'd done this kind of thing another nine or ten years and it had gone over pretty well.

It was supposed to be funny and what the posters still called *heartwarming* at the same time. The tired old plot of the tomboy who hates being a girl and goes swaggering about in jeans playing baseball (or riding broncs or driving racing cars or flying airplanes) until Love Enters Her Life and overnight she becomes a demure clinging vine . . . Of course the photography wasn't so good, but it was interesting to see what she had been: he had an idea, now, of the goal she was aiming for with all the effort put out. This vapidly pretty girl with blond curls and spontaneous adolescent giggles.

The dramatic action was jerky, everything drearily spelled out. She waded in a stream, casting a line with what even Hackett could see was inept awkwardness. She rode in a horse show, smart and boyish in jodhpurs. She went skeet-shooting with her distinguished sportsman father, in—

Suddenly he heard his own voice, loud and shocking in that place, 'My God!'—and found he was standing up. It couldn't be—but it was, he'd swear it was!

He sidestepped out to the aisle and ran up it. And as he ran, a few pieces fitted themselves together in his mind, and he thought, So that was it. The coat, the damned coat—but—

'Telephone?' he gasped to the doorman, who gaped at him and pointed out the public booth in the lobby. Hackett fumbled for a dime, slammed it into the slot . . . 'Jimmy,' he said when he got Sergeant Lake, 'let me talk to him —I don't care if he's in conference with the Chief, I've got—'

'He isn't here, Art, you just missed him.'

Hackett said a few things about that. 'Know where he's gone?'

'If you'll let me get a word in edgewise. He was just back from somewhere, looking like the dealer'd handed him a royal flush first time round, when that Miss Weir called and out he goes again in a hurry.'

'Oh, O.K., thanks.' Hackett hung up. It was twenty past five. He seemed to remember that that school of hers closed at three-thirty, four, around there: she was probably at home. Try, anyway. He found another dime, looked up the number.

'Miss Weir? Art Hackett. Is Luis there? . . . Luis, listen, I've got something, something so—'

'Well, well,' said Mendoza, 'have you limped up to the finish post, *chico*? Congratulations. You'd better come round, we've got something here too.'

At about the same time that Hackett was brooding over nis drugstore sandwich, Alison was saying helplessly, 'Now drink your tea while it's hot,' and wondering why it was that in the American mind, apparently, tea was connected with trouble. Could it be still reverberations from the Stamp Tax? When someone was in trouble, a little under the weather, or having a crying spell, automatically you made them a nice hot cup of tea.

She had found the girl outside her apartment door when she came home, a forlorn stranger who told her numbly, like a child repeating a lesson, 'Sergeant Hackett said to come and see you. I'm sorry, I didn't know where else to come. I didn't know what to do. But I had to get out of that house. I had to. I'm Angel C-Carstairs.'

She was shaking and cold, and she'd had some kind of bad shock, Alison saw. Having heard a little about this case from Mendoza, she recognised the girl's name; she made her come in and sit down, she made the tea and gave her soothing talk, and then all this began to come out. Incoherent at first.

'I didn't know—I thought I'd never seen it before, but it must be hers, because—because she kept saying—Like, you know, if you keep on telling a person he's stupid, he *will* be. She *did* that with me, I know it, I know it in my mind but I c-can't seem to do anything about it—telling me I'm too big and clumsy. You know. It was like that, about this—as if she thought, if she said it to me enough I'd begin to believe it—the way everybody else would. And it's not *true*, it's silly. That I could ever—be in love—with somebody like that! Like Brooke! I didn't even think he was handsome, I mean he was *too* good-looking—you know—'

'Yes.'

'Oh, I don't *know* what I'm doing here—perfect stranger to you. I'm sorry, I'm sorry, but I didn't know—I just had to get out of *her* house—You see, it was so funny, the way she kept insisting it *was* my coat, as if after a while I wouldn't be sure about that either, and say it was—and then after they'd g-gone, she got onto this, kept saying she *understood* how I'd loved him, felt jealous—and then I thought *why* it could be. I didn't believe it—I don't know if I believe it—but if she did—! Oh, I've hated her, I've hated her so—you can't understand that, how anybody could—my own mother, but you don't know, *you* probably have a n-nice mother—'

'Drink your tea,' said Alison. She was beginning to understand what this was all about, and automatically made quiet responses while she thought, I'd better call Luis. Persuade her to talk to him, if she will. 'Actually I don't remember my mother at all, she died when I was two, and my father brought me up. Not much of a bringing-up, I expect, either, because he was an engineer and we lived in Mexico mostly, travelling around from one godforsaken spot to another—construction camps, you know. But people are just people, no better or worse for being mothers or fathers. And hating doesn't do any harm except to you—'

'I know, I don't *want* to, I—I don't think I do, any more, It's all *over*, all of a sudden, and I don't know what to do—but I shouldn't be here, I'm sorry. I've g-got money, and in the bank too, I mean I'm all *right*. I expect I'd better go to a hotel. It just *hit* me all of a sudden, the reason. And I don't know—now—how I *do* feel about her. Doing that. Not him—but trying to—wanting to—'

'Yes. I think the only way to feel is sorry for her, don't you? Not resentful. It's just a thing you have to face up to.'

'I—I guess I'm not very good at that.'

'Then now's the time to start,' said Alison firmly.

Angel had calmed down a little; perhaps the kitten had helped, curled up beside her purring. 'I always wanted a c-cat. She never— But I *could* be different, couldn't I? I could learn better. To cope, sort of, you know. You know what I always wanted to do? It's silly, I guess, *she* said . . . But I liked it better than anything else at school, even than poetry. I l-like to *cook* . . . She kept *on* at it, until I suddenly saw, that was all. And they think it was me, that's what she wanted them to— Not Sergeant Hackett, he's nice, but the other one. That I *was* in love with Brooke. But does she think I'm c-crazy, not to *know* how I felt—and didn't feel? Oh, I don't understand—and—'

'You'd better tell Lieutenant Mendoza about this.' And then Alison spent ten minutes persuading her.

'I *couldn't!* Don't you see—even if—even if I don't feel anything—like that—for her, she *is*—! I couldn't—like t-telling tales—'

'Don't be childish,' said Alison. 'This is serious, you know it is. And I doubt very much if it'll come as a surprise to Luis, when—' even you know about it, she finished in her mind, but Angel was rushing on.

'And besides *he's* the one thinks I—! He *looked* at me when he left—I knew what he was thinking—'

'That I doubt too,' said Alison. 'If he looked at you one way, it probably meant the opposite. I'm told that's the secret of his success—experience at the poker table. Now you go and wash your face—you've been crying and it'll make you feel better—and you'd better take an aspirin too, and lie down on the bed and rest quiet until he gets here. You can trust Luis not to jump to any wrong conclusions, and it's much better in his hands.'

Angel went meekly to do as she was bidden, and five minutes later Alison, looking in, found her sound asleep, curled up on the bed like the kitten.

She left her thoughtfully, shutting the door, and was sorry Mendoza arrived so soon. He listened to her rather incoherent account and said, 'Awkward. I'm not quite ready to break this yet, I want a bit more information, and I hope her—mmh—precipitate flight doesn't scare Mona. No odds if it does, though, she'd only do something else damn silly. No finesse at all.'

'But what an awful thing, Luis—her own mother—'

'Physical sense only. She's never had a thought in her head besides herself. In this case, anything expedient to get out from under. Now I wonder if that was why she took that laundry bag away? Just in case.'

'Will Angel have to testify against her? She's just about at the end of her tether now—'

'*Es poco probable*, I don't think so. Not if we get a nice tight legal confession, which I'd like. She'll have a rough time for a little while, the publicity, but these things die down—something else'll come along to make gossip.'

'There's good stuff in her, I think—she'll take it, and maybe be the better for it. My Lord, how I long to get *at* her and fix her up—she could be a good-looking girl, you know. And what a time to think of that . . .'

'Any time's the time to think of a good-looking woman, *chica*. You do just that, and earn Art Hackett's gratitude. I'd heard the one about beauty being in the eye of the beholder, but I never believed it before. Another good man gone wrong . . . Yes, I'm afraid so, *lo siento en al almo*, to my deep regret. Many a man ruined for life by marriage, I only hope he'll have better luck.'

Alison said, 'Yes?' She watched him relax on the couch, stroking the kitten.

'Well, where is this girl? I've got other irons in the fire—'

'Count five and start pretending to be a human being,' said Alison dryly. 'I'll get her.'

And he gave her his one-sided smile, caught her hand as she passed and kissed it. 'Sorry, *querida*, it's routine to me, sometimes I forget it isn't to everybody. I'll be nice to her.'

But she hadn't taken another step before the phone rang, and it was Hackett . . .

Angel looked a little better for the rest, with her face scrubbed, her hair combed. She sat erect on the edge of the couch like a child in school, with Alison beside her, and only gradually relaxed under their quiet voices, their reassuring phrases.

'It was,' said Hackett, 'a picture made before you were born, so you wouldn't know anything about it. But what startled me was that there's a scene of her shooting —target-shooting—and the way it was taken, I don't see how it could have been faked. She was doing it, not someone doubling for her—and she wasn't missing a shot. Quite a little exhibition.'

'I don't know anything about the picture. But I can tell you a little about that, I guess—' She stopped, looked stricken again, and again Mendoza was patient.

'Miss Carstairs, I'm not lying to you when I say we'd get all this elsewhere if not from you. There's only a few little things I want to ask you right now. I knew about your mother this morning, when I looked at that coat and saw it was brand-new, and heard her trying to convince us all that it was yours, and that you'd had it for some time. You're not betraying her in any sense, believe me—you're only filling in a little for us that we could learn from others.'

'I see that,' she whispered. 'I—I don't like it, but you'd

only—find out anyway, and I don't suppose—this'll be as bad as—if there's a trial and so on.' She stiffened her shoulders, took a deep breath. 'Mr Howitz could probably tell you more about it. I know I was awfully surprised when he mentioned it once—it was the first I'd ever heard of it—it must have been that picture he meant. He said everybody had been surprised to—to find she was a second Annie Oakley. You see, she was brought up on a farm, or anyway a very small town, I'm not sure which, in South Dakota, and she used to go out hunting with her father. She got to be q-quite a good shot. Later on she—I think she felt it was unwomanly, you know—she never mentioned it or *did* it any more. My father—I've heard Mr Horwitz say—was a sportsman, he liked to hunt, and I don't know but maybe she used to go with him then. But that'd be twenty-five years ago, and so far as I know since then she's never— But Brooke wasn't *shot*, was he?'

'Not Brooke,' said Mendoza. He took the old Winchester revolver out of his pocket and laid it on the coffee table. 'Have you ever seen this before, Miss Carstairs?'

She looked at it for a long moment. 'I—why, yes, I think—I think that's the gun Brooke stole . . . She wasn't really angry about it, just a little put out. She never could have refused him anything, you know,' and faint contempt was in her tone. 'She was terribly silly about him. I knew—even I knew—he just fawned on her, flattered her, because she—gave him presents, and I think she used to pay too, when they went to some awfully expensive place. I—it was *shameful*. I wouldn't have liked him anyway but when he did that—'

'Yes. He stole this gun?'

'He called it borrowed. He was going to be in some play where they had to have a gun,' she said dully. 'I said my f-father liked to hunt, he had some guns, and two or three of them she never sold. This was one of them. It's not the kind you hunt with, of course—the others are rifles—but she kept this on account of burglars. She said. He saw it one day, it was in the den with the others in a case, and he took it. She said he should have asked, of course she'd have lent it to him. He never gave it back—I don't know if she asked, or maybe gave it to him to keep. I do know it was loaded when he took it, she always kept it loaded. In case she needed it in a hurry, she said, if someone broke in.'

'Twenty-five years,' said Hackett to Mendoza, meditatively.

'I don't know, it's a thing you don't lose entirely. If you've had a lot of practice. You'd get rusty, sure, but—in an emergency—you'd instinctively do what old experience told you.'

'Probably. A great help, anyway—the old experience—in that particular target shot.'

'*Claro está*. Miss Carstairs, I've got just two more questions to ask, and then we're going to see that you're settled in a hotel. Miss Weir'll go along and I expect lend you whatever you need, and we'll stop bothering you for a while. Can you tell me anything about Miss Janet Kent?'

Angel's eyes hardened a little. 'Yes, I can,' she said steadily. 'She was a—a sort of nurse-supervisor for me for about ten years, from the time I was five. I don't think she meant to be—unkind, but she was awfully—oh, strict and old-fashioned, and crotchety. She was old then, and looking back now, I can see she used to—to fawn on *her* and pretend to admire her so much, because she was afraid of losing her job, not being able to get another. But—*she*—swallowed it all whole, you never can give her too much flattery, she never sees through it. And when I got too old for Miss Kent, *she* gave her a sort of pension, just because it makes her feel magnanimous to have someone dependent on her that way. I—I feel sorry for Miss Kent now—once in a while *she'd* get me to go with her there, you know, and it's just sickening—to me anyway—the way Miss Kent kowtows to her, you almost expect her to say "my lady" and curtsey—oh, you know what I mean—like a whipped dog—because she's old, nearly eighty, and she hasn't got anyone or any money, and if *she* ever stopped giving her this little bit to live on, Miss Kent'd have to go on the county. *She* just revels in it, of course, the funny thing is she thinks Miss Kent really means it—'

'Yes. Now I want you to take your time and think about this one,' said Mendoza. 'You know, of course, that your mother had made a very inept effort to cast suspicion on you. She didn't choose you deliberately, but when we found the body, you see—which hadn't been intended—and began finding out a few things close to home, she got nervous. She had a few things she hadn't got rid of, to link her with it, and now she was afraid to try to dispose of them, that we might see her doing that. So it had to be someone in the same house, in case of a search warrant. And that meant you. You know about the coat. There's something else. Something about two feet long or a bit more. Fairly heavy, but partly flexible. Is there anywhere in that house where she could put such a thing, where it would be definitely connected with you and still you wouldn't come across it right away?'

She didn't think twenty seconds; she said simply, instantly, 'Why, of course. My old trunk. That is, it's—it was my father's, there were some old family pictures in it and odds and ends. She was going to throw it away once when I was about seven, and I begged to have it. I—I never knew anybody in either of their families, you see, my grandparents or aunts and uncles—and it made it seem I had more of a family somehow, those old pictures. I used to t-tell myself stories about them . . . I keep it way at the back of my closet, it's locked, and there are things in it I expect it's silly to keep, but the kind of things you don't throw away. My high school graduation dress, and the school yearbooks—and a c-couple of letters—things like that. I don't open it once in six months, now.'

'Locked,' said Mendoza. 'Where do you keep the key?'

'In the top drawer of my dresser.'

'And where were you from six o'clock on last evening? At home?'

'Why, no—for once I wasn't,' she said without

bitterness. 'I felt I had to get out—away—I went to a movie by myself . . . No, of course I haven't looked in the trunk since.'

'Thank you very much,' said Mendoza, smiling. 'That's all for now.'

And as they waited for Alison to pack an overnight bag for the girl, over Angel's protests, Mendoza suddenly asked, 'You didn't pick up a traffic ticket on your perambulations today, by any chance?'

'A— No, why?'

'Neither did I. Oh, I don't know—round out the case,' said Mendoza vaguely. 'Traffic tickets, they've had quite a lot to do with this case, one way and another. If Frank Walsh hadn't given me that ticket and subsequently found I'm a tolerably reasonable individual to talk to, he'd probably have done nothing about his doubts on Bartlett. Let Slaney convince him he was just being over-conscientious. And if Madame Cara hadn't got a ticket that night at—as we now know—the corner of Avalon and DuPont at seven minutes past eleven, I might easily have decided to use that warrant and charge them with the murder. And in the first instance, if Walsh and Bartlett hadn't stopped to hand out a traffic ticket right there, she wouldn't have had such a good chance to spot the squad-car number she was looking for, and take those shots at the driver—the wrong man. Funny how things work out sometimes. If she hadn't done that extra kill, nobody might ever have known a thing about it. Twelvetrees-Trask quietly moldering away there with his suitcases. Woods would have gone on looking, and finally filed it under Pending, and that would have been that . . . It was the extra kill—and the traffic tickets—that tripped her up in the end.'

And Hackett asked, 'But why? What possible motive—'

'*Eso tiene gracia*,' said Mendoza, 'that's the funny thing. I don't know. I've got a little idea, but I don't *know*. Maybe she'll tell us.'

CHAPTER SEVENTEEN

And it was a curious ending to a curious case, how readily she told them, eventually.

When they brought her in the next morning and confronted her with the green plastic laundry bag and its contents, which had been locked away in Angel's old trunk, she went on talking for a while about her poor misguided child, so frantic with unrequited love.

She sat in the chair beside Mendoza's desk, which she had unobtrusively moved to put her back to the light from the window, and smiled at him, and at Hackett, at the silent policewoman and the stolid police stenographer, in perfect confidence. She was in black today, as glossily turned out as ever—and the little loose fold of skin at her throat shaking a little as she turned her head from one to the other, the little strain lines about the eyes (because she should wear glasses) showing deep, and the raised blue veins on her hands; the thick, skillful cosmetic mask could not hide the lines and hollows and shadows.

'Miss Ferne,' said Mendoza finally, 'it's really no use, your going on like this. Sooner or later you'll have to listen to me and believe it. We know Miss Carstairs had nothing to do with the murders. We know who did, and we have evidence on it. The salesclerk where you bought that coat on Monday remembers the incident very clearly—do you know why? Because, as Mr Horwitz told us, you never were much of an actress and you can't do character parts. You overplayed it quite a bit, with that black hairpiece fastened to a turban, and the fake accent that puzzled everybody because it was partly French and partly German and partly just your own idea of how any foreigners talk English. You didn't fool anyone—the cab driver that night, or the man in the shop where you bought the serape, or the clerk on

Monday—they all knew you were putting on a very crude act—'

'That's a *lie!*' she exclaimed. 'I can! I'm a great actress, everyone always said so—it's only jealousy, I'd be showing these snippy young things today if—'

'We have the whole story from Miss Janet Kent, too. You make a mistake there in believing she really was devoted to you. All she was interested in was the money you gave her. Just as Brooke Twelvetrees was—wasn't he? That's why she fawns on you and flatters you—that's why she was afraid not to oblige you, when you came to her last Sunday and asked her—told her—to be ready to back up an alibi for you for the night of Friday the thirtieth. You hadn't thought you'd need one up to then, but after we'd found the body you thought you'd better have one. Miss Kent didn't like it, though I'm afraid she thought it was an illicit love affair—'

She smiled and smoothed her hair. 'Of course. And that's a lie too, she *is* devoted to me—simply devoted. Servants always like me. You probably forced her to tell.'

'It's always a mistake to count on other people in a business like this. They just haven't the incentive, you know, to go on telling lies. And when she heard that it was a murder case, she told us all about it. You made quite a few mistakes that night, and not the least of them was in overlooking all those odds and ends on the bureau. His hat, and the medicine bottles, and his watch and pocket-knife, both monogrammed, and the half bottle of Scotch and so on. It was convenient that you'd also overlooked that laundry bag on the chair. Into that it all went. But you couldn't face going down that trap again, so you took it with you.

'You thought you'd covered your tracks so cleverly, with the act you put on for the cab driver, for the salesclerk—' Mendoza laughed and shrugged. 'You have a most unfortunate love of wild Gothic melodrama, Miss Ferne—no appreciation of dramatic subtleties at all! As I daresay directors have told you—many years ago.' He let some contempt show in his eyes.

'A lie,' she said in automatic reaction, 'it's all lies.'

'But things went on going wrong, we found the body, and that brought you into it—when we'd identified him—if only on the outskirts of the case. And when you talked to your dear friend Cara Kingman on Monday, she told you that the police had connected with the murder a woman wearing a light-coloured coat with dark bands of trimming on the cuffs and front panels. That really frightened you, because you still had the coat—'

'*Angel* had it. You found it.'

'I mean the real coat,' said Mendoza patiently, 'the one you were wearing that night.'

'You don't know,' she said almost slyly. 'I never owned a coat like that in my life. You *don't* know.'

'But I do,' and he smiled gently at her. 'I had to do a little serious thinking on it, but it came to me. It was your fur coat you were wearing that night, wasn't it? That specially made brown mink with the white satin lining. It was the one halfway clever idea you had—to turn it inside out and wear it that way when you needed a quick disguise. People could see what you'd done in good light, of course, but in the dark like that, it was quite effective. Only the fur on the inside borders still showed, to look like trimming in the dark. And the rain ruined the lining, didn't it? You were afraid to send it to the cleaners, they'd be bound to ask questions and remember. When we searched your house last night, one of my men examined it, and we've gone back just since you've been here, to impound it as evidence.'

'You can't do that—'

'I'm afraid it's quite legal. As I say, you were frightened when we got that close to home, and you went on making mistakes by most unnecessarily trying to cast suspicion on your daughter. And most ineptly! The rawest new rookie in uniform could have followed the trail you left. You had a long hunt for a coat made just like that, you spent most of the day at it, in your crude disguise, and we've found several clerks who remember you and your specific request. You finally found what you wanted at a small shop called Betty Jo's, on Beverly Boulevard, at about four-thirty. You paid thirty-seven-fifty for it. You hid that damning laundry bag in your daughter's trunk that evening, put the coat in her wardrobe. Had you kept the bag in case you needed a scapegoat? I think so. You didn't have a chance to plant them in Miss Carstairs' room until she decided to go out to a movie. You knew where she kept the key to her trunk—but you'd decided to be bold about the coat, which was a very stupid mistake too . . . Once you'd gone to all this trouble, you were really hoping we'd come with a search warrant: I saw how pleased you were, yesterday morning, when we walked in and saw that coat lying there. But your daughter's an intelligent grown-up woman, Miss Ferne, however much you hate to acknowledge it, and you couldn't have forced her to admit owning that coat and forgetting it, or to believe she'd been in love with Brooke Twelvetrees.' Suddenly he got up and stood over her. 'You were the one in love with Twelvetrees—weren't you?'

She looked up at him for a long minute, wide-eyed, a little smile still on her painted mouth. Then she said, 'You're much cleverer than I thought the police were. You *do* know, don't you?'

'We know. We know all about it, Miss Ferne. But maybe you'd like to give us your version.'

She fitted a new cigarette into the jewelled holder and he leaned to light it for her. 'I wonder—it might be good publicity.' She laughed. 'You know what they say about publicity?—it doesn't matter what you get in the papers *for*, just get there! I daresay,'—and her tone was complacent—'I'd have a number of contract offers, afterwards . . . I don't believe Stanley's been *trying* to do anything, just spite, and besides he's getting old, losing his grip. I'll get a new agent . . . Because of course I'll get *off*, nobody would say I was guilty—when they know why. Not if there are any women on the jury,' and she giggled, and then looked thoughtful. 'Or perhaps men would be better.

Yes. I must remember to tell my lawyer. I'll have someone really good, to put on a good production . . . It might be interesting.'

'I'm looking forward to it. You were going to give us your version.'

She smoothed her hair, looking up at him sideways, coyly. 'He insulted me, that was why, really. And a *lie*. Yes, I did love him—dear Brooke—and I'd been kind to him, awfully kind. I felt sorry for him, you know, the poor boy hadn't any money but the *pittance* Martin could afford to pay him. And he was proud, really he was, I thought—he didn't like to take presents from me, but he always gave in so charmingly! And he spent too much money on me, at quite nice, expensive places—'

'Like the Voodoo Club.'

'Oh, yes, we went there a lot. It was only fair I should try to make some return. But he was shy too—I thought—' she gave a little gasp. 'I was sure he loved me too, only he was too shy and proud to say—because I had more money, and then there was just the *tiniest* difference in our ages—'

'Just twenty-eight years' difference,' said Mendoza crudely.

For one moment her face was convulsed with rage. 'You—! It doesn't matter, it doesn't matter—it was a lie, a lie, a lie! He was going away, he was packing—when I came—he let me in, we were in the living room but I could see into the—I'd made up my mind to smooth matters out *for* him—you know—and tell the dear boy I *returned* his love—I'd be proud and happy to marry him—I knew he'd been hestitating to—you know—try his fortune with me. And he—and he—it was a lie, of course, he was drunk or he'd gone mad or something! I told him—and he *swore* at me, he called me—'

'An old hag,' said Mendoza softly. (And this was it, the offbeat little idea in his mind.) 'He said you're an old desiccated bag of bones, a wrinkled mummy, he'd as soon go to bed with his grandmother—a silly old painted bitch pretending to be sixteen—' And he stepped back quickly from her clawing fingers, and Hackett and the policewoman took her by the shoulders and forced her down to the chair again.

She sat rigid for a minute, and the mask of rage smoothed out to her usual vapidity. 'You see, I nearly killed *you* then. Any woman— And he was mad, it's a wicked, *wicked* lie, all anyone has to do is *look* at me,' and up went the manicured hand, gracefully, to the perfect coiffure. '*Real* beauty doesn't fade, of course. And I *do* have enough self-respect to keep myself *up*, retain the youthful *outlook*—that's the great secret. You remember that, dear,' she said condescendingly to the policewoman. 'But even though I knew *it was a lie*—as anyone can see—I, well, I suppose I lost my temper. Just for a minute. I slapped him, I know, and he must have been frightened—of me, imagine!—because he stepped back and picked up that gun. I'd given it to him, you know—silly boy, it made him feel like an adventurer or something, I think—it was an old one of Bill's. He couldn't ever have *shot* anyone with it, he didn't have the courage for that. I reached for it and got it away from him—really you could say it was self-defence!—and I must have hit him with it, because he fell down and when I *felt* him, well, he was dead. It was his own fault, he shouldn't have *lied* to me like that! You can see how it was.'

'I can see. So you started to leave.'

'Well, there wasn't anything else to do, was there? He was dead, and while it *was* his own fault, I didn't want to be connected . . . It was raining quite hard then, and when I opened the door—I'd left my car on the street that time, very foolishly—there was this sudden great flash of lightning, it lit up everything—'

'Including the police car sitting right outside. And the driver. And its number. Yes, I know all about that too. And several people have identified the gun. It was that extra kill that was your biggest mistake, Miss Ferne . . . You thought the driver had seen you, and you decided—shall we say—you might as well be hung for a sheep as a lamb? So you thought it over, and went back to get the gun, and then you found the car had gone. You spent quite a while hunting it.'

She looked down and then up through her lashes, demurely. 'I know that whole thing was foolish, I realised it almost as soon as it was over. But I *was* frightened, and not thinking very clearly—and of course women haven't logical minds, have they? There wasn't any way to be *sure* I'd really killed him, that was the trouble. It was awful, driving all over looking for that car—I passed several police cars, but I couldn't always read the number, and I was frantic—and then, it was like a miracle, I saw it just ahead, stopped, and the roof light showed up its number, the right one. Seven-four-seven it was. So I went around the block—of course I'd made sure the gun was loaded . . . You know, I hadn't fired a gun in years, and I was always better with a rifle too, but it *came back*, if you know what I mean. But I couldn't be *sure*. So then—I was thinking *much* more clearly by that time, of course—I thought, well, Brooke was leaving anyway, why not just make it look as if he'd gone away? And then it wouldn't matter about the policeman, no one would know Brooke was dead. So I went back, and that time I parked behind the building. I hadn't any trouble getting in, you see, he'd already put that note for the landlady, with the key in it, on the front door. And at first I thought of putting everything, Brooke and the suitcases, into the car, and going down to the beach—but it would have been awfully difficult, being a woman I'm *not* very strong, of course. And then I thought of that funny trap door. I'd only been to his place once before, you know—he was ashamed of it, I think—but he'd shown it to me then, because I noticed the hinges on the floor, such a funny place, and asked. I think it was clever of me to remember and take the time to *bury* him. Dead things begin to—to—you know, have an *odour*, after a while. I didn't think it needed to be very deep, just *enough*. And it was the oddest thing, very lucky, there was a trowel, just lying there on the couch in the living room—I can't imagine why. Very lucky, because of course you couldn't use a spade down there, there wasn't room. It took *ages*, after I'd pushed him down there, and I was terribly frightened once when some people came in—I don't know who. They knocked, and I knew the door was unlatched—they might come in—so I just closed the trap and waited. I'd left my purse in the car. I knew there wasn't anything damaging for them to see. They stayed an awfully long time, I could just barely hear the voices, you know. I thought they'd never go—'

'Weren't you,' he asked of private curiosity, 'at all nervous down there in the dark with a dead man?'

She stared up at him. 'I was waiting for them to go, so I could get on with burying him. No, why? You said, about later on, I couldn't face going down again—how silly—it wasn't that, it was my shoes—I'd almost ruined them, quite expensive shoes, and I didn't want to get them dirty again after I'd . . . And I *did* think, those things—to *plant* on someone else, if . . . I remembered to wear my gloves all the time, except just at first, and I wiped off things I remembered touching then. Only I lost a button from one of them, somewhere—'

'Yes, we have both the button and the glove.'

'Oh—have you? You *are* clever . . . And, you know, when I slid him down the trap—I *have* been a little worried about this—there was a lot of money, all in a great roll, fell out of his trouser pocket, *and* the bankbooks—for the Temple accounts, I mean. I've been worried about those, I didn't know what to do—Martin should have them back, but— Oh, and I kept the money, of course— You needn't say I stole it, the way Brooke did, because you know, I'd spent that much and *more* on him, it was only fair! . . . And I cleaned everything up tidily, the last thing—that was *after* I came back in the cab, of course. I emptied the ashtray and put some scraps of waste paper into the wastepaper basket, an empty pack of cigarettes and torn paper, there on the bureau—' (Yes, of course, Kingman's note, and Mrs Bragg emptying the basket.) 'The car was an awful nuisance. Of course it had to go too, and I thought if it was found near the station people would think he'd gone away on a train. *That* was stupid—I didn't think until I was almost there—I should have left it at the airport, much closer to the apartment, so much easier. I took along the smallest suitcase because I thought that would look to a cab driver as if *I'd* just got off a train—but then I realised I couldn't take a cab right at the station, in the light. You know,' she simpered at him, 'people always do look at me, and they'd be bound to remember. So I thought, something to put over my hair, and I put on a lot more make-up too, heavy eyebrows and so on, like that, as a disguise. And, oh, that suitcase was so heavy! I walked and walked, looking for some place I could get a scarf, something like that—but everything was going right for me that night, I found a place open—and you're lying when you say that man, and the driver too, knew I was acting a part! I always said I could do character work, though it's not *necessary*, of course—I *am* better, I admit that, at ingenue types. And when I did get back, such a time it took too, I put the note back on the door where it had been, and the key, and—I never thought anyone would find out, and what did it *matter?* But you were cleverer than I thought—I can't imagine how you came to find him . . . All the same, I don't think I mind, because I really believe this might be the great turning point for me, you know? Some really *useful* publicity—and of course a good new agent, someone *young*—'

'Maybe so, Miss Ferne,' said Mendoza. 'Thank you very much, I think that's all we'll ask of you right now. You can sign a typed statement later.'

'Come on, dear,' said the policewoman.

'Oh, may I go now? I must see about a lawyer, I suppose. Goodbye, Lieutenant.' As she was led out the door she was saying again, to herself, 'Someone *young*—with the *youthful outlook*—that's the main thing, the important thing—'

* * *

Hackett said angrily, wonderingly, 'She never asked about Angel at all. Where she is, how she feels. And, my God, this is going to be tough on Angel . . . Even without a trial, if the lawyer persuades the Ferne not to try denying that confession—'

'She'll probably try,' said Mendoza. 'Claim the brutal police forced her to sign it. Rather odd business altogether, but then—as Madame Cara said to me—people *are*. And, speaking of clichés, that's one we always come back to in our business, don't we?—you look far enough, there's a woman at the bottom of every piece of mischief. For me, *nada de eso*, thanks. Too dangerous.'

Hackett looked at him there, leaning back in his swivelled-around chair, looking out the window. Hackett said, 'There's another one says the most accomplished and wary Casanova meets his downfall sooner or later and gets led to the slaughter. I'm just waiting for the day it happens to you—I'll be there to cheer on true love.'

Mendoza swung around and laughed up at him. 'A lot of people are waiting for that day, boy. You'll all wait a long, long time. Maybe forever.'

'*Cuanto apuestas*, how much do you bet?' asked Hackett.

Mendoza looked interested at once. 'At what odds, friend? If they're long enough— But what'd we make the *terminus ad quem*? Retiring age, maybe?'

'I was just talking,' said Hackett hastily, 'no bets. Not with you, Retiring age? My God, you'd get up out of your coffin to chase a pretty woman—'

'Probably,' said Mendoza, 'probably. But not so headlong that I'd run into the trap.'

Hackett laughed a little shortly and went out. Mendoza looked after him and shook his head: a pity about Hackett, if he was really serious over this girl. However, these things happened. '*Eso allá el*,' said Mendoza to himself, 'his own business.' But very probably he'd be of little use for a while until he recovered from temporary lunacy . . .

At which point Sergeant Lake came in with a sheaf of new reports, and Mendoza sat up, demanded coffee, lit a cigarette, and began to go through them with interest. Always another job coming up, in this business.

This accidental poisoning, for instance, had it really been accidental? Sergeant Galeano thought not. Better hear what he had to say, and begin to think about it . . .

A FEW CLUES ABOUT MORE GREAT TITLES YOU'LL SOON BE SEEING IN KEYHOLE CRIME

STAR TRAP
Simon Brett

When someone attempts to sabotage the rehearsals of a new musical, Charles Paris, actor/amateur detective saves the show with a mixture of luck, experience and sheer talent.

THE BEAUTIFUL GOLDEN FRAME
Peter Chambers

Mark Preston, Private Eye, is hired to protect a portrait, framed in gold, of millionaire Bernard Rivers' dead wife. But stopping the madwoman who threatens to burn down Rivers' house proves almost impossible.

THE FAMILY VAULT
Charlotte Armstrong

Did the skull encrusted with blood-coloured rubies discovered inside the Kelling's family vault belong to night club queen, Ruby Redd who had disappeared 30 years before? Who could have buried her there and why?

Look out for them wherever you normally buy paperbacks

If you have any difficulty obtaining any of these titles, or if you would like further information on forthcoming titles in Keyhole Crime please write to:-

Keyhole Crime, PO Box 236, Thornton Road, Croydon, Surrey CR9 3RU.